nF420735

ALSO BY SIERRA SPENCER

Standalone Novels

Developing Feelings

Troped

Eastern Standard

Standalone Novellas

A Very Standard Christmas

Bad for Business Series

Model Behavior

Grove Meadow Witches

Something's Witchy

eastern standard.

Sierra Spencer

Copyright © 2026 Sierra Spencer

All rights reserved.

No part of this book may be reproduced, stored in a retrieval system, or transmitted in any form or by any means, electronic, mechanical, photocopying, recording, or otherwise, without express written permission of the publisher.

This book is a work of fiction. Any references to historical events, real people, or real places are used fictitiously. Other names, characters, places, and events are products of the author's imagination, and any resemblance to actual events, places, or persons, living or dead, is entirely coincidental.

Cover Design by Parker at Author's Best Friend

First Edition Editing and Proofreading by Lauren at Author's Best Friend

Printed in the United States of America

To all the Lover and evermore girlies, this one's for you.

A NOTE FROM SIERRA

Hello dear reader,

Thank you for venturing into the small town of Connor Bay, Massachusetts. I love these characters, and I hope you will, too.

Before you read, I wanted to let you know a few things. This book has depictions of grief, anxiety, and some situations that you might find to be unsettling if you have recently lost a loved one. I would love for you to meet these characters, but not at the expense of your well-being.

With love,

Sierra Spencer

PLAYLIST

1. marjorie - Taylor Swift
2. Wendy - Maisie Peters
3. Miserable at Best - Mayday Parade
4. CHRONICALLY CAUTIOUS - Braden Bales
5. Alone Together - Dan + Shay
6. The Sound of Letting Go - All Time Low
7. I Can See You - Taylor Swift
8. things i wish you said - Sabrina Carpenter
9. Cruel Summer - Taylor Swift
10. evermore - Taylor Swift

Scan this code in the Spotify app for the full playlist!

DIVE BAR ON THE EAST SIDE

Before

The bar is so loud I can't hear myself think. I'm not entirely sure why he wanted to come here in the first place. New York, I mean, not the dive bar. Two boys from Connor Bay, Massachusetts know their way around a dive bar.

Well, maybe not one on the Upper East Side. Even in a bar with Christmas lights hanging from the ceiling in the middle of September, we're vastly underdressed.

This city has always been confusing to me—advertising its culture and diversity but only allowing the elite to truly succeed in navigating it. It's full of self-important social climbers married to their jobs for better or worse.

Not that the two of us were any better. This is the first time we've had the same weekend off in months.

Oh. Right. New York is the halfway point between us. That's why New York.

He's telling a story about something that happened on the

drive into the city, but I can't hear him anymore. Not that I really could before. Now he's just background noise. I can't even see anything clearly because *she* is the most beautiful thing in this room...in any room I've ever been in.

She looks as uncomfortable as I feel, but I know she's not. I can tell she belongs in the city from the way she's sitting. At the bar, her back is ramrod straight. Delicate fingers rest against her glass. One leg crosses neatly over the other at the knee. Every so often, she tucks an unruly strand of red hair behind her ear.

Even more occasionally, she double-taps her cell phone on the bar beside her.

To check the time?

Is she waiting for someone?

"I'll be right back."

1

NO JOHN HUGHES MOVIE

My husband died in the middle of the last argument we ever had. I'm not even sure who would have won it. I guess *he* did, considering the circumstances.

"Not an argument." He'd probably say to me now. "We don't argue. We have lively discussions."

I'd been thinking a lot about what he might say if he were here. Maybe he would say Connor Bay wasn't *so* bad, and everyone would come around soon enough. He might say that the starlight and the sound of cicadas in mid-June were better than the lights and sounds of the city.

But he wasn't here to say those things, and in my opinion, Connor Bay was *that* bad. I seriously doubted anyone in this godforsaken town would come around to me any time soon, and I hadn't had a full night's sleep in over a month because the cicadas were louder than a traffic jam on Fifth Avenue.

The worst part about Connor Bay was that it was a place that lived for the days. It thrived on breakfast dates, afternoons at the lake, and all the interactions between sunrise and sunset. But I was a New Yorker, born and bred. I lived for the moment the sun dipped below the horizon, and the city came alive.

All of the best things in my life happened at night.

But then again, so did all of the worst.

Once again, I could see the light flash over his face, but I couldn't see after that.

There was no after.

There was only then and now. As if that split second in time was the end of Olivia Carrington: The Origin Story and simultaneously the birth of Olivia Carrington: The Sequel. Everyone knows the sequel is never as good as the original.

In the movies where the city girl moves to a small town and falls in love with a lumberjack, the credits always roll before you can see how it plays out in the long term. Well, I can tell you that it's not always a fairytale ending. Not that I moved to Connor Bay and fell in love with a lumberjack. No, my small-town love interest came to the city. He found his way to *me*.

Just a few months ago, I lived in a loft on the Upper East Side across from Central Park. On weekdays, I carried heels in my bag to change into at work after my walking commute. In the evenings, I had a husband who met me outside of my office building. He smelled of espresso beans and pastries from the coffee shop where he worked. Cradling my face in his hands, he would kiss me once on the tip of my nose, "For the good things that happened today," and once on my forehead, "for all the bad things," and finally on my lips, "for everything in between."

Pain rang through my chest, sharp and immediate, and I rubbed at it with the heel of my hand. I wasn't supposed to think about him during the day. I only let myself remember him at night.

When the cicadas got too loud, and the weight of his absence pressed against every cell in my body, I let myself think about my husband.

Some days, I hoped I'd wake up and breathing would suddenly feel easier. On other days, I relished in the grief because it meant we had something so potent that losing it left a permanent handprint on my soul.

I rubbed at it again. Perhaps it would have been easier to think about him now if I wasn't in Connor Bay, a town with less than 500 residents, wiping down a counter covered in Crayola crayon markings from one of the Erickson twins.

This was what the ~~argument~~ lively discussion that night in the car had been about. His parents needed his help back home, but I didn't want to leave New York, and he didn't want us to be apart.

We'd been married for six months at the time. I hadn't even met his parents yet, and he was asking me to move to Connor Bay for them. I was supportive of him going to help out his family, but I didn't want to move my entire life. Clearly, I had lost because I was standing in their restaurant.

"Olivia, table six needs more bread, and table 3 needs a drink refill," Marjorie said from behind the register, pulling me out of my thoughts.

I gave her a grateful smile, even though I knew she hadn't done it because I looked upset. No, she probably just thought I didn't have anything better to do.

"On it," I replied, ignoring that both tables were hers and not mine.

I wasn't sure what I was doing in Connor Bay exactly. I'd come because that's what he would have wanted, but it was clear I didn't fit in, and the people didn't like me. They didn't know me, but they didn't like me.

Privacy in this town was non-existent. Everyone knew everything about everyone and made judgments based on what they heard. It took me longer than I would have liked to find an apartment here because no one wanted to rent to the woman who stole Marjorie's son away to the city under the cover of night. As if I were some siren who lured him into a bar that Friday night in mid-September. As if I had been the one to approach him. As if I had been the only one who fell hard and fast.

I had two great loves of my life: him and my work. He used to joke that he was my side piece, coming second to my job. He never said it in a way that made me think it bothered him significantly, but he said it with enough frequency that I stopped working on the weekends...at least after he woke up in the morning.

When I told the firm I would need to work remotely for a while with odd hours, they were more than supportive, but sometimes I wished they denied my request. At least then I would have had a reason not to come here.

"Can I grab you anything else?" I asked, placing two plates of Marjorie's peach cobbler in front of the customers.

They weren't local; I'd have recognized them by now. I'd been here a little over a month, and I already knew every person's name, where they lived, and where they worked.

I knew that the bookstore owner was engaged to the florist's daughter. They'd have a wedding in the late summer before she started to show. I knew that the Tomlinsons and Garners were engaged in an epic battle of who would have the best booth at the Summer Festival at the end of July. I also knew that Caroline Stenson would never miss an ounce of gossip. If something happened at 9 a.m. on the dot, Caroline would know by 9:01. I was pretty sure she had the whole town tapped.

"That's all. Thanks." The woman on the left replied. I

smiled at them and returned to the counter to refill salt and pepper shakers.

"Olivia." Marjorie's voice rang out from further down the counter. "It's pretty slow. You can head out if you have something better to do."

I wanted to say that I didn't have anything better to do but that I appreciated her letting me go early. I wanted to ask her if she wanted help prepping the desserts for tomorrow—pies and cobbler made fresh daily, that was their thing—or mention that I was going to stop at the market and I could pick up anything for her if she needed it. But we didn't have that kind of relationship. She didn't want it.

I saw him again in that moment. Five o'clock shadow on his jaw, blue eyes sparkling with mischief from one too many stouts from the pub down the street. The woman at the counter pushed a form toward us.

We'd gotten married so quickly. The time between a dive bar on the Upper East Side and an Atlantic City speedy chapel was shorter than a college spring break trip.

No one told you that if you wanted to elope in AC, you needed to wait 72 hours for it to be processed, so that added a few days, but the pace we were moving was unparalleled.

I looked over the form and began to fill it out, pausing at the second question—a new married name.

"What's your last name?" I whispered, embarrassed at the thought the woman in front of me might overhear and find out that I didn't know my soon-to-be husband's last name.

He let out a laugh that made my heart flutter. A deep one that only surfaced when someone was truly and irrevocably happy.

"McCleary."

My eyes widened as I looked back down at the form. "Absolutely not. I will not be writing that." I shook my head, checking the box indicating I would not change my name.

He didn't seem offended in the slightest when he asked, "What's your last name? Maybe I'll change mine."

"Carrington," I replied, looking him over with a smile that contained nothing but my own unadulterated bliss. He laughed again.

"Oh god. My mom's gonna hate you."

And sure enough, Marjorie McCleary hated me without a shadow of a doubt. If she and her husband didn't so desperately need free labor in their restaurant, I would have been run out of this town by a pitch-fork-wielding mob.

"Alright. Thanks." I said, finishing up the last shaker and untying my apron. I tossed it in the laundry hamper under the counter and grabbed my bag from the cabinet beside it. "See you tomorrow."

She didn't acknowledge my goodbye, and I didn't press, but she called to me just as I reached the door.

Every time we made eye contact my breath caught. He got his eyes from his mom, and I could see him in her smile, not that it was ever directed at me.

"I won't be home until late tonight. Levi thought it would be a good time for you to stop by the house and take a look around his old room. See if there's anything you might want."

I blinked at her. Levi and Marjorie McCleary had never so much as invited me over for dinner, and now they were offering me...something. Some part of their son that I'd never experienced before. I nodded at her slowly. "Thanks. I'll come by."

"Okay." She said, looking back down at the receipts in her hands. "That'll be all."

I pressed my lips together in a firm line and nodded slowly again. Processing. My mouth opened to say something else, to carry on this olive branch, but I didn't have anything.

Her head snapped up at me with an unamused expression on her face. "In or out, Olivia? You're blocking the door for customers."

My mouth went dry.

I'll try another time.

"Right, sorry. Bye."

2

YEAH, ME TOO

The town itself wasn't that bad. In fact, I could see how someone not like me might fall in love with it.

It was humid in the summer, and they didn't believe in cell phones, from what I could tell, but it was vibrant. Kids ran around and lined up outside the candy store owned by Matt Dillard, whose father owned it before him and his father's father before that.

Next door at the flower shop, Amelia Haverford, the bookstore owner's fiancée, paid the kids each a dollar to help water the plants. The shop owners had to be in cahoots because as soon as the watering was done, there they went—right up to the crooked door with the bell that clamored when the line of children stormed in to buy their sweets at a criminally discounted price.

Connor Bay had all the basic necessities. *The Bean* was a coffee shop around the corner from the diner and had the best scones I have ever had, though the espresso quality was severely lacking.

When I first arrived in town, I wasn't sure how *The Bean*

ever made money. Every time I walked in, they'd give me an extra scone for free and a discount on coffee.

"The newcomer's special," Sidney, the barista with the dark brown bob and front bangs, said the first time I visited as she shoved the paper bag and to-go cup at me with a smile.

It was short-lived.

Word got around that I was the widower who came to cause trouble in their small, quiet New England town. Now, I was pretty sure I paid double what everyone else did. Mostly because I was trying to bribe Sidney into liking me again by tipping her 100% of the bill. It wasn't working.

I didn't linger in the shop to finish my breakfast anymore. I just took the bag and the paper cup and hurried over to the diner, as if being seen less might make me less noticeable.

The next block over, the old movie theater played three movies—something old, something new, and something weird. That decision, I was sure, was made just so they could use the name *Oddly New Oldies*. Now, *that* was a place I was welcomed in. A nice, dark theater where no one would be able to tell it was me. They had to warm up to me at some point... right?

Walking down a house-lined street that would take me past the theater and then onto my apartment, I considered stopping in for a movie. It wasn't like I had anywhere I had to be right away. I definitely wasn't ready to go to the McClearys'.

The one-bedroom apartment I was renting from a man named Nando was sparsely furnished, with uneven floorboards that creaked no matter where I stepped. It seemed like I spent all my time either in the diner, my apartment, or traveling between the two.

What felt the most strange was that it was not like the New York version of Olivia had been much different. I'd head to the office and then home. *This* was different somehow.

Even if I remembered a time before him, I knew *this* was different.

Maybe it was because I felt like I belonged to New York.

I did not feel like I belonged to Connor Bay, and it most certainly did not belong to me.

"Are you Olivia?"

I stopped abruptly. I hadn't noticed anyone around me, but then I realized the voice had been hidden in the shadow of a porch awning.

"Excuse me?" I turned to the small yellow house with the porch swing that currently rocked back and forth. His voice called out again from the shade.

"I said, 'Are you Olivia?' Your hearing can't be worse than mine. I have a hearing aid in each ear, and I ain't getting any younger."

Donald Sanderson. Thirty-two Elm. Retired in the yellow house with the porch swing and white trim.

I bit my tongue to keep myself from arguing that I had not been expecting anyone in this town to address me as...well... anything at all, to be honest.

"That's right. I'm Olivia." I replied, heading up his walkway so we could stop shouting.

"You married the McCleary boy," he said, continuing to shout anyway.

I ran my tongue over my lips, suddenly aware of how dry they were. "Yes, sir."

"Helping out his parents, I hear."

I adjusted the bag on my shoulder and wrapped my arms around myself. A reflex, like bracing for impact. I couldn't meet his eyes because they looked too much like mine. He didn't have to tell me he was like me; I just knew.

"Yes, sir. Down at the diner."

Of course, if you asked Marjorie whether I was technically

"helping," I'm sure she'd laugh. I wasn't even sure how to help them. To be of any real help, I'd need to know about their expenses and business plan, but I was confident that Marjorie did not want me to know about any of that.

"They don't like you much."

He adjusted the square glasses on his face and scratched the stubble along his jaw. His brown hair was still full at the top, though it thinned near his forehead.

I didn't respond. I wasn't sure how.

"It's okay," he added. "This town don't like me much either."

I met his eyes then. "Why not?"

He shrugged. "Probably on account of me being grumpy. But I think there's lots to be grumpy about."

"Like what?" A ghost of a smile crossed my features. I was sure it didn't meet my eyes, possibly just a slight turning of the corners of my mouth.

"I figured you'd know all about things to be grumpy about. Considering your situation."

He took a long drink of whatever was in the glass on the stool beside him. I tracked his movements carefully like one of us would spook if we made any quick movements or said something that cut too deep.

"My situation?" I asked. I wasn't sure if I'd ever asked so many questions in a row.

"Well, you're not here because you want to be here." He made a sound that was remarkably close to a scoff. "Heard you're a city girl. My wife was a city girl. Dragged her back here with me when we were around 20."

I sat on the top step of his porch, my back resting against the railing.

"Did she get used to it? Being in a small town?" I knew the

answer. Women like us didn't blend into places like this. We disrupted them.

We weren't the standard here.

He gave me a ghostly smile of his own. "No, she hated it. Hated Connor Bay."

I looked away from him and down at the warped wood of his porch.

It probably would have been the same for us if he'd lived and we came here. Would I even have come? Would we have tried long-distance? For how long? How long until we'd start to resent each other? Before we missed FaceTime calls and went to bed without hearing each other's voice?

"I didn't understand it when she was around. Now I do."

I turned back to him. "What do you mean? You don't love Connor Bay?"

I'd just met him, but he must have loved this place if he had made his wife come here—at least *before*.

"I did once. Back when I wanted a family with a picket fence and a good job. Now my kids are grown and never call. My wife is gone, and I live in this big house with nothing but memories of her. And there's no place in this town for an old man who wants to live in the past a little longer."

My heart ached for him. For his wife, who probably loved busy streets with crowded sidewalks and too loud music. For his kids, who probably just didn't know what to say to him.

"What do you miss most about her?"

My head lolled to the side against the wood, looking out at his yard.

"It changes from day to day. Today, I miss her sun tea because this tastes like garbage."

A laugh slipped through my lips, unexpected and brief, like something stolen.

Driven by curiosity alone, I stood from the stairs. "Can't be that bad."

He picked up the glass and held it out to me. Taking it from him, I inspected the beverage. It looked right. It smelled right. It must—

"God, that's awful, Donald. Don't ever drink this again. I'll bring you some of Marjorie's from the diner tomorrow."

He laughed, and I could tell by his expression afterward that it felt foreign to him—surprised him even. Maybe it'd been a while for him too.

"Tomorrow? Well, that'll be just fine with me, Olivia. I'll see you tomorrow."

He stood from his chair and nodded his head at me before going inside.

As I continued on my walk home, guilt rang through my body.

I shouldn't have promised him tomorrow when I wasn't sure I'd make it through today.

3

I WATCH YOUR LIFE IN PICTURES

After some work and dinner alone in my apartment, I gathered enough courage to head over to the McClearys'. It was only a four-minute walk toward the center of town. They lived on a street covered in sycamores, and all the houses sat in a uniform row, though each one looked different from the last.

The McCleary home was one of the only ones with a fence. A white picket one you'd see in a movie. I let my fingers drag along the pointed tops of each panel before I reached the gate, as if touching it might steady me.

I knew the house would be empty. Levi's Chevy wasn't in the drive, and only the porch light was on, even though the sun had yet to set.

It was there that I wondered if people in small towns were afraid of the dark. Afraid of endings. Afraid of what lingered after beautiful summer days and the people they loved. It seemed as though they fought the dark any way they could in their starlit town.

The wood porch creaked under my feet as I approached the screen door. A note was taped to the front.

Olivia –

Sorry we couldn't be here when you got here. Busy day and all. His room is at the top of the stairs, the first door on the left.

–Levi

My interactions with Levi weren't as terrible as my interactions with Marjorie. Levi had visited the city a handful of times, but I always missed him. He'd drive in early in the morning, get breakfast with his son, and leave before I got home from work to beat the traffic out of the city. We'd offered him to stay the night in our guest room, but he'd wanted to get back to Marjorie. Sometimes, I wondered if she even knew he came.

No one locked their doors in a town of five hundred people, so it opened immediately when I twisted the handle to the front door. The McCleary home smelled like cinnamon and lemon, and I thought about how warm it must have felt during a holiday. I imagined a time when we might have visited them and been overwhelmed by the sounds and fragrances of Marjorie and *him* in the kitchen together.

I didn't linger near the door. I took the stairs straight up. I knew if I looked in any room other than his bedroom, Marjorie would find out, and I'd never be invited back. There already wasn't a guarantee I would be.

I paused on the stairs when a photo on the wall caught my eye. My hand lifted of its own accord and pressed against the glass.

A wedding photo.

Our wedding photo.

Well, a wedding photo taken much later than our wedding.

"We should take pictures," he said in the kitchen one evening while he made pancakes. A typical dinner in the Carrington-McCleary loft.

"Pictures?" I asked, pulling the syrup from the fridge and setting it on the table.

"Like wedding pictures. For my parents. I think they'd like it."

He didn't look at me as he prepared to flip a pancake in the air. It turned once and landed back in the center of the pan. He made perfect pancakes. *He* was perfect, and it made me feel like we were, too.

"You'd have to buy a suit," I said, resting my head on his shoulder, watching him finish plating.

"I own a suit, darlin'." He laughed and turned his head to press a kiss on my cheek.

"Well, then, I guess we'll take some pictures."

Later. I could think about this later.

I dropped my hand and continued up the stairs. I could do this. I *would* do this.

When I entered his room, I wasn't hit with the wave of grief I thought would wash over me. I assumed being in his bedroom would feel harder than this, but this was a piece of him I didn't know. In some ways, it was like learning something new about him—a bit of his history frozen in time where there was an after.

Being in the loft had been hard because he was frozen there in a way that didn't continue anywhere else. His coffee cup from that morning was still in the sink. His work boots were thrown haphazardly near the door.

I leaned against the doorframe, my body folding slightly under the weight of my thoughts.

His room was simple. That made sense. He was never one to own many things. I was the one who took up a closet and a half with too many handbags and pairs of shoes. I had sunglasses for every day of the week, and many of my clothes still had tags.

When he moved into the loft, I was worried about how to make all of our things fit in the small space, but he showed up at my door with a duffel bag, and that was it.

"Don't need much, darlin'. Already got everything I need."

"Surely you're joking," I said, opening the door wider to let him inside.

I must have been making a face because he laughed. "Name one thing I need that's not already in this apartment or this city."

"But you must have *things*. This can't be everything you own."

He dropped the bag by the couch and scanned the room. His eyes narrowed at the corner. "What are those?"

"Well, they were boxes so I could make space for your *things*," I said, a hint of exasperation coating my words.

He gave me a crooked grin as he walked over to me. "You were gonna make space for me?"

I frowned at him. "Of course I was."

"Don't need space, Liv. In fact, there's too much of it now."

He lifted me, and my legs wrapped around his waist. He carried me to the bedroom and showed me exactly how little space he needed.

I wondered what he was like as a kid. His room didn't convey much personality. No little league trophies on the shelves or decathlon awards hanging on the walls. There were some photos pinned to a corkboard over the desk that was nestled into the corner of the room.

I wasn't sure if I was ready to see him in a photo again, so I sat on the edge of his bed and looked around, trying to see it all from his eyes.

I shifted to lying on his childhood bed and staring at the ceiling. One breath in, one breath out. Connie, the yoga instructor at Soul Sculpt back home, would be so proud of me. I was transported into a sea of calm I hadn't felt in a long time.

Did he do this when he was younger? Did he stare at this ceiling and count the faded glow-in-the-dark stars contrasted against the white paint?

I reached out with my left hand, closing one eye for precision, and traced one of the stars with my index finger.

When I couldn't hold my arm up anymore, I rolled onto my left side, facing his window. Did he keep the curtain open so he could see the stars while he fell asleep? I wish I asked him questions about his life here. I *should* have. I should have taken every scrap of history he'd given to me and committed it to memory.

Sometimes I felt like an intruder. Like I had barged into his life and taken what I wanted with no regard for anyone or anything else. I hadn't offered to visit Connor Bay in the six months we were married. I didn't ask him about his childhood or his friends.

My eyes flitted to the corkboard again. If I wanted to know him, I had to try. I had to take advantage of being in this town. He grew up here. His soul was embedded in Connor Bay.

I held my breath as I stood and moved toward the desk, preparing myself to see him again. Mostly, they were pictures of places without people in them. It didn't look like he took them. I didn't know how I knew that. He didn't take many pictures when we were together. He was a live-in-the-moment kind of guy. *Maybe they were places he wanted to visit.*

There was one picture of him. He looked like he might have been 9 or 10 in it. He wore a baseball uniform. His face was pointed at the camera, and he had his arm around the boy beside him. The other boy's face was occluded by his baseball cap, the bill drawn low over his face.

I unclipped it from the corkboard and flipped it over.

The inscription read that it was taken in June of '04, and the boy beside him was named Keating.

I tried to remember if I'd heard that name before—if he'd mentioned the boy in the cap in those six months, but nothing came.

This room didn't hold anything for me. Maybe it could have if we'd come here together. If we'd visited for Thanksgiving, and I wore a dress. If I carried a lukewarm green bean casserole from the car that he made before we left the city, and waited as he rang the doorbell. If he leaned over to me after dinner and asked if I wanted to see his room.

If he hurried me up the stairs, pressed me against his bedroom door, and kissed me.

Maybe if we'd been different, I'd want more than this one picture.

But we hadn't done those things. And there was no rewriting them now.

So I slipped the photo into my bag and left the McClearys' house no more whole than when I arrived.

4

HE WAS SUNSHINE

"Olivia, go on your lunch. It's pretty slow right now," Marjorie called from the window connecting the counter area to the kitchen. If this were my job in New York, I would have reminded her that it was always slow. That was why I was here in the first place.

"Sure. Be back in thirty," I replied as I finished wiping down the counter.

I'd taken to having my lunch in the grassy picnic area across from the diner. It had the perfect amount of shade from the maple trees, and the ground sloped, so it overlooked the mini-golf course at the base of the hill. I typically used this time to answer the growing amount of emails in my inbox, but I didn't have any desire to do that today. The emails could wait until the evening...or even tomorrow.

Last night, after I'd gotten home from the McClearys' and stared at the photo of the two boys for far longer than I should have, I decided to take advantage of being in his town. I wanted to love this town because he loved this town. He loved this town, and he loved me. I kept turning that over, trying to make it add up.

Or maybe he loved me because I was the antithesis of it all.

I was not Sunday strolls down Main Street, freshly baked pies, or reading by the fire. I was early-morning hot yoga, takeout containers, and pencils twisted in my hair, answering emails at 3 a.m. because I was on a deadline.

Maybe he loved me because he wanted to add a piece of sunshine to endless midnights.

Focus.

I forced my attention back to the mini-golf course, my eyes tracking the slow movement of people below. There was a couple down by the batting cages, and before I could stop it, I was there again.

The sound of the machine was a hum in the background. His arms were around me, and his hands gripped my own as he helped me get used to the position. His breath tickled my neck. I squealed when the machine let out a ball, and his body tensed against mine as we maneuvered to hit it together.

We missed, of course. I was too rigid. Too afraid of getting hit. The sound startled me every time.

"C'mon, Liv. It's okay. Just relax." His voice was patient and understanding.

I shook my head. "No, I don't want to."

"Okay. Take a break. Watch me for a while," he said, putting a finger under my chin and tilting my face towards his to kiss me.

I did watch him.

And I fell more in love with him.

His arms flexed under his long-sleeve shirt as he prepared to swing. He didn't shift around, not like me. He was sure of himself as the bat collided with the ball again and again. He made it look easy. After a while, he looked over his shoulder, a toothy smile just for me.

"Want to try again?"

I shook my head.

He nodded and winked before turning back toward the pitching machine. He reminded me later that was what it was called, over pizza and beer from the place attached to the cages. I asked him if he played much when he was younger.

"All through middle and high school." He told me he played with some friend of his.

"Like for fun?" I wrinkle my nose at him.

He laughed as he reached over to wipe something off my cheek with his thumb and said, "Yes, Olivia. For fun. Maybe you've heard of it." But I don't react because he doesn't remove his hand from my face.

His hand stayed where it was.

His thumb slid across my bottom lip, tugging it down slightly. My breath caught.

"You're so beautiful, Liv. It hurts sometimes."

I looked away because I understood exactly what he meant. Loving him had felt like standing too close to something bright.

His hand slid to the side of my neck. His wedding band was cool against my skin, pressing into my pulse. I was sure he could feel how fast it was racing.

My phone buzzed in my pocket, and I jumped. Eric. I declined the call.

I wasn't in the mood to talk about work or how many deadlines I'd missed since coming here. I was well aware I'd worked considerably less since coming to Connor Bay, only opting to address the most overdue tasks. The only reason I still had a job was likely because Eric had been holding down the fort back in New York.

It wasn't like me to avoid work or Eric. I often found a lot of validation in my work. I was good at what I did, and I loved doing it. Lately, it was starting to feel meaningless. *Who cared if my marketing campaigns helped make a multi-million dollar company an extra million a year when my husband was dead?*

"I saw that, Olivia Carrington. You can not just decline my call."

I whipped my body around so fast I was sure I pulled something.

If I thought I stood out in this town, Eric was a Broadway marquee. His suit was finely tailored, likely costing more than three months of my current rent.

"Don't look so happy to see me, Livie," he said. "Wouldn't want you to sprain something."

I stood abruptly. "What are you doing here?"

Eric looked me up and down but didn't say anything about my appearance. That was kind of him; I knew I'd seen better days. He, of course, looked immaculate. His brown hair styled and coifed atop his head. Clean-shaven. Nary a dark circle to be seen under his hazel eyes.

"Well, you haven't answered my calls in days, so naturally, I needed to confirm that you were alive...or something akin to that."

"Well, you saw me. You can go home now," I replied, sitting back down on the grass and unwrapping my sandwich.

Eric laughed. "Oh, Livie, I'm not going anywhere. I told Clark that I'd be working remotely with you in Connor Bay. He thought it was a great idea."

"Clark said that you had a great idea?" I asked skeptically, wiping my hands off on a napkin.

Clark never thought anyone's ideas were "great." They were "adequate" at best and "abysmal" at worst. I was sure those were the only two adjectives Clark knew.

Eric grimaced. "Well, he said I could, which is basically the same thing. We're a little behind on the Fiedler campaign, so we both agreed that you might need some extra in-person hands on deck. So here I am. Put me in coach."

Yeah, that made more sense. I was behind at work, and they'd sent Eric to get me back on track. Clark probably even made Eric think it was his idea. *Clever.*

Usually, the sight of my best friend after long periods away induced a wave of dopamine, but I couldn't find it in me to be happy about his arrival.

"I'm sure you've been working on the campaign, Eric; just keep doing what you're doing. I'll get back into it tonight after the diner shift."

And, of course, by "get back into it," I meant "start it" because I had no idea what we were even trying to help Fiedler market right now. A new set of luggage, maybe?

"Oh, I'm here to help with that, too," Eric said, running a hand through his hair. "I'm team Livie all the time. 24/7. Whatever you need, babe. Well maybe...16/7, I do require a full 8 hours."

At that, I laughed. "Eric, you can't work at a diner."

"Why not?" I just looked at him. "I have clothes other than suits, Olivia."

Did he? If he did, I'd never seen them. I shook my head at him. "Marjorie won't—"

He gave me a sympathetic look. "You leave Marj to me, okay? Parents love me."

And I'll be damned. When we returned to the diner, Eric and Marjorie hit it off. I guess she liked people who...weren't me. At least, that's what it seemed like from my end of things. Eric took to the diner gig easily. So easily that it inspired what he thought was a superb idea.

"Hey Marj, since you and I've got it handled here, why

don't we let Olivia call it a day? She's got a big campaign we're working on. She could use the extra time." Eric gave her one of his wine-and-dine smiles.

Marjorie smiled back at him. "That sounds like a great idea. We wouldn't want Olivia to fall behind, now would we? Go on now."

Rolling my eyes, I filled a to-go pitcher with her sun tea and headed out the door with a wave.

I should have been more excited that my best friend had come to stay here, especially now that he'd taken some of Marjorie's attention off of me. The problem with having only one friend was that they knew you on your best and worst days. My worst day and Eric were intricately connected in my memory.

Hospital lights overhead. A beeping from my left side that made my head pulsate. A fuzzy version of Eric to my right. I asked him something, and he shook his head slowly. My stomach bottomed out. His hands gripped mine. A scream from somewhere...someone...me. I had been screaming.

I squeezed my eyes tight, trying to make it stop. I couldn't go there right now. I knew it would come eventually. If not now, I would see it all again in my nightmares.

As I rounded the corner that would take me down Elm, I saw Donald on his swing with the paper.

"I bring sustenance," I called, unlatching his gate and inviting myself onto his porch. He placed his paper aside and gestured to the two glasses he'd brought out. "Have you been out here long? Sorry, I should have given you a time," I said as I filled the glasses.

"Not too long. I figured it'd be later in the day. Marjorie's probably working you hard."

I didn't feel like I had to pretend with Donald. Maybe that was crappy of me. He and his wife had kids. A whole history together. I was only married six months and had only known him less than a week before that. Despite that, it seemed like Donald didn't mind. Maybe he was glad he had someone to talk to now, too.

"We're both just hard workers, is all. We're growing on each other." I said, clinking my glass against his and taking a sip. *Her tea certainly is growing on me.*

"People don't grow on Marjorie. She either likes you or she doesn't," he said confidently.

I laughed. "Gee, thanks, Donald. That's real helpful. Got any other sunshiney tidbits in there for me?"

"They're probably underpaying you," he offered, taking a large drink of his tea.

I laughed again. "They're not paying me at all. Family is free labor."

His expression turned sad, but he smiled at me. "Does Marjorie know you think she's family?"

I'd called them family just now. *Have I done that before? Do I think of them like family?*

Part of me wanted to. I wanted to so badly I could feel it in my bones. I wanted somewhere, someone, anyone to belong to right now. Especially someone that *he* had belonged to—even if that someone was Marjorie.

"I suppose not," I said, taking my seat from yesterday.

Donald nodded. "Your parents are okay with this move from the city?"

"I'm not sure if my parents know I moved. We don't talk much. They work a lot overseas." Growing up, my parents traveled together constantly and with me, never. I had an endless supply of nannies and drivers to ensure I got to where I needed to go. I was often lonely but never alone—sort of like being in this town.

We were quiet after that. A companionable silence. I appreciated it. A silence that was interrupted suddenly.

"Olivia? Is that you?"

Apparently, if I wanted people to talk to me, I just needed to hang around Donald's house.

If you asked me if Levi McCleary could pick me out of a police lineup, I'd say the odds were 30/70 not in favor, but there he was. He stood in front of Donald's fence in a red plaid shirt over a gray T-shirt, dark blue jeans, and a blue ball cap.

"Levi! Hi. You know Donald Sanderson," I said, quickly getting up and wiping off my now sweaty palms on my jeans.

As much as it hurt for me to look at Marjorie, it hurt even more to look at her husband. He was a spitting image of what I'd expected *him* to look like in 20 years. He was at least a whole foot taller than me, just like his son. A light brown beard covered his jaw. There were wrinkles in the corners of his eyes because when *he* smiled, he did it with his whole face.

"How's it going, Don?" Levi nodded at him, coming up the walkway. The man on the porch gave a nod back. "Diner slow today?" I nodded, crossing my arms over my chest. It felt like protection.

I was broken, but I was sure that Marjorie and Levy McCleary were the only two people in this world who could find a way to break me some more.

"Did you stop by yesterday? Sorry I wasn't there to show you around," Levi apologized.

I shook my head. "No problem. Yeah, I...I took a picture off his corkboard. I hope that's okay." Levi nodded and took off his cap, rolling it between his palms. I shifted my weight to my back foot. "I saw that you hung up our wedding photo."

He stopped rolling his cap and nodded again. "It's a real nice photo of you two, Liv. Thanks for sending it."

Neither of us dared to look the other in the eye. I ignored

how my chest tightened at the sound of my nickname coming out of his mouth.

Maybe only one of the McClearys hated me as much as I thought. Though after that night at the bar, Levi probably had his own reasons to judge me. I didn't want to think about that right now.

"Well, I'm just gonna head on down to the diner. See if Marjorie needs anything," Levi said, bringing the cap back to his head and flexing his hands at his sides once it was on.

"Okay." I nodded before turning away from him to resituate myself on the porch. I fought the urge to down the entire glass of sun tea.

Levi's voice startled me once I'd sat down, expecting him to have already been gone. "On Sundays, we barbecue. Starts around 4. I think it'd be real nice if you came."

I looked up at him, but he had turned away, too. Levi McCleary was inviting me to a barbecue at his house. *Did I fall into an alternate universe?*

"Does Marjorie think that's a good idea?" I asked.

"Don't you worry about Marjorie, Liv. Leave her to me." Levi said, finally looking at me. He broke eye contact almost immediately. "You too, Don. 4 o'clock."

Levi didn't wait for a response before walking quickly down the path toward the diner.

"You ever been to a Sunday barbecue in a small town, Olivia?" Donald finally asked me. I shook my head, staring at the place Levi had stood. "It ain't for the faint of heart. That's for sure."

I licked my lips, preparing myself to say...anything. "So you won't be coming then?"

"Sweetheart, nothing can keep me away from a Sunday barbecue invitation." He paused briefly before continuing. "Then again, I won't be the one getting roasted."

I turned to him with a glare. "Thank you for that. I'm going to go home and never come back here."

He let out a hardy chuckle before standing up with his paper and the pitcher of tea. "See you tomorrow, Olivia."

"See you tomorrow, Donald."

5

____

SWEET TEA IN THE SUMMER

Before

I lay on his chest late at night, so late it was almost technically morning. His fingertips ran through my hair. My hair had gotten tangled earlier, so his fingers caught in the strands now and then.

"What do you miss about home?" I murmured against his skin. My voice sounded different in the dark. Softer. Like I was asking for a story.

He was quiet for a moment. I felt him breath in. "My mom's sun tea. She serves it in the diner. Some people come in just to buy a pitcher of it during the summer."

"What's sun tea?"

His throaty laugh made his chest vibrate against my cheek. "You don't know what sun tea is?"

I looked up at him and raised an eyebrow. "Am I supposed to?"

He lifted a shoulder. "It's tea that gets brewed in the sun. My mom has this secret ratio of tea to water to time in the sun that I think she'll take to her grave." I hummed in response. "Maybe we should go visit them soon."

I yawned. "Yeah, maybe."

I meant it the way you mean things when you believe you have all the time in the world.

6

OVERLOADED SERIAL STRESSER

onald's words did nothing to ease my nerves about this whole situation. I almost wished Levi hadn't invited me because now I had approximately three and a half days to prepare for this barbecue and for Marjorie.

Before I left, Donald had informed me that most hospitalizations in this town resulted from a Sunday barbecue rivaled only by the 4th of July barbecues and Thanksgiving dinner. I took that to mean that gathering people in the town and forcing them to interact was largely a death trap.

I paced around my bedroom, chewing on my thumbnail anxiously. *Why would Levi invite me anyway?* Since being here, we'd only interacted twice; both times had been brief and faltering.

Maybe they wanted me gone so badly that they were going to make my death look like a barbecue accident. And it would be something humiliating probably...like death by hot dog.

I picked up my phone to dial Eric, but he was already calling.

"What do you wear to your dead husband's parents' barbecue?" I blurted, resuming my pacing and nail-biting.

Eric barked a laugh. "Open your door."

"My closet door?" I asked, walking over to it and yanking it open, hoping he had pulled some rom-com makeover stunt and the perfect outfit would already be hanging in my closet.

"No, your *front* door, Olivia. *Honestly,* what is wrong with you?"

Honestly, a lot was wrong with me right now. Between Eric showing up, not sleeping, falling behind at work, and dealing with Marjorie, my dance card of problems was full.

I closed the closet door, actively ignoring the box in the back corner like it might bite, and hung up on him.

When I peered through the peephole, I saw a less-than-pleased Eric holding a bottle of wine and a takeout bag. I quickly unlocked the door.

"What took you so long?" I asked as if we had predetermined plans.

Eric rolled his eyes and brushed past me into my less-than-company-ready apartment. "I brought Italian. You look like you need to eat a carb. Or a thousand."

"You don't need to worry about me."

He gave me a look, the kind that said he absolutely did not believe me, and went into my kitchen. It was smaller than the one I'd had in New York, which was impressive in a bleak sort of way.

He used to joke that when we bought a house, the kitchen would have to be the biggest room in the whole place to make up for all the times he had to cook in our microscopic one.

I had no need for a large kitchen now.

Once the wine had been poured and we were sitting on the floor of my living room, because it was comfier than the futon that came with the apartment, Eric dove into the tumbleweed that was my life.

"First," he said, counting on his fingers, "Marjorie hates you. Second, we're behind on the Fiedler campaign. Third, you and your apartment look like crap." He glanced around like the walls might personally offend him. "Anything else I should be aware of?"

I twirled my fork into my pasta noodles. "That about covers it."

Eric and I tended to be curt with each other. We didn't glide past hard things. We dragged them into the light and dared them to survive.

It was probably the second reason I avoided him. Now that he was here, there was no turning a blind eye and waiting out the storm.

Eric DiCarlo was a storm-chaser.

"I missed you, you know," I said.

His frown deepened. His grip on his fork tightened.

"You suck, you know that Liv? You ghosted me for weeks. I have to come to this shithole town that doesn't even know how to pull a proper espresso shot to get you to talk to me." He stabbed a noodle like it had personally betrayed him. "It sucks. You suck."

He wasn't trying to be cruel. I could tell because his face wasn't tightening the way it did when he was angry at someone.

He was being honest. I was the one who hadn't been.

I nodded. "I do suck. I am the suckiest." I pointed my fork at myself like I was presenting evidence in court. "My only friends are you and a seventy-year-old man named Donald. If that doesn't scream 'suckiest,' I don't know what does."

Eric's mouth twitched. "I hate you."

"Hate you more."

For the first time since coming to Connor Bay, I laughed

during dinner in my apartment and didn't think about *him* once. Not his face. Not his hands. Not the way grief lived in my mouth like an aftertaste.

I met Eric when I started at the marketing firm right out of college. We were hired as interns together and worked our way up. Eric handled client relations. I covered finances. We both did marketing plans, scheduling, mock-ups. Somewhere along the way, we became best friends.

I knew I had done a shitty thing by temporarily pushing him out of my life, but I couldn't see him. It was too hard.

I couldn't even begin to think about how to explain that to him.

One key difference between the two of us was that Eric dealt with emotions as they happened and I was prone to bottling them up until I exploded.

I refused to let the guilt of avoiding him eat at me tonight. I'd just gotten him back.

"You know what I think, Livie?" Eric asked after dinner, scrolling through the selection of sofas listed on my laptop through Article's website with one hand and holding a mostly empty wine glass in the other.

One bottle of wine turned into two. Two turned into three. Somewhere between bottles two and three, he'd decided to help rectify his third problem.

Me and my apartment.

I placed an order for a new bed frame from West Elm on my phone. "What do you think, Eric?"

"I think we give this town the old DiCarlo-Carrington one-two punch."

I gave him an amused look before returning to my phone to search for a coffee table that wouldn't need to be stabilized with a piece of cardboard under one leg.

"I just mean," he said, softer now, "you're going to be here a while. Which means I'm going to be here a while. You can't hide away, Olivia." He leaned back, eyes half-lidded from wine and sincerity. "You're meant to shine. Even here. In this very dull town where everything closes at 6 p.m."

He clicked his tongue and finished his wine.

I didn't want to remind him that he was the one who shined, not me. That I was the workhorse behind his charisma.

But my heart was warm for the first time in months, and I didn't want to argue with him. Not right now.

"What did you have in mind, Eric DiCarlo? I draw the line at tractor parades."

If Eric wanted to help me figure out how to fit in here until I came to my senses and moved back to New York, then I would let him. I was wrong to come here alone; I think he knew it before I left.

An "I told you so" was bound to be on its way.

"Well, for starters," he said, "maybe you could try bringing something to the barbecue on Sunday. Three days and change should be enough time for you to learn to make something at least partially edible."

I laughed. "It will have to be edible, or Marjorie will tell the town I've tried to kill her in her own backyard."

Eric gave me a pitying look, putting a hand on my shoulder. "Sweetheart, Marjorie would never eat anything you brought. You'll be fine."

"Oh fuck off, DiCarlo." I laughed. "How's Leo? You two doing okay?"

His jaw ticked.

Ah.

There is was.

"Well," he said carefully, "look at us. A newly single bachelor and a widow in a town with only five hundred other people and no good espresso." He held up his wine glass like he was making a toast to bad life decisions. "Is this what *Will & Grace* was about?"

I poured the rest of the third bottle into our two glasses.

"Livie," he said, looking at me like I was the world's most exhausting charity case, "you're no Debra Messing." He tilted his head. "But I do know one thing for certain."

I raised a brow.

"We're going to burn this couch as soon as the new one comes. Also, I'm sleeping with you tonight. My chiropractor will kill me if he finds out I slept on this thing."

I snorted but didn't protest.

Maybe Eric's snores would drown out the cicadas, and I could finally rest.

7

LOOK AT YOUR FACE

I sat on Donald's porch again the next day, leafing through his wife's cookbooks.

"Sonya," he told me, "was the best cook I'd ever known."

Who was I to argue with him when he placed three of the books beside me after I relayed Eric's plan. To his credit, he didn't think it was a bad idea, but then again, he'd never had my cooking.

Eric was covering for me at the diner, which was probably for the best. I was having a good day. Despite my cover-hogging best friend, I did manage to sleep through the night.

All the way through. No waking up gasping. No clock-checking. No staring into the dark like it might open its mouth and say his name.

When I woke up, Eric had just returned with coffee and scones from *The Bean*. Sidney must not have known that Eric was in an alliance with me because he was over the moon about the *Newcomer's Special*. I didn't have the heart to tell him it would all end once he was seen with me.

I sighed and closed the book in my hands, resting my head on it.

It was useless. There was absolutely nothing I could make that would win them over. Couldn't Eric have suggested a marketing campaign for the diner? A new town budget? Anything I was *actually* good at.

I highly doubted any kind of dish would win over Marjorie anyway. It was more likely that my leaving Connor Bay would be the best thing for our relationship, but I'd come here to help the diner. And I wasn't leaving until I did.

"Seems like he did all the cooking?" Donald said from his spot on the swing.

I let out another deep sigh. "What gave it away?"

He laughed. "He was a good cook. I'll give him that much." His voice softened as he stared out at his yard, like he could see the past sitting in the grass. "Always in trouble. Could sweet-talk his way into and out of anything with a plate of sweets or a dinner invitation. He was good in the diner."

I smiled. These bits about him didn't hurt to hear. Maybe it was because, despite the barbecue situation, it felt like a good day. My first good day since coming here.

And maybe that meant it was a good day to ask.

I rifled through my bag for the photo.

"I found this in his room," I said, standing and passing it to Donald. "It was the only one with someone else in it. Do you recognize the name?"

Donald adjusted his glasses. His mouth twitched like the answer amused him.

"Well, now. That would be your husband and Keating."

He passed it back, and I studied the picture again, as if it might reveal itself differently this time.

"I'm not sure," I admitted. "I can't remember him mentioning Keating at all."

Donald chuckled. "Ah. Well, he wouldn't use that name. That's probably why you're confused. Your husband called him Whit. Keating Whitaker."

My throat went dry.

Whit.

Whit and I used to play ball together.

Whit's coming into town next week. Do you think you'll be able to go to dinner?

Look at what Whit just sent me.

Whit. Never Keating.

You're supposed to know your husband's best friend's name.

"They've been best friends since the Whitakers moved to Connor Bay," Donald continued. "Good kid. Just finished medical residency in Baltimore."

I swallowed hard.

"His parents moved him here when he was around seven or eight. The McClearys and the Whitakers were thick as thieves." Donald nodded like he was reciting town scripture. "Once Keating went to college and his younger sister, Daisy, moved to the West Coast after finishing school, their parents moved to North Carolina." He lifted his brows at me. "He's Keating to most everyone here."

It was like he knew I'd already begun tearing myself apart. Like he could see the thread of guilt winding tight around my ribs.

"No reason for your husband to have called him that," Donald added gently.

"They grew up together," he went on. "Good boys, those two. Well, McCleary had a mouth on him, but Keating kept him grounded." He glanced at me. "You talk to him much since...?"

I shook my head. "I don't... I don't talk about him much. I don't talk to people much right now, period."

Donald nodded once. No pity. Just understanding.

"Well," he said, "if anyone can tell you about your husband's life in Connor Bay, it's Keating Whitaker."

My good day collapsed in on itself.

I could feel the guilt rising, thick as bile, clogging my throat. Donald must have noticed the shift because he cleared his throat and said, "Why don't you just buy something for the barbecue instead? Something you can assemble."

Relief loosened my shoulders. "Maybe that's a good idea. Assembling is much more my speed."

AFTER TALKING TO DONALD, I ended up going to the diner to check in on Eric. He seemed surprisingly right at home behind the counter, chatting with Marjorie in a dress shirt and slacks—an improvement over yesterday's suit. However, I had a feeling they were newly purchased, and he did not have them in his closet prior to the move.

"Hey, Liv! How's Don doing?" Eric asked when I walked in.

"Pretty good," I replied, dropping my bag behind the counter. "Where do you need me?"

I tied my apron around my waist and slipped a pen and pad into the front pocket. Marjorie had already retreated to the back to begin ignoring my existence, so I waited for Eric to give me instructions.

He frowned at the still swinging door to the kitchen. "I thought I made some progress on this situation."

I laughed. "Don't be disappointed, I always think that. The barbecue is progress, though."

Eric's gaze darted back to mine. "Right. How's the planning going?"

I turned away from him, grabbing the sanitizing spray and a fresh rag. "Don and I think a nice fruit platter would be the best option."

"Olivia Carrington," Eric scolded me, "you can't show up to your in-laws' barbecue with a fruit platter."

I snorted, picking up a napkin dispenser on the corner table by the windows to wipe underneath it. "Well, a *charcuterie* platter hardly seemed like the Connor Bay vibe, Eric."

He slid into the booth against the wall for no other reason than to ensure I could see him glare at me.

"Olivia. Be serious. Just try to make something. I'm not asking for a holiday dinner here."

I sat across from him. "Eric, I can hardly heat soup without causing some sort of disaster. Assembling something is my best option."

He rolled his eyes, then his attention snagged on something outside the window. A slow smile appeared.

"Well," he said, voice dropping, "aren't you just a tall drink of water? Who is that, Livie?"

I turned.

And my heart stopped.

A baseball cap and a black T-shirt. It was nothing special, but how his shoulders filled out the shirt and the Red Sox logo on the back of the cap.

I blinked.

I'd lost it. I was seeing a ghost. My husband was dead, and this was an imposter sent from the depths of hell to torture me.

At least, I thought so until he shifted away from the blonde woman he was talking to, and I could breathe again...*kind of.*

He was certainly not my husband back from beyond the grave, but *god* was he beautiful.

I didn't think I'd ever thought that about anyone the first time I saw them. Not even *him*. My husband was beautiful. But not like this. Not stop and stare beautiful.

The man outside looked sculpted, angular, like someone had carved him out of stone and then made him walk around in a T-shirt like that was a reasonable thing to do to the general public.

Dark stubble shadowed his jaw and curved around his mouth, and my brain short-circuited at the sight of it.

He must have sensed us staring because he started to turn toward the window.

Eric and I jumped back and pivoted our bodies toward the counter so fast I nearly knocked my spray bottle over.

After a silent count to ten, I glanced at Eric.

He was trying very hard not to laugh.

I let out a breath. "No idea who that was."

Eric smiled, his eyes twinkling with amusement, "But you'd like to find out, I bet."

I felt my cheeks heat, and I cleared my throat. "So, fruit platter."

At this, he finally laughed. "Better be the best damn fruit platter this town has ever seen, Livie. Get back to work."

I gave him a lazy salute and worked my way down the tables, trying to get the picture of that man's mouth out of my head.

After my fourth table, I froze.

Oh god.

Was I supposed to feel that way about someone?

He'd only been gone three months. Was it normal to be attracted to someone like that?

I tried to remember if I'd felt that way about other men

when he was alive. If I'd ogled them like the way I just had. I couldn't remember. I couldn't remember so much as talking to a man who wasn't my husband or a coworker.

My chest panged again, and I rubbed at it as I began clearing the next table.

Was I feeling guilty for finding that man outside attractive or because, for just a moment, I forgot about my husband?

For just a single moment, I had forgotten why I was in Connor Bay and who owned this diner. I knew *he* wouldn't fault me for finding someone else attractive, but forgetting him, even for a second, felt like a betrayal.

It wouldn't happen again.

8

SLIGHT MALFUNCTION

Eric was right, of course, about more than I'd like to admit. We were way behind at work. He'd been keeping us afloat, keeping *me* afloat, by doing some of my job for me while I was here.

It was time to get back to reality, which felt easier said than done in this small town where I was balancing two lives. I knew it wasn't sustainable, but I had to keep trying.

In New York, I was a multitasker. I was the expert on doing too many things at once, and Eric was the pretty face that convinced the client my madness was genius. I created the campaigns, and he sold them. I was the half-mad Michelin star chef, and he plated my eccentricities and turned them into something exquisite.

We were a good team, and I was letting him down.

For three days, I'd thrown myself into work. Work-work, not diner-work. That was still a problem I needed to figure out, but if the barbecue later today went well, maybe it would be easier to talk to Levi and Marjorie about their situation.

Eric and I were finally back on schedule for the Fiedler

campaign, so on my way to the grocery store for much-needed essentials and the fruit for Connor Bay's most elaborate spread, I called Clark's assistant, Kelly, and brought her up to speed on the campaign's progress.

Kelly, bless her heart, was not the sharpest person I'd ever worked with, so what was supposed to be a brief update turned into a twenty-five minute phone call that had me wandering aimlessly through the store.

Naturally, I'd found myself in this one.

"Right," I said, adding a bottle of red wine to my basket. "The Winter campaign needs to launch in October."

I looked between my cart and the shelf, angled the phone between my ear and shoulder, and grabbed two more bottles.

"I know it's the *Winter* campaign, Kelly, but for people to buy the things from the Winter campaign for the Winter, we need to advertise *before* the Winter." I stared at the label like it might save me.

Maybe one more.

My fingers had only just gripped the neck of another bottle when I saw him again.

I jerked at the sound of a crash against the floor. For a beat, my brain couldn't process it. Sound first. Then scent.

A sharp, sour-sweet bloom of red wine.

It was only when the man in the cap turned around with wide eyes that I realized three things.

The first was that the man from outside the dinner was not just passing through.

Second, I was sure I had never stopped and stared at a stranger like this.

Third, likely related to the first, was that I had caused the crash, and the floor was covered in a 2021 red blend.

"Shit. Kelly, I have to go," I said quickly, hanging up before she could ask me another question about seasonal ad copy.

I shoved my phone into my bag and looked down at the mess, then up at him, then down again. My face burned. My stomach rolled.

"You okay?" The man in the cap asked, walking down the aisle toward me.

"Depends on who you ask." I crouched instinctively, as if I could scoop wine back into the bottle with my bare hands. "I should clean this up."

How do I clean this up?

My heart beat too fast. I wasn't sure if it was his presence or the humiliation, but either way, it was starting to feel like a medical event.

I didn't think I asked about cleaning up the mess aloud until he responded.

"I think they'll come to do it for you, but you might be out a few dollars. You break it, you buy it, and all that." I let out a stark laugh and looked at him, but his gaze was poised on my basket. "You planning a party?"

"A party?" I repeated.

His gaze met mine again, and I almost faltered. His green eyes were cloudy in a way that could only be described as concerned amusement.

The other day had not been a fluke. This man was undeniably gorgeous. Between the wine spill and the way my pulse had apparently decided to audition for a marathon, I couldn't bring myself to feel guilty for noticing him.

"Three bottles of wine," he said. "A box of Nerds. And a party-size bag of Cool Ranch Doritos." He nodded toward the basket as if it were evidence in a trial. "That screams party."

I looked down.

I was only sixty percent certain I put the box of Nerds in there, but indeed, the other items did allude to some kind of gathering. I found myself nodding.

"Uh...sort of. I'm supposed to go to a barbecue and..."

And what, Olivia? And what?!

Say something, or he's going to have you committed.

He grinned. "And you're going to bring a bag of Cool Ranch Doritos?"

God, what a *good* grin it was.

The things he could get away with when it happened were probably considered acts of terrorism in some countries.

"Stop saying it like that."

His dark brows pinched together in confusion, but the grin stayed firmly on his face. "Like what?"

"*Cool Ranch Doritos.*"

He frowned and fuck me if it didn't make his lower lip jut out ever so slightly.

"How am I saying it?"

"Like it's derogatory."

"Well," he said gravely, "it's insulting to assume all of the guests will like *Cool Ranch Doritos. And* it's especially insulting to assume they like them so much you need a *party* size of them."

I crossed my arms and frowned at him. If I focused on how rude he was towards my snack preference, I could stop thinking about how beautiful he was.

"I didn't realize you had a copy of the guest list."

He opened his mouth to say something, but a grocery store worker with a mop entered the aisle.

"Hey, Keating! Didn't know you were in town already."

It felt like someone dumped cold water over my head.

The aisle blurred at the edges. Sound dropped out, leaving only one word, beating like a pulse in my skull.

Keating.

Hey, Keating.

Keating, as in my husband's best friend. My dead

husband's lifelong best friend was the man I ogled in the diner with Eric three days ago.

And then again just now.

I went completely still.

My mouth filled with saliva, sudden and sickening.

I was going to throw up.

9
____

A LONG TIME COMING
WHIT

You're not supposed to look directly into the sun, but I couldn't help staring at Olivia.

She was here. Here in Connor Bay. Here in this grocery store aisle. Here in front of me.

Alive. Breathing. Real.

Well, physically, she was here, but I knew the second Braiden said my name, I'd lost her in every other way. No conversations from now on would be easy. They'd be guarded. *He* would hang in the background of all of them.

I'd never be *just* Whit, and she'd never be *just* Olivia. Not that she'd ever been *just* anything.

"Yeah," I said. "Just got in. Ran into Olivia."

It was like she couldn't decide if she was in fight or flight. Her hands kept lifting from the bar on her shopping cart like a steering wheel that was too hot to hold onto right away.

She looked much better than when I'd last seen her. Today, she wore her long, coppery red hair down and curled around her shoulders. Her blue eyes were icy and bright against her skin.

I refused to let my eyes drop past her chin because the sundress she was wearing was criminal. If I looked again, it would be impossible to pry my eyes away. Her sunglasses rested lazily at the top of her head, and I knew she'd just thrown them off her face when she walked into the store. Freckles dotted across her nose so profoundly I had to actively ignore the urge to count every last one of them.

"Olivia?" Braiden asked.

I glanced down and raised an eyebrow at him. Surely Olivia had been here long enough for people to know who she was. Her name, at the very least.

Braiden looked at her like he hadn't realized she'd been standing there. How could anyone *not* notice her?

"Oh, Da—"

Like she sensed his name about to be uttered, Olivia blurted, "I have to go." Her hands finally decided to rest on her cart. "Barbecue and all that. Lots to do."

"Olivia, wait." I began to move toward her, but I wasn't sure what I'd say even if she did wait.

She looked at me, but her gaze was detached. Dissociation from what was happening if I'd ever seen it.

Then she did the most peculiar thing.

"You should come," she said quickly. "To the barbecue. It's today at four. At the McClearys' place." Her words stumbled over each other like they were trying to outrun her panic. "You're probably not free. No pressure. But if you're free. Come whenever. If you come too late, I might be out of the chips. Bye."

I blinked at her retreating back.

"What was that about?" Braiden asked.

I shook my head, looking away only when she turned the corner. "Nothing. I'll see you around. Sorry about the mess."

"Whit, oh my god."

Daisy's voice pulled me away from Braiden and back to where Olivia had just vanished.

My sister hurried down the aisle in a way that was intended to not draw attention, but her bracelets clinking together on her arm really weren't doing her any favors.

"I think I just saw her. I think I saw *Olivia.*" She whisper-shouted, dropping the pack of hotdogs Marjorie asked me to pick up for the barbecue into the basket she was carrying.

The same barbecue that Olivia had just invited me to, it seemed.

"I just ran into her," I said, walking around Daisy to get out of this too-small aisle, in this too-small store, in this too-small town.

Why was it suddenly so warm? Why wasn't the AC on? It was the middle of June.

"You did? What did she say? What was she like?" Daisy peppered the questions too quickly for me to field them one at a time. "Did she look okay? Is she going to the barbecue?"

I ground my teeth together as I loaded the conveyor belt with our items. "Yes, Daisy, she'll be at the barbecue."

Unless she decides to run. Unless she sees me there and decides it is too much.

But she had invited me.

"She's going to need patience," I added, quieter now. "She doesn't know us. Don't spook her."

Daisy clicked her tongue at me. "She's not a horse, Whit. People like me. And what do you mean, 'she doesn't know us'? She's had to have seen pictures of us. We can't be total strangers...right?"

"Just," I sighed, "go easy on her. She looked like she'd seen a ghost when we were talking. It might be hard to be around so many people."

Daisy rolled her eyes. "She's from *New York,* Keating. If

she dislikes being around people, she sure picked a strange place to live."

Daisy was stubborn. Nothing would stop her from trying to attach herself to Olivia.

I was grateful that Daisy had missed the funeral back in March because Olivia kept to herself the whole time. The only person she talked to was the person she came with...Eric, I think Levi said his name was—a friend from work.

I told myself I didn't approach her because she probably needed space, but I knew that was a lie. The worst kind of lie because it was covering up a much bigger problem.

A problem I had long before my best friend died.

The mere existence of Olivia Carrington enthralled me so much that I couldn't bear to be around her, let alone talk to her.

I had a thing...a crush...a fascination with my best friend's wife, and now he was gone.

It was a secret so horrible that I couldn't help but think his death was somehow my fault.

Because what kind of man looks at his best friend's wife like that? Even once. Even accidentally.

10

CAN WE JUST GET A PAUSE

OLIVIA

I called Eric after I'd abandoned my shopping cart in the middle of an aisle to tell him that he needed to pick up the things for the barbecue. I hung up before he tried to fight me on it. He wouldn't be at the apartment when I got home, and that was the best gift I could have received right now.

I needed to calm down. I needed to think.

He would forgive me for finding his best friend attractive. I shouldn't punish myself for that. It was normal.

In, one, two, three.

Out, one, two, three.

I turned my key in the ignition. He'd probably think it was hilarious, honestly.

In, one, two, three.

Out, one, two, three.

What he wouldn't think was hilarious was bolting out of there. He would have expected me to talk to his best friend. To ask him how he was doing. To think about someone other than myself.

In, one, two, three.

Out, one, two, three.

I needed to apologize to him, and I had to do it before the barbecue. Otherwise, I was sure there was a special place in hell for people who ruined Marjorie's barbecues with their personal problems.

I could get Whit's number from *his* phone. The one that's sitting in the box in my closet. The box I'd been avoiding but couldn't seem to leave behind in New York.

In, one, two, three.

Out, one, two, three.

I parked my car on the street with no recollection of the drive back and ran up the stairs to the duplex that didn't feel like home, shoving my key into the lock. My hands shook as I turned it.

I dropped my bag on the floor and tossed my keys on the counter. I didn't bother locking the door behind me. On autopilot, my legs carried me to the bedroom.

The pounding in my head only worsened.

Pulling open the closet door, I dropped to my knees.

The box on the floor of my closet had remained untouched in the time I'd been in Connor Bay, but I spared no second thought ripping off the tape that held it shut.

The first thing my fingers touched was a flannel shirt that somehow found its way around my shoulders. Holding the collar against my nose, I breathed in a stale version of him.

An old version of the scent that had been so overpowering in our New York apartment that I needed to stay in a hotel for a week after the funeral.

His phone was the next thing in the box.

I closed my eyes and pressed the power button. Part of me hoped it needed to be charged, but it vibrated in my hand.

No such luck.

I kept my eyes closed.

It continued to vibrate. Chimes and alerts. They kept coming.

In, one, two, three.

Out, one, two, three.

When I was sure it was done, I moved from the closet to my bedroom floor.

Leaning against the bed, I stared at the lock screen.

The one that alerted me to his voicemail box being full and dozens of unread text messages. The notifications covered a photo of us, but I knew what I'd see if I cleared them. Me, flushed from the cold. His lips pressed against my cheek. Snow speckled the lens. *Christmas.*

He hadn't come home.

Now that his phone was in front of me, I wasn't sure I could do it. I wasn't sure that I could call Whit.

What would I even say?

Sorry for freaking out when I heard your name.

Sorry, you caught me off guard because I was too busy staring at your mouth.

I didn't know. I didn't know. It's a mental plea, but I'm not sure who it's for.

I tapped the phone icon and froze.

At least a dozen missed calls from Whit, but not from *before.*

They're recent over the last two months. I tapped the voice-mails tab.

Whit's name covered the screen. One after the other. Sometimes weeks or days apart. Sometimes hours.

I pressed my fingers to my mouth as my thumb hovered over the very first voicemail after the accident.

I held my breath as I pressed play.

> *Davis. Hi.*

There was a pause in Whit's message.

My body tensed as it prepared for the pain of hearing *his* name to seep throughout my body. I hadn't heard it in a long time.

I'd read it. I'd written in on paperwork. I hadn't said it.

Not here.

"Davis," I whispered in the solace and silence of this bedroom in a small town that didn't want me, against a bed that wasn't ours.

I had said it.

11

____

I'M NEW YORK CITY
OLIVIA

Before

"**H**i!" He shouted over the noise. "I'm Davis."

"You're *famous?*" I shouted back, narrowing my eyes at him.

The man didn't look familiar to me. Maybe he was some *B*-list actor? The statement didn't throw me; New York was filled with social climbers. I saw more than I heard him let out a laugh.

"Davis," he repeated.

I nodded in clarity. "Ah. *Davis.* Like the school."

Like the school? This was probably why I did not go to bars like this. I could not make small talk to save my life. I was used to bars where the main activity was dancing or drinking in between dancing. It left no time for chatter.

Like the school? I wanted to smack myself.

He leaned in closer, so close that I could smell his cologne. The bergamot hit my nose, and I wanted to bury my face into his collar. He smelled expensive. Like confidence. Like trouble.

"Say that again."

"Like the school."

His grin was crooked. "No. My name. Say it again." I laughed. A real head-tilted-back laugh. "Nevermind. Do *that* again."

I noticed him then. *Really* noticed him. His dark blonde hair and blue eyes. The chiseled nose and single dimple on his left cheek. The single dimple on his left cheek. The way he held my gaze like it was the easiest thing in the world.

"Are you meeting someone, or can I sit here?" He asked, already pulling out the chair before I could answer.

I smiled. "Just a friend, but he's late."

I didn't do this. Not usually. Maybe it was the two Vodka sodas I'd already consumed or how he laughed, but I wanted him to stay.

He ordered another round of drinks and then another. I couldn't remember the last time I'd laughed so hard. My cheeks started to ache from smiling.

My phone buzzed on the bar. *Eric.*

In my haze, I did recall that I was supposed to be mad at him. He was the one who convinced me to meet him for drinks to celebrate a perfectly executed ad campaign.

"One sec," I told Davis as I answered the call, covering my other ear with my hand to hear Eric better. "Oh, hello, Eric DiCarlo. Did you get lost on the way to the bar?"

Eric laughed. "How mad are you?"

I glanced at Davis, who was already looking at me like he'd devour me right here on the bar top.

I smiled wider. "Furious."

"You sound like it," Eric said. "Perhaps you can take your anger out on whoever is sitting in front of you. He looks like he'd be okay with it." I didn't turn to search for Eric in the bar; I didn't want to look away from *him*. I didn't think I could. "Should I interrupt or go home?"

"See you in the office, DiCarlo," I said before ending the call and dropping my phone in my bag.

Davis's smile widened, too. "Emergency at work?"

"Not at all."

His smile was almost predatory as he finished the last of his drink before leaning close to me. "I don't do this often."

I knew whatever he was about to say was a lie, but I could pretend it wasn't. I could pretend for him. For tonight.

"Do you want to get out of here?"

I wet my lips and looked over his shoulder at one of the neon signs with a beer name illuminated. How long did I have to pretend like I was considering rejecting his invitation?

I let out a breathy laugh when I realized something.

"You don't even know my name. You don't think that's a problem?"

For some reason, I didn't, but it bought me time to think about this.

The more I looked at him, the slower my thoughts became. The rational part of me tried to dig its way out of the Davis-induced haze I was experiencing, which was surely made up of one-third vodka soda and two-thirds blue eyes.

I *never* hooked up with guys I met at a bar. That was Eric's thing. I dated friends of friends or people I met at work functions. I didn't—

"Oh, I think it's a huge problem," Davis replied, "but not for the reasons you think." His eyes dipped briefly to my mouth. Like he couldn't help himself. "But if you told me your name, it wouldn't be a problem anymore, darlin'."

I looked him over again before finishing my drink.

Standing, I stepped toward him so I stood between his legs.

His blue eyes sparked as they tracked me. My hand snaked around to the back of his neck, and I pulled his mouth to mine.

Davis didn't hesitate. His hands gripped my waist and pulled me closer to him. My body nestled against his as we made out in some bar called Ethyl's on Second Avenue.

When I dared break apart from him, his breathing was ragged.

"Olivia," I said.

He gave me another crooked grin. "Olivia."

12

TALKING TO YOUR MEMORY
OLIVIA

I tried it again. "Davis."

The edges of my body only prickled in pain. It was not at all the scorching inferno I had expected to spread across my skin. It was quieter than that. Worse in a different way.

I held my breath again when Whit continued.

> *Or maybe Liv's listening to this. God, I hope not.*

I used this pause to inhale an unsteady breath.

> *I don't even know why I'm calling. You're not going to answer. Maybe I thought Liv would, and we could talk. I don't know. Does she have anyone to talk to Davis? Did you leave her alone when you...*

He let out a shaky sigh.

Well, if you're listening, Liv. Give me a call.

I struggled to think *his* name, but it didn't hurt so much now that I had said it out loud. I only had to lightly press against my chest to soothe it.

He had probably mentioned Whit a dozen times, but I couldn't remember anything specific about him. He'd come to town once, and Davis went to dinner with him when I had to work late.

He called me Liv on the voicemail. That meant *he* talked to Whit about me.

Of course he did, you are his wife.

You were *his wife.*

I never knew what tense to use.

My favorite and my least favorite game to play was *What If.*

What if I had listened to this message three months ago? Would I have called him? What if I'd gone to dinner with them? What if—

Before I could think about it anymore, I clicked another message mindlessly.

Whit's voice was heavier than the last time. It felt confessional. The kind of breathy speech that reverberated in still and silent rooms shrouded in darkness. Secrets you couldn't bring yourself to whisper anywhere but the comfort of your empty bedroom.

> *Davis, I never told you this. And I don't think*
> *I'd ever be brave enough to say it to your*
> *face...*

I paused the message there.

Whatever Whit was about to say was not for me. It wasn't even for my husband.

It was for him.

I may not have been thinking straight, but my head was clear enough to know that listening to that message, whatever it was, would be crossing a line I couldn't come back from.

I clicked another message instead. One closer in time to the first message.

> *I don't think Liv's checking your messages.*
> *Maybe it's too hard for her to go through*
> *your stuff. Maybe she respects your privacy.*
> *Who knows? Anyway, I'm just calling*
> *because I'm going to a Red Sox game tomor-*
> *row, and I was thinking about when I*
> *pitched you that curve ball in middle school*
> *and gave you a black eye.*

Whit laughed so deeply that it felt like the speaker on the phone vibrated in response.

> *I still don't think it was fair that you had to give*
> *me one in return.*

I laughed at that. Davis had been an eye-for-an-eye sort of man. Figuratively, and apparently, literally.

> *Of course, that was nothing compared to wiping*
> *out wakeboarding and slicing my chin on*
> *that rock. I still have that scar, you know?*
> *What am I saying? You just saw me last*
> *month... Thinking about growing out this*
> *beard. It would hide it for sure.*

He'd certainly done an excellent job of growing out that beard.

My thumb hovered over the following message.

Should I be listening to these?

I didn't even know Whit. There were so many voicemails. The durations and amount of time that separated the messages were inconsistent—days between some that lasted seconds, weeks between the longer ones.

I shook my head and locked the phone.

I couldn't bring myself to listen to another one. Not when he might show up at this barbecue I haphazardly invited him to.

Even if I did give myself a boundary, I didn't have a good reason to listen to them. Not really. Other than for the possibility that Whit could have said something about Davis I didn't know.

I turned off the phone and placed it back in the box. Davis's shirt went in next.

Saying his name was like unlocking Pandora's box. I couldn't stop thinking about it now that I'd done it. Couldn't *not* say it.

Once Davis's box was back in the closet, I leaned my forehead against the doorframe and took a steadying breath.

Between mentally preparing myself for seeing Marjorie outside the diner, meeting Whit, and hearing his voicemails, I was exhausted when Eric returned.

13

JUST BREATHE, JUST RELAX, IT'LL BE OKAY

OLIVIA

Eric turned to me on the porch, brows raised. "Ready?"

I gave him a tight smile. "Remember when Clark told us we'd be out of a job if we didn't land that handbag campaign with Chloé?"

He let out a laugh.

"I feel like that," I continued, "but maybe ten percent worse."

Eric lifted his chin. "There's a bush over there in case you want to reenact what happened before that presentation."

I tightened my grip on the platter that held Eric's professionally carved fruit slices. "Marjorie would murder me if she found out I threw up in her azaleas."

I needed to get a grip.

We'd go in, exchange pleasantries, sit for dinner, and then Eric would explain that he wasn't feeling well—after insisting that my fruit platter was likely to blame for it and not Marjorie's exceptionally delicious food. Then we'd leave.

I could do that.

After another minute of staring at the screen door, I nodded slightly, and Eric raised his fist to knock.

"Olivia?"

Eric turned to see who it was before I did. I didn't recognize their voice, so whoever it was knew me, but I didn't know them. Not that big of a surprise in this town.

I let out a breath in an attempt to compose myself before turning.

I was right.

I didn't know the blonde woman who called my name, but I'd know Keating Whitaker anywhere now. His face was tattooed permanently on my brain, and the sound of his voice played on a loop in my head.

I could feel Eric's gaze burn into the side of my face. I hadn't told him about Whit or the voicemails. I wasn't sure how to even begin that conversation.

Thanks for picking up the fruit. I had a breakdown over the fact I drooled over Davis's best friend. Then, when I got home, I listened to some voicemails he left him detailing his most intimate thoughts about Davis's death.

Yeah, that wasn't going to go over well.

"Whit," I said, voice thinner than I meant it to be. "You came."

Whit gave me a slow smile as they joined us on the porch. He changed his clothes since the grocery store. Tan shorts and a well-fitted white T-shirt. The cap remained, though it had been turned backward.

"If I'm being honest, Liv, I was already invited." He gestured to the plastic bag with the store's logo on it.

My nickname on his lips was *almost* enough to distract me from the horror of inviting this man to a barbecue he had more of a right to be at than I did.

I was the one who didn't fit here.

I nodded and looked at the woman beside him. She looked ready to jump into action, constantly bobbing from one foot to the other. Her blonde hair was chopped into a shaggy bob, and her bright green eyes and pouty pink lips made me consider the possibility that she may have been half-fairy.

I'd never described anyone as ethereal, but she fit the word well.

"I don't think we've met," I said. "Olivia Carrington." I readjusted my grip on the platter and held my hand out to her.

She glanced at it, her brows raised in confusion—disgust even—before she launched herself at me.

I stiffened, prepared for an assault, but her delicate arms wrapped around my shoulders. I braced myself and the food I held.

"Daisy Whitaker," she said brightly, no end to the hug in sight. "So good to finally meet you."

I glanced at Whit, who just shook his head at his... My eyes drifted down his body, but his left hand was in the pocket of his shorts.

"I'm sorry I wasn't at the funeral," Daisy continued. "I was traveling, and I... She pulled back slightly, then waved a hand as if she could physically erase the sentence. "Well, it doesn't matter."

"Daze," Whit interrupted, "I think you should probably let her go now."

Daisy released me immediately.

"Right. Sorry. I'm a hugger," she said, holding me at arm's length as she looked me over. "Beautiful. Davis knew what he was doing."

Eric laughed, and that got her attention. It gave me a moment for my heart to restart from hearing Davis's name in real life, in sunlight, in someone else's mouth.

"Daisy, Whit," I said, gesturing, "this is Eric DiCarlo." Eric held his hand out to Whit. "Eric's keeping me company while I'm in Connor Bay."

Daisy hooked our arms together as she turned to open the screen door—Eric all but forgotten. "Where are you staying, Olivia?"

She looked at me like I hung the moon, but I was sure she did that with everyone she talked to. She seemed like one of *those* girls. The nice ones with lots of friends that didn't make sense as a group unless she was at the center.

"Uh. A one-bed off Elm," I said, trying not to look too hard at the pictures on the walls of the McCleary household.

Daisy wrinkled her nose. "Nando's probably ripping you off. That man was born to be a con artist. Landlord is a close second, I suppose." She nodded decisively. "Whit will talk to him."

She added that last bit as we crossed the threshold into the McClearys' front door.

"Sure thing," Whit said quickly.

I didn't know if I should protest. Nando was most definitely ripping me off, but what New Yorker wasn't used to being ripped off? Plus, I made decent money and had an inheritance from my grandparents, so I wasn't exactly strapped for cash.

I also wasn't sure if Whit would actually say anything to Nando on my behalf. Daisy gave me the impression that she talked a big game, and it may have been easier to appease her in the moment.

"I would have thought you'd stay with Marjorie and Levi, actually," Daisy said, leading us to the right of the house.

"Daisy." Whit's voice was a warning, and it made my chest tighten.

She glanced at him over her shoulder before her head snapped back around.

He knew.

I didn't know if he'd pieced it together from Braiden's reaction to me, or if he'd already known about my relationship with this town. But despite whatever Daisy was to him, he hadn't told her.

The kitchen was to the right of the entryway—a small but functional space, currently overrun with barbecue fixings and food prep items. The kitchen wasn't our destination. The house was too quiet; everyone was already outside.

Daisy led us out the back door into a spacious yard that bled into their neighbor's, the air thick with June heat and the smell of charcoal, meat, and cut grass. Laughter floated from somewhere behind a line of trees.

Before I could take stock of who was at the barbecue, Daisy pulled me to a picnic table with food spread across. I found an empty spot for the fruit and placed the platter down carefully, as if setting it too hard might shatter my last nerve.

"Hey, Jim. How's Carol?" Daisy asked Jim O'Malley—*lives on Church St. and runs the paddle board rental on the shore.*

He smiled down at her. "Daisy Whitaker, as I live and breathe. What brings you back to Connor?"

Jim's smile faded ever so slightly when he glanced over at me.

I prayed Daisy didn't notice.

She did.

"Oh, a little of this, a little of that," Daisy said lightly. "You've met Liv, right Jim?" She squeezed my arm. "Isn't she just the sweetest? Davis would be so happy to know she's spending the summer in his hometown, don't you think?"

Her tone was pure sugar, but her face was pure challenge.

Jim scratched the back of his head, looking anywhere but the two of us. "Of course. Hi, Olivia. We're so happy to have you here." His eyes flicked to Daisy like she might bite. "Glad you and Daisy are getting on well. I have to bring this over to Carol."

Then he fled so fast his speed rivaled a cartoon road-runner's.

"Daisy," I said softly, tucking a piece of my hair behind my ear. A nervous habit more than anything else. "You don't need to do that."

She looked over at me. "Do what?"

I raised an eyebrow.

"Did you know I grew up with Davis McCleary? Had a crush on him all my life, actually."

I stiffened.

"Sorry, that came out weird. It was totally a brother's best friend thing. Nothing of substance there."

I wasn't sure what that meant, but she didn't seem like I'd stolen the love of her life, so I relaxed slightly.

"The point is," Daisy continued, her voice softening, "I knew Davis." She swallowed, just once. "And if he saw what was happening here, Olivia..." Her eyes flashed. "It would break his heart."

I didn't breathe.

"You're family," she said simply, "and I'm not going to let Jim O'Malley, or anyone, make you feel like you aren't."

I swallowed and nodded.

Having an insider on my side in this town other than Donald was a strange feeling. It was likely because somewhere in the past month, I'd convinced myself that the feelings they held toward me were warranted. Perhaps I was to blame for their loss.

That the only reason Davis McCleary wasn't here today was because I existed.

Daisy unthreaded our arms and turned to grab a plate.

"Besides, Marjorie and Levi would feel just terrible if they knew Jim looked at you like that."

My throat dried instantly.

Daisy thought Jim was a one-off, but I didn't have the heart to tell her that my biggest obstacle was Marjorie McCleary.

Once she'd assembled a plate of food, Daisy put a hand on my shoulder and gave me a small smile before walking over to a group of older women sitting at another large picnic table in the center of the yard.

I took my time assembling my own plate. The more time I spent here, the less time I'd need to spend out there.

"Hard decision?" Whit's voice didn't startle me the way someone else's might have. "Sorry about my sister. She's a handful. Sisters think they know everything."

I laughed. "Don't they?"

I didn't want to look at him because I knew I'd be forced to think about how beautiful he was if I did. How I could tell that beneath the dark scruff was a perfectly chiseled jawline. How depthless that shade of green in his eyes was.

How...

I guess I was already doing it, so I might as well not be rude.

I looked at him.

Yep, it was definitely worse to have looked at him.

"Yeah," he said, "but don't tell her that. She'll never let me live it down." He grabbed one of everything and piled it on his plate. "Do you have siblings?"

I turned back to the table. He watched me as I chose between a scoop of something with an illegal amount of mayonnaise and something deep-fried.

"No siblings," I said. "Though Eric and I are pretty close. He occasionally acts like he's my younger brother. If that counts."

Whit shrugged. "Sure. Anyone can be family."

"Right."

Except that my actual family felt more like colleagues, and Davis's family wished we were strangers.

"I know it doesn't feel like that right now, Liv, but trust me. Marjorie and Levi will come around."

I could feel his sincerity, but I knew it was a long shot.

I think the rejection from the McClearys hit hardest for me because of how much Davis loved them. Part of me hoped that whenever I got married, I'd have in-laws who treated me like their own. I had a feeling that a therapist might tell me that I was hoping to fill the void my own parents left, and in my imaginary counseling session, I had no rebuttal.

Before I could respond to Whit's optimism, he looked down at the table and grinned, "Man, this spread could really use some *Cool Ranch Doritos.* "

14

RIGHT DOWN THE RABBIT HOLE
WHIT

I held back a laugh as Olivia grimaced while putting a scoop of potato salad on her plate. I imagined that watching her eat it would be equally humorous, possibly even more so.

Olivia didn't stick out as much as I thought she might, but I bet it wasn't for lack of trying. She'd switched out of her sundress and now wore fitted jeans and an oversized top. Her hair was down, copper catching the sun whenever she moved. The sunglasses, which I was certain were permanently attached to her head and not her face, remained.

The backyard buzzed with barbecue noise. The hiss of the grill. The clang of tongs. Laughter that rose and fell like a tide. Everything smelled like smoke and summer and something sweet in the air that might have been Marjorie's sauce.

"Are you visiting?" she asked.

"No. Just moved back, actually."

She nodded, her eyes drifting back to the table. "I heard you finished your residency in Baltimore."

I inclined my head to one of the empty tables Levi and I

had brought out last night in preparation for today. "You been asking about me, Liv?"

Her cheeks turned the slightest shade of pink, and I fought a grin.

"Not directly," she said. "I found this picture of you and Davis."

A picture?

I tried to recall what picture of the two of us Davis might have had readily available. Unless she'd found it on his phone.

I swallowed a lump in my throat as we made our way over to the table. If she had gone through Davis's phone, she would have heard the voicemails, or seen that they existed at the very least.

Once we were sitting, she dug through her bag and pulled out a Polaroid.

I nodded at it, suppressing a sigh of relief. "Those were some good summers. Davis had an arm on him. We thought he might go pro."

"Why didn't he?"

The truth would probably hurt her, but she wasn't mine to protect. "Marjorie and Levi needed help at the diner. He couldn't go off to play college ball."

She paled. I could practically hear her thoughts because they were the same ones everyone here had when they heard about what Davis had done.

He couldn't go off to college, but he could *marry a girl he just met and move to New York without a second thought.*

I couldn't blame him. I *hadn't* blamed him. Not for *that* anyway.

Olivia pushed the food around on her plate. "What are you doing back here?"

"Taking over the clinic for Pete," I said, watching her scowl after putting a forkful of potato salad in her mouth. "My dad and Pete ran it, and Pete's retiring. He's pretty much stopped coming into work."

I took a breath. Olivia watched me, waiting, that same controlled stillness she wore like armor.

"The Whitakers have a strange history with this town," I continued. "A few of us always tend to find our way back here, whether for short bits or our whole life. My parents moved once I finished college. They aren't too fond of small-town living. But we came here when my grandparents were getting too old. Dad worked with Pete. Mom helped her parents. Daze and I grew up here most of our lives."

I glanced around the yard.

Connor Bay. Familiar faces. Familiar rules. Familiar judgment.

"My parents were always busy, so we spent a lot of time at the McClearys. Connor feels more like home than anywhere else."

We ate in silence for a while. It wasn't uncomfortable, just quiet.

"Olivia, do you mind getting me a glass of that sun tea?"

I raised my eyebrows in surprise at Donald Sanderson's arrival at our table.

According to Davis, Donald had been scarcely seen since his wife, Sonya, had passed away. By the confused faces around the backyard, I was sure that hadn't changed much...until now.

Olivia moved her napkin from her lap to the table and nodded. "Sure, Donald. Be right back."

Donald leaned his head over the table and whispered, "Marjorie doesn't know Olivia's here."

My mind stalled. "What do you mean? How do you know?"

I'd rather ask how he and Olivia met and found themselves in a friendship I'd only seen depicted in Pixar films.

"When I got here about three minutes ago, Marjorie had just gotten back from the store with more ice. She was talking to Caroline Stenson about Olivia."

His gaze darted toward the table where Olivia poured drinks into cups.

Checking on her or making sure she couldn't hear what he said next?

"They were saying some hurtful things that don't really need repeating," he continued, "but I gotta figure that Marjorie doesn't know her daughter-in-law is in her backyard."

Ah, the latter.

He leaned back, looking at me with wide eyes.

My brain felt sluggish, trying to catch up with what Donald was saying. It cost me seconds I didn't have.

"Three sun teas." Olivia smiled at Donald when she returned with three plastic cups balancing precariously in both hands. "What are you two whispering about?"

What were we going to do? If Marjorie saw Olivia here, it might cause a scene. If we told Olivia that Marjorie didn't know she was coming—that she was already here—it might also cause a scene. It was only a matter of time before Marjorie came outside and saw her, so whatever we were going to do had to be done quickly.

I glanced at Donald, who looked at Olivia with so much concern my heart squeezed.

I didn't know what brought them together, but whatever it was, it had formed a bond. One that made Donald want to protect her from an altercation she wasn't prepared for.

Before I could concoct a plan, Donald contorted his face into a look of discomfort.

"Olivia," he said, voice strained, "I'm sorry, but I'm not feeling well. Do you mind helping me home?"

Olivia's eyes widened, and she nodded furiously. "Yes. Yes,

of course." Then she looked at me. Right at me. Her eyes contained the same concern Donald had moments ago. "Maybe Whit should look at you."

She hovered beside him as he maneuvered out of his seat.

Donald waved off the suggestion. "No. Just tired. Being old does that." He glanced at me. "Whit should stay."

I assumed he said it because people would notice if I disappeared, but if two people Marjorie didn't even know were invited left, she might be none the wiser.

Of course, people would certainly ask her about it later. Connor Bay was home, but it was also home to the worst gossip I'd ever heard.

"Olivia?"

And it was too late.

Olivia didn't turn. Her focus was on Donald, who, the moment Marjorie's voice rang out, sat back down as if his legs had quit on him.

"Donald, are you okay?" Olivia knelt beside him. "Do you need help getting up?"

He gave her a small smile. "No, darlin', I was just trying to avoid this, but I'm good now."

Olivia's brows came together. "Avoid what?"

Marjorie's gaze met mine as she led a small charge over to the table.

I stood immediately, moving to act as an obstacle between the two women—one of whom didn't even know she had walked into a lion's den unarmed and chairless. As soon as I reached my place in front of Olivia, I was joined by Eric and Levi, who had seen what was about to happen.

"Marjorie, the food is great. Thanks for having us." I said, taking a few steps to head her off.

I glanced back at Olivia, still oblivious to the scene her

presence was causing. She continued to fuss over Donald Sanderson.

We were out of earshot of our table.

"What's she doing here, Keating?" Marjorie said in a low voice that she only used when Davis and I had gotten into so much trouble that yelling wasn't worth her breath.

Levi stepped up beside me. "I invited her."

"Why on God's green earth would you invite her to our home, Levi?"

To his credit, he didn't falter. "Because she's family, Marjorie. You're drawing attention. Just be civil for a few hours."

"Why should I be?" Marjorie snapped. "I see her every day at the diner, and now I have to see her in my own home?"

"Marjorie." Levi's voice was tired.

They'd had this fight before.

"I want her gone."

Marjorie turned on her heel and stormed back into the house just as Daisy came outside with a fresh pitcher of lemonade.

"What'd I miss?" Daisy called, her gaze flitting across Levi and me.

When I'd convinced Levi to call Olivia for help with the diner, I never thought this was how it would be. I never thought Marjorie would be this hostile toward her.

She wasn't just angry that her son was gone; she *hated* Olivia. She hated Olivia, and she wanted everyone to know it.

I looked back to where Olivia was, but Eric was standing in front of her. He looked over his shoulder at me like he knew I was checking on her.

He shook his head, which I took to mean that Olivia hadn't seen what had just happened, and for that, I was more than relieved.

Davis would have killed me if he knew I had feelings for Olivia. We'd gotten into fights over girls in high school. They were typically settled over one good sparring match back then, but if it happened now...with Olivia. There would be no reconciliation.

So when he was alive, I could bury the *what-ifs*. I could hide them in secret compartments of my life and only open them at night.

I was able to do that because I knew Davis loved her, and she loved him. I knew that he wanted to do right by her...be the best version of himself *for* her.

It was the only thing that kept me from resenting him when it came to her.

The problem now was that he was gone, and he left a mess.

Marjorie could blame Olivia all she wanted for her son not staying in Connor Bay, but Davis had never really asked Olivia to visit. Not until that night when he said he would ask Olivia to move back home with him to help his parents.

We'd talked about it before. We'd talked about Davis inviting Olivia home for the weekend to see his parents and the diner. Maybe I would go home that weekend too and see everyone.

Each time, the conversation always ended the same way.

He didn't think his parents would like her. He didn't think the town would impress her.

I hadn't pushed him. I hadn't said, "Maybe you should have thought about that before you *married* her, Davis."

I didn't argue that maybe Olivia would love the town because *he* loved it.

I'd seen her with Donald.

I knew that if Connor Bay gave Olivia Carrington a chance, she could love this town.

And she would love it with her whole, goddamn heart.

15

TIMELESS

OLIVIA

onald insisted he was fine, but I didn't entirely believe him. Eric had come over to check on us, and in his "expert opinion," the seventy-year-old man just needed more tea. I rolled my eyes at that.

When Donald seemed to get annoyed with my fussing, I gave up. I righted myself and turned to see Whit in what looked to be a very heated discussion with Levi. Their voices were low, their bodies angled inward, the kind of conversation that felt private even from across the yard. One I thought better of interrupting.

Donald excused himself to talk with Levi, and I tried to explain to my best friend that tea is not a fix for ailments. No matter how much he insisted.

It seemed like there was never a dull moment in this town, and the thought of Donald being legitimately ill with someone as old as Pete being the only doctor...I was glad Whit was here.

When Whit returned to the table, he looked plagued by something. His forehead was creased, but it softened when he looked at me.

"You two up for a trip to Duke's?"

"Duke's?" Eric asked.

I grimaced at a memory the name evoked. "It's a bar off the highway right before town."

"This town has a bar, and we haven't been there yet? You've been holding out on me, Olivia." Eric said, wrapping an arm over my shoulders. "And to think, we've been getting drunk in your apartment every night."

Whit raised an eyebrow at us.

"I've only been once. The weekend I got here," I clarified, my gaze dropping to the table, as Daisy appeared in our semi-circle.

"What was that about?" she asked.

"Oh, Donald just wasn't feeling well," I explained, trying to spot the old man to check on him.

Her brows furrowed. "Donald?"

"Yeah, he—"

"We're going to Duke's. You coming, Dais?" Whit asked.

As much as I didn't want to be *here*, I had to make an effort. I should at least thank Marjorie for letting me come in the first place.

"Do you think Marjorie would be upset if we all just left?"

It was Levi who answered, joining our group. "Actually, Duke's is a great idea. You all go on. No need to spend time with the old folks."

Levi was the last person who should be encouraging me to go to Duke's.

I frowned. Something felt wrong. Eric had been insistent that I make a good impression today, and now we were going to leave before most of the food was ready. Whit slipped his hands in his pockets but shrugged his shoulders in a way that felt more resigned than casual.

Daisy seemed just as confused as I felt, but the three men around us didn't look like they intended to elaborate.

Then it clicked, and I looked for Marjorie in the backyard. I didn't see her, but I did see Caroline Stenson watching me like a hawk from the steps of the back door, her arms crossed tight against her chest.

I gritted my teeth. "She didn't know."

Daisy looked at me. "Who didn't know what?"

I ignored her and looked at Whit, who gave an almost imperceptible dip of his chin.

"Nothing. Let's go to Duke's."

THE FIRST, and I had hoped last, time I'd been to Duke's, I found myself in a heap of trouble.

It was the first weekend in Connor Bay, and I had been searching for a place to live the whole week. There were undoubtedly apartments to rent, but not if your name was Olivia Carrington or Marjorie McCleary had blacklisted you.

I'd been staying at a hotel just outside of town, the *Juniper Breeze*. I expected more gingham prints from a hotel named after a discontinued *Bath & Body Works* fragrance, but it would do.

I had gone to see the McClearys at the diner the day I got in, and I had never been so thankful that their business was drowning because Marjorie gave me an earful about my audacity. Her voice had carried, sharp and unrestrained, and the only saving grace was that no one had been in the diner to see it.

I didn't dare try to go back that week. Levi had called and apologized, asking me to give Marjorie space while he worked on it. In the meantime, I explored the town.

It had been three days before I found myself at Duke's. I hadn't heard from Levi, no one would rent to me, and I'd visited every store in town twice. I was avoiding Eric's calls, and I missed my husband.

Saturday night, I remembered seeing Duke's off the interstate and drank way more than I should have. I wasn't sure if the bartender had called Levi or if he was already there, but he cut me off and dropped me off at the *Juniper Breeze*. I wish I could say that we never spoke of it again, but that would have been far too easy.

Duke's obviously hadn't changed at all in the month since I'd seen it last, but it did make my stomach roll uncomfortably.

"Keating! Good to see you!" The bartender called. "I'll bring over a round."

Daisy saw someone she knew, so she went to sit with them while Eric, Whit, and I slid into a booth. Unfortunately for me, the bartender was the same one from a month ago, and I had to pray he didn't remember me, or care. I would take not caring over having to explain myself.

However, I relaxed when I realized no one at this table would judge me for getting a little too drunk one night in my husband's hometown. Eric certainly wouldn't, and Whit probably did his fair share of blackout nights when he heard about Davis.

"Angus, you're a good man," Whit said when the drinks arrived.

Angus let out a hearty laugh. "Good to have you back. The clinic could use someone with decent eyesight again." Angus looked over at Eric and me. "Olivia." He nodded his head at me. "Good to see you again. Glad you brought friends this time."

I shrugged and gave him a small smile. "Seemed like a better option."

Angus smiled and gave us a two-finger salute against his forehead before bringing Daisy her drink at the other table with her friends.

Eric nudged me. "Care to share with the class, Olivia?"

"It's old news. Got a little too drunk one night...Levi had to pick me up."

Eric laughed. "Davis would have loved to see that, I bet."

In a twisted way, he was right. My husband loved giving me a hard time about drinking too much and singing karaoke, or ordering way too many chicken nuggets once we were home.

Of course, had he been there, had he been alive, I wouldn't have been in that situation to begin with.

Whit looked between the two of us seriously. "So, how are we going to fix this?"

I frowned. "Fix what?"

"As much as I love narrowly escaping arguments with Marjorie McCleary..."

"That wasn't my fault! Levi said I should come, so I came. How was I supposed to know he didn't tell her?"

"It's not your *fault*, Liv," Whit agreed. "But if you're going to be here, we have to find a way to make this okay for you two. Do you have any friends other than Donald Sanderson and Eric?" I bit my lip. "I thought so. You have Daisy and me now, so that'll help some. You should also get out of your lease with Nando."

Eric nodded in agreement, a little more enthusiastically than I thought was necessary.

"I would, but he was the only one who would rent to me. I'm pretty sure Levi had to talk him into it."

I was more than pretty sure. I'd only gotten that call the day after Levi had picked me up from the bar, and Nando had already told me no the day before.

"My parents bought one of the houses on the lake to rent

out to tourists, but they're having trouble finding an extended stay this year. You and Eric could take that. Rent is probably better than whatever Nando's charging you if you're really on Marjorie's shit list."

I nodded. "That's nice of you, Whit. Thanks."

"What's in it for you?" Eric asked, and I elbowed him. "What, Olivia? You just met him."

He was right. I had *just* met Whit, but it felt like I'd known him forever. I didn't know if it was the voicemails or his connection to Davis, but we felt old. Not like we'd grown up together or knew everything about each other, but he felt timeless.

I couldn't explain that to him...to anyone. So, instead, I said, "You're going to turn down a lakehouse?"

"Fine." Eric relented. "But I've got my eye on you, Whitaker."

Whit shrugged. "Wouldn't have it any other way." He picked up his glass, and our eyes met. "Now that that's settled, we need to integrate you into the town."

"I already live here. How much more integrated can I get?"

Whit laughed and shook his head. "You don't even know the half of it. I'll call Paula at the dance school to see if she could use more volunteers for the summer recital. If you're going to stay, Olivia, you're going to have to do more than work at the diner. You'll have to convince this town you're a sure thing."

I wasn't convinced I *was* a sure thing, but I nodded anyway. "Okay, sure. I can do that."

Whit gave me that slow smile again. The one that started on the right side of his face and blossomed across the rest. "I know you can."

Something shifted at this moment...maybe it had already been shifting from the moment I saw him in the grocery store.

Keating Whitaker was more than just my husband's best friend. He was my salvation.

Hey man. Sorry I missed your call, I just got off a 24-hour shift. Sounds like whatever you have to tell me is a wild ride. Surprised to hear you're still with Olivia. She must be something special. Talk soon.

16

LOW-KEY, NO PRESSURE
OLIVIA

The following day, I reported bright and early to Paula's Dance School to do whatever she needed.

It seemed like everyone in town owed Keating Whitaker a favor. I liked to think of it that way, rather than admitting that Whit was willing to collect those favors on my behalf.

Regardless of which it was, he was right. I was getting nowhere with Marjorie, and while she may have been the key to getting this town to like me, she was on a level I wasn't ready to attempt again.

When we'd gotten home from the bar, Eric looked up the lakehouse Whit offered to rent to us and deemed it adequate. Based on the photos, it was more than adequate. It was gorgeous.

Whit asked for a day or two to have the cleaners come in for a deep clean, but we could move in on Wednesday.

I considered returning the newly purchased furniture, but decided that leaving it for Nando's next tenant might get him to warm up to me. He could charge them more if he touted newly purchased furniture.

Though that hadn't stopped him from charging me an arm and a leg for an apartment with bad furniture.

The dance studio was already buzzing. Small children darted around in glittery costumes while parents gathered along the edges of the room, coffee cups clutched tightly in their hands.

Whit didn't give any indication of what he agreed to with Paula, only that I should plan to be there at 6:30 a.m.

My entrance hadn't gone unnoticed by the adults along the walls. I could tell because their once audible chatter had dipped into low whispers.

I found Paula coming out of a small closet she'd turned into some version of an office. I wasn't sure what I expected, but Paula looked tiny enough to fit in my pocket.

Her deep brown skin contrasted beautifully against a lavender leotard and matching tights. She wore her hair in a tight bun on top of her head.

Most unexpected of all, she looked surprised to see me.

"Olivia! You're here." She checked her watch. "And you're early."

I nodded and widened my smile, though I had a feeling Marjorie had gotten to her at some point and told her I was chronically late.

Then again, maybe I was just paranoid.

"Of course. Happy to help. What can I do?"

"Whit said you're in marketing? Is that right?"

"Yes, ma'am. I handle campaign finances and design."

Paula nodded and began digging through the piles of paperwork on her desk.

"I'm afraid this won't be the most exciting task," she said, "but Whit said you'd be okay with that."

"Yes," I said quickly. "Definitely. Whatever you need. I'm your girl."

Her shoulders visibly dropped, as if I'd lifted a weight she hadn't yet told me she was carrying.

"I'm in over my head here. My books are a mess. Maybe my desk gave that away," she admitted with a breathless laugh. "I've been meaning to digitize everything, but I don't have time between classes and preparing for the summer recital."

"No problem."

"I don't have the extra funds to pay you," she added, her eyes growing more frantic. "But Whit said you'd be happy to do it for free."

"Mrs. Sullivan—

"Paula. Please."

"Paula," I said gently, "I'm happy to do whatever you need. My friends joke that spreadsheets are my love language."

Well. Eric joked. *Once.*

"I can absolutely get everything up and running for you. Can you tell me how comfortable you are with digital records? I want to make sure I'm setting you up on something that's your speed."

I followed Paula around the room like a puppy as she explained what would be the most helpful, and I scribbled it down on my iPad. Honestly, as far as volunteer gigs went, this was a dream.

I asked her how people paid for sessions, if she managed her own website, and a myriad of other things as she set up mats for the 7 a.m. class.

By 6:55, I decided I had everything I needed to get started, so I went back into her office to sort through paperwork and get things squared away.

Working had always been a solace.

I could quickly lose track of time when I was focused on a

task, as evidenced by my startle when someone knocked on the office doorframe. My heart rate increased when I saw it was Whit.

I didn't think I'd get used to how good-looking he was, but if I was going to live in this town for any extended amount of time, I'd need to get over it.

"Paula said you were still here," he said. "I just ran into her at the coffee shop."

I looked at my phone. It was noon. I'd been in here for 5 hours sorting files and trying to make sense of chicken-scratch notes and receipts. There were a few things to confirm with Paula, but for the most part, I was ready to start scanning things and logging expenses.

"Want to get lunch?"

"Thanks, but I shouldn't."

The list of reasons that I shouldn't be alone with Keating Whitaker wasn't long, but it was thorough.

For one, he knew more about my husband than I ever would. He knew the parts of him I never saw. I was certain that, if anyone had the right to judge me, it was him.

His best friend was dead because he'd married me and moved to my city. It took him away from his family, his friends, and the town he'd grown up in. If I'd been in his shoes, I'd expect me to know more than I did about my husband.

Whit had done nothing to make me believe he judged me. If anything, he'd gone out of his way to be kind. To help. To welcome Eric and me without hesitation.

Still, no one in our New York circle did anything for free.

The other reason I didn't want to go to lunch with him was simpler.

I was hiding the voicemails.

I tossed and turned all night, trying to stop thinking about the fact that there were so many voicemails that might have details about Davis that I could keep for myself. Pieces that I could add to a small but growing stash of momentos gifted to me by other people.

"Why not?"

I gestured weakly at the piles of paper surrounding me. "I've got a lot of work to do."

Whit's eyes scanned the stacks. "I didn't send you to Paula to burn yourself out. You can take a break, Liv."

I wondered if this was one of the things Davis told him about me. Sometimes, I'd get so wrapped up in work that I wouldn't eat or take a break until I felt I was at a good place to stop. Davis tried so many nights to coax me to bed, but I'd wave him off.

I put a lot of pressure on myself to be the best at everything. To work the hardest.

I knew it wasn't sustainable, but I kept telling myself I'd pull back one day. When I felt like I was where I wanted to be in my career and my life, I'd pull back.

And I kept telling myself that it was fine. That everyone in New York was like that. It was a city with a standard, and if I wasn't meeting it—*exceeding* it—I was failing. I had been failing since I got to Connor Bay.

I'd felt that way until this morning. Until I'd seen Paula visibly relax, trusting me to take care of this. It was enough even if she'd only trusted me because she trusted Whit, for now.

"I'd really rather stay," I told him, turning back to my computer.

Whit sighed...deeply.

"It's like this, Liv. If you finish all this work for Paula too quickly, you won't get to know her. If you don't really care about that, fine. It's not the point of all this, but if you want to cross people off your list like a guest book, then fine."

His voice wasn't angry. It was more sad than anything. I couldn't tell if it was for me or because of me.

"If that's the case," he continued, "then you'll need another person to work for, and finding that person for you is my job until you get some more friends."

I glanced up at him without raising my head. He raised an eyebrow at me.

"So the way I see it is you need me for whatever the next step is, and if I think you're not really holding up your end of the deal, then..."

Shrugging, Whit blew out a breath and shoved his hands in his pockets. I narrowed my eyes at him and leaned back in my chair, which was definitely not ergonomic or good for my back in any way.

"Sounds an awful lot like blackmail, Keating Whitaker."

He shrugged again and leaned against the frame. "Blackmail is such a dirty word, Olivia. I like to think of it as...incentivizing. Besides, what's 30 minutes with me? You'll be back in that god-awful chair in no time."

We stared at each other.

He looked smug, and I hated it. I hated that he was right and that I needed him. I shook my head in defeat and closed my computer.

"Fine, but you're paying."

He turned his body away from me. "Meet you outside. There's too much glitter in here."

I smiled to myself as I picked up my bag and let my hair out of the pencil-held bun.

Whatever I'd been expecting from my husband's best friend, this wasn't it.

Whit wasn't like Davis, and he wasn't like his sister.

Could it be that Whit and I were most similar to each other?

So Jeremiah called me yesterday and asked if I thought your parents would rent him your room. I tried to explain to him that I didn't think it was likely, and he somehow took that as an invitation to help them clean out your room and begin the grieving process. He thinks that living there will really comfort them.

I should probably remind him that Marjorie threatened to have him arrested if he even so much as knocked on her door after she caught him digging through their trash.

17

YOU'RE THE WEST VILLAGE

WHIT

I wasn't supposed to be here.

I told myself I'd keep my distance until the rental was ready, but I wanted to check on her. The problem was that the more time I spent with Olivia, the more time I wanted to spend with her.

When I walked into Paula's, I knew the person I was seeing was the old Olivia.

The one Davis used to gripe to me about. The first time it happened, I almost hung up on him.

He was on speakerphone in my car as I drove from the hospital to my apartment in Charles Village. At a stoplight, I rubbed my forehead and tapped my other hand on the steering wheel.

"She just works all the time, y'know?" His voice crackled through the phone. "I thought I was marrying this girl who was about adventure and spontaneity and...and...I don't know. Not this workaholic."

I could hear him moving around his kitchen, their kitchen. The sounds of chopping and sizzling filled the car.

"Whit? You there?"

"Yeah, Davis. I'm here. Have you talked to her about it?"

From what Davis told me about her job, it wasn't surprising that she worked all the time.

Her role was split between marketing analyst and coordinator. She had a partner at the company she worked for...Eric? Maybe. Davis had complained about him before, but once he found out Eric had a boyfriend, those complaints fizzled out.

I'd Googled her once.

Luxury brands. Names I only recognized because of Daisy and her jet-setting.

I'd thought Daisy and Olivia might either be best friends or hate each other. Daisy made friends everywhere she went.

She'd gone to school for journalism and didn't make much money, but her articles always sold, so she always had travel and money to live off. There was always something to write about when you traveled the world and had fashion models for friends.

"Yes? No?" Davis said. "I don't know what counts. I try to talk to her when she gets home, but it's like there's a wall up. I'm convinced she's married to her job and not me."

He let out a laugh, but I could hear his frustration.

I tried to see it from his side.

He'd left his family. His town. His entire life to move to New York for her.

I didn't think he was lonely. He'd gotten a job at a coffee shop near their apartment. He went out with coworkers. Davis was like Daisy. He made friends everywhere.

"Do you think it's forever?" I asked. "Like, is she trying to move up?"

"I don't know. She hasn't said."

"She hasn't said, or you haven't asked?"

"Whose side are you on, Whit?"

My brows rose, not that he could see it. "I want to be on yours," I said carefully. "But I get it. I work insane hours, too. If she's trying to get to a place where she can breathe, that makes sense. Just talk to her."

The line went quiet.

He hadn't wanted solutions. He wanted to complain.

The problem was that he was preaching to the overworked choir. Med school and residency had me working killer hours, and there were many times when I'd come home, pass out, and do it all again the next day.

But it was temporary. I'd finish here in Baltimore and move back to Connor Bay.

"You're right," Davis said eventually. "I'll try harder. She's just so intense."

I laughed. "I thought you liked that about Liv."

"I did...I *do*," he corrects himself. "I just thought we were intense about the same things."

"You mean you thought the week-long couple's trip to Atlantic City and bar hopping on the Upper East Side would be your whole life."

He laughed. "I mean, yeah. Kinda."

Watching her now, bent over Paula's desk with her brow furrowed in concentration, I didn't know how he could have thought that. One look at Olivia was enough to know she gave everything she had to whatever was in front of her. Especially when someone depended on her.

It wasn't my job to make her life easier, and it would have been better for me to avoid her altogether.

But I couldn't.

Not now that I'd seen her gaze linger on me when she thought I didn't notice, and how much she cared for Donald when he said he wasn't feeling well.

No, staying away from Olivia wasn't a possibility.

She emerged from Paula's with her hair down, sunglasses holding it back on her head. Her bag looked big enough to hide at least half a body inside. I was surprised she wasn't in danger of tipping over.

"You look too New York," I said, opening the driver's door. "You know that, right? Get in."

Olivia rolled her eyes but walked over to the passenger side. "I'm from the city, Whit. What would you prefer I wear?"

That was a loaded question if I'd ever heard one.

A Top 20 hit filled the car, and I turned the radio down to an acceptable volume. "I'm just saying, if you want to fit in, you could try looking like you're not in an entirely different tax bracket."

Her jaw ticked as I pulled out of the parking spot.

"Where are we going anyway? Everything in town is within walking distance."

"We're not going somewhere in town."

"What happened to a thirty-minute lunch?" I gave her a look. "This is kidnapping, you know?"

"You got in the car willingly," I reminded her. "It will never hold up in court."

She turned her body in the seat to face me. "A doctor *and* a lawyer. Your parents must be so proud." It was my turn to roll my eyes. "Did you always want to be a doctor?"

"I guess so. I wanted to be like my dad, and my dad is a doctor. There wasn't a moment when I woke up and wanted to be a doctor. I think everyone just assumed that's what I would do, so I just did it."

"But you like it?"

"I'm not sure yet. I think I will," I said honestly. "I always knew I'd end up here, so I tried out an internal medicine residency at Hopkins, and that kept me busy, but it wasn't my favorite. You know I was pre-med at NYU."

I offered the information to her to establish a common ground, and she took it like a fish on a hook.

"Where in New York were you? Near campus in NoHo?"

I nodded. "Little shoebox studio in Greenwich Village. Davis said you were on the Upper East Side?"

From the corner of my eye, I could see her tuck her hair behind her ear and look out the window.

"A two-bed on 5th." I let out a low whistle; she made a disgruntled noise that was cuter than it should have been. "Don't start."

"I didn't say anything." Davis mentioned Olivia came from money, but 5th Avenue money was another story. "Did you always want to go into marketing?"

"No, I was a business major in college, but had to take a marketing elective my junior year. I interned at a marketing firm that summer, and it just felt right."

Olivia leaned over and turned up the radio, which I took as a sign she didn't want to engage in small talk anymore. Then she started to hum to the song playing and rolled down her window.

I would have given anything to know what she was thinking.

She was less than pleased to talk about money. Maybe this had been a sore subject for her and Davis. It wasn't particularly unusual. Talking about money made lots of people uncomfortable.

I glanced over at her. She had moved her glasses to her face for the first time since I'd seen her in the grocery store, and her hair whipped around her face wildly from the wind. Her elbow rested on the window frame while her hand drummed against the outside of the car. I didn't want to take my eyes off her.

It seemed like the more distance we put between us and the

town, the more she relaxed...and the more she relaxed, the more I had to try not to fall in love with her.

Our brief road trip ended a few minutes later as I pulled into a restaurant parking lot off the highway.

"This was Davis's favorite place," I told her as she twisted her hair into a clip and shoved her glasses to the top of her head.

"Davis knew his parents owned a diner, right? That wasn't a secret?"

Stones Pub was a bar off MA-127 in the town beside ours. "Marjorie would never serve pub food, Olivia. Don't be ridiculous." She held her hands up in defeat.

Once we sat and ordered, Olivia looked at me expectantly.

"So, you obviously brought me here to tell me something... or ask me something. I'm not sure about that part."

I raised my eyebrows. "Why do you think that?"

"C'mon, Whit."

She was mostly right. Though I had really intended to check on her, I wanted to talk to her away from the prying eyes of the town and Caroline Stenson.

Of course, I was sure she'd already heard that Olivia had been seen getting into my car at 12:07 p.m., and that our return arrival time would be extensively documented in the official town gossip magazine.

"How long are you staying?"

She blinked at me. "I'm not sure."

"The diner's not doing too hot, Liv." She nodded. "I'm talking maybe three, four months unless we can come up with a plan."

"We?"

I rolled my eyes at her. "Yes, Olivia. *We.*"

"Marjorie won't talk to me about the finances, so I can't

exactly weigh in there, but I think this is a bigger issue. The whole town needs a boost in tourism. I can find ways to cut down the menu, maybe strike some deals with their suppliers, but unless we get the town revenue up, there's not a lot we can do."

I nodded. She was right. Helping Levi and Marjorie would require addressing more systemic issues within the town. "Have any ideas?"

She shrugged. "I mean, we could definitely be doing more to generate tourists. There's no reason that lakehouse of yours should have to go to me. It's beautiful. The summer festival should draw some people in, but people kill for small-town activities. Hug a goat, watch a movie in a theater with one screen, and get berated by grumpy old men on their porch. It's all part of the charm. If we started social media campaigns or asked some companies for sponsorships, we could probably get the revenue up relatively quickly."

"You have been thinking about this."

She frowned at me, and I wanted to run my thumb across her bottom lip. "Of course I have. I came here to help the diner. The best thing for it is to get more customers."

I waited for the server, who'd just arrived with our plates, to walk away before continuing.

"Speaking of the lakehouse. Cleaners were able to get in there today. You and Eric can get settled tomorrow if you want."

She dipped a fry in the house cheese sauce. The one I recalled Davis all but smothering over his food.

Olivia frowned at it before grabbing the ketchup bottle at the end of the table.

"That sounds great. Eric is probably building some kind of shrine to you and your family as we speak."

After lunch, Olivia paused, getting into the passenger seat. "Oh my god, Whit. Look."

She shut the door and jogged across the street. When I realized where she was headed, I swiftly made my way over, lest she do anything too rash under my supervision.

"Look at them, Whit!"

Except, I didn't look at them; I was only looking at her. I tried to memorize how her cheek dimpled when she smiled that wide, and her eyes sparkled as she picked one up.

"I could get a dog. People love people with dogs, right?"

I finally looked down at the pen of dogs up for adoption outside the pet store. "I don't know if it's such a good idea, Olivia. I mean, you've got a lot going on."

She pressed a small golden puppy against her face and laughed. "I know, but look at them." She put the dog down. "Oh, Whit, what about this one?" There was an older golden who trotted over to our side of the pen. Olivia crouched down and stroked the top of its head. "An older dog would be less work than a puppy."

I looked back at the dog, and there was something in its eyes that screamed mischief, so I wasn't sure how true that was. The thought was further supported when the dog tried to jump out of the pen to reach her.

"Maybe you should call Eric."

"Why would I need to call Eric?" She asked, smushing the dog's face in her hands.

"For one, I have no idea if this is normal behavior for you. Eric would most certainly be a better voice of reason here."

She sighed and stood. "You're right. Eric would agree that this is a bad idea."

I swallowed, feeling guilty that I'd deflated her joy so quickly.

"We should head back," Olivia said, giving me a tight-lipped smile before putting her glasses on her face and heading back to the car.

Nice going, Keating.

18

OH MY GOD, SHE'S INSANE

OLIVIA

In bed that night, pillow pressed against my ears to drown out Eric's snoring beside me, I continued to ruminate over my lunch with Whit.

He was right. I had too much on my plate.

I couldn't even consider getting a dog or doing anything for myself until I moved some things off my shoulders. I needed to regroup and reprioritize. Marjorie needed help at the diner whether she wanted it or not, but I didn't have to be there every day. I could work out a schedule with her.

I wasn't getting anywhere with her, and my efforts to not be a social pariah were best spent winning over the other people in town. But to what end?

Whit asked me how long I was staying, and I didn't know. I didn't know how long it would take me to figure out why I came here.

Was it to get closure? Was it to help my husband's family? Or was it something else entirely?

There were two things I *did* know.

First, Marjorie was unlikely to come around anytime soon,

and if the rates of tourism in this town didn't change, the diner would go under.

Second, I had extensive experience in getting people to buy products they didn't particularly need. That was what I did for a living. It should not have been this hard.

I could see it then. In the darkness of the too-small apartment, I could see it all come together.

Connor Bay was like a luxury item; getting people to visit was just another marketing campaign. I swung my legs out of bed and crept into the living room, shutting the bedroom door behind me.

"Oh my god." Eric's voice startled me from the doorway of my bedroom. "What is happening in here?"

It was then that I noticed the light streaming in from the windows.

Eric took inventory of the place as he walked further into the room.

The boxes we packed up yesterday with my sketchpad and color swatches sat empty beside the couch. Pages from my pad were strewn about haphazardly. I'd run out of Post-its and had taped takeout napkins to the wall. It was a mess, but Eric looked at the wall covered with half-formed ideas and smiled.

"You're insane."

I stood from my place on the floor, knees cracking as I unfolded myself, holding my iPad to my chest. "I think we can help them, Eric. Not just the McClearys, the whole town."

He held out his hand without looking at me, and I handed over the tablet.

He was quiet for a long time as he read through the proposal, the checklists, the logo designs...everything.

Finally, he said, "You know I can't legally agree to anything before 8 a.m., but this...this is good."

I let out a breath that felt like I'd been holding it since last night...maybe even before that. Since New York.

"I'm glad you think so because I need you to do something." He clicked off my screen and raised an eyebrow at me. "Well, obviously, the town can't afford something like this on its own, and we can't keep doing our job full-time *and* work on this..."

"So you need me to pitch this to Clark." It wasn't a question.

If we were going to do this, we'd need money, and the town didn't have that. It would be an impossible pitch, but if anyone could convince Clark, it would be Eric.

Saying no to Eric was like saying no to Harvey Specter. No one said no to Harvey Specter.

"Okay, I'm still not saying yes, but hypothetically speaking, we could see what's in the philanthropy budget," he says. "I think saving a small town could fall into some category of charitable expense."

I could practically see the wheels turning in his head.

"We could try to drum up some traction before the pitch by reaching out to a few of the tourism magazines we've worked with recently. I might still have that *Coastal Living* contact. Anyway, *hypothetically*, we might also want a representative from the town there at the pitch. Have you thought about the best way to approach them about this?"

Another sigh from me. "I think Whit's our in here. We should pitch to him first and see what he thinks. Then maybe we could try to get all the business owners to come together." I chewed my bottom lip. "I don't want to promise them anything. If we promise and can't deliver, it'll be bad."

Eric nodded. "Okay, then maybe you keep working on this stuff. Get Whit involved, and I'll reach out to a few journalists, maybe some bloggers, and see if they'll run a piece about Connor Bay. If they can run it before the summer festival, that would probably help a ton. Regardless of what happens with Clark, all press is good press."

He was right; we couldn't dive into this project headfirst. It needed to be executed carefully. "I'll talk to Whit."

"Good. Now, go to bed and get at least an hour or two of sleep because I will not deal with a cranky version of you on a moving day. I'll go get breakfast and send off some media inquiries."

This could work.

It *had* to work.

WHIT SAID he would meet us at the lakehouse at noon. Eric had let me sleep until 10 a.m. before he demanded that I help clean up the mess I made in the living room.

The drive wasn't long by any means, but I wouldn't be able to walk to work anymore.

For a second, it felt like I wasn't in Connor Bay anymore. Just taking a scenic drive along the coast.

My chest ached at the thought, but I also felt some relief emotionally. Being in the town, even now that I had people looking out for me, came with a pressure to act a certain way... *be* a certain way.

It didn't go unnoticed by me that the longing in my chest for my husband had lessened now that my days were busier. In the moments between the chatter, I thought of him, and all that pain came coursing back.

I turned up the radio in the car and tried to find a station playing a song I knew.

I had a feeling I was not doing this grieving thing the right way. If I let it keep building, I'd break one day, but I couldn't afford to let it be now. Not when I was less than a minute away from seeing Whit.

He was on the porch when I pulled into the drive. Eric followed in his car behind me. Whit was casual today: black gym shorts, a white shirt with a Connor Bay logo, and that damned backward cap.

The house was beautiful with its wrap-around porch. It was pretty secluded, other than the house next door, which shared a yard with it.

White shutters and trim against a coastal blue paint. How quintessential small-town New England.

Whit smiled as I got out of the car.

"Need a hand?" He jogged down the steps and waved to Eric, who stepped out of his car.

"Nice place."

"Yeah, Whit. It's really something." I said, walking around to the trunk of my car. "Thanks for letting us rent it." Whit waved me off and grabbed my suitcase. He frowned at me when I grabbed my other suitcase.

"This is everything?"

I tilted my head at him. "Yeah, that's all."

"Davis mentioned that you were an over-packer," he explained. "I was expecting—"

It was the first time that Whit admitted he'd talked to Davis about me.

"A car filled to the brim with stuff? Usually. I just...I didn't give myself time to pack much." Whit nodded like he understood and didn't press it further.

"If you two are done chatting, I could actually use some help over here," Eric called, surrounded by suitcases and garment bags.

"You can go help him. I've got these two," I told Whit, who looked like he wanted to protest. "Trust me, Eric will throw a tantrum if you don't go help him. It's best to do it. I can manage."

After Whit helped Eric carry in the bags, he showed us our rooms on the second floor of the house.

I was most excited to have some privacy again. It was sort of hard to cry yourself to sleep at night listening to your dead husband's best friend's voicemails when you have a roommate, let alone someone sharing your bed.

The best part of the house was the view and the backyard that led to the water, separated from the house by a large stretch of grass. The lake wasn't vast by any means, but it was beautiful, surrounded by greenery, and reflected the smattering of clouds in the sky.

Whit excused himself to go to the clinic an hour after we arrived, and Eric, to my surprise, invited him over for dinner.

"What?" he asked when I shot him a look after Whit was gone.

I shrugged. "Nothing. You just seem to be changing your tune."

"Olivia, he just gave us a house. Surely, that warrants a meal. Now I'm going to get some work done. I looked over the notes you left on the Dior pitch. Can you get to the Tiffany campaign before the diner?" I nodded, pulling out my phone. "I think the new Hailey Bieber photos are in. Kelly emailed me an attachment this morning."

I paused my scrolling. "Why would she send them to you?"

Kelly always sent me campaign documents first, and I organized them before sharing them with Eric. It was *my* job.

"I asked her to send me anything time-sensitive." I frowned. "This is just temporary, Olivia. I don't want anything falling through the cracks, and I want you to be able to focus on getting better. You don't need annoying emails from Kelly in your inbox."

My heart squeezed. For all the support Eric had given me... *tried* to give to me despite my resistance, he was hurting too.

He'd lost Davis, sure, we all did. But that night in the hospital, he'd lost me too—not in the most absolute way, but in ways that mattered.

"Eric."

He gave me a sad smile. "I know, Liv. I know. We'll get there."

I think I finally convinced Levi and Marjorie to ask Olivia for her help with the diner. I'm not entirely sure that she'll say yes, but maybe being around the town will be good for her. I know you thought Olivia wouldn't like it in Connor Bay, but I think she'd appreciate being around the place you grew up.

I'll be there in late June, and I'm trying to get Daisy to come home for it. My parents are unwavering in their refusal to visit. I'll probably go see them in the Fall. Do you think North Carolina will become the next Florida? Like that's where everyone will go when they retire? I'll have to let you know.

19

BLOOD MOONLIT

OLIVIA

I finished the priority tasks on the campaigns Eric needed and worked the afternoon shift at the diner. Marjorie didn't talk to me, and I didn't make an attempt.

Things had been tense since the barbecue. We'd regressed from her passive-aggressive comments about my wardrobe and work habits to nothing at all.

I stopped by Donald's to bring him sun tea and planned for breakfast on his porch sometime this week. Since his appearance at the barbecue, Donald had been venturing into town more and coming back with all sorts of gossip.

Apparently, Sidney the barista at *The Bean* had started dating a barista at a rival coffee shop in the next town over. I wasn't entirely sure why our coffee shop needed a nemesis when the coffee wasn't great, but Donald said the scone recipe was a well guarded secret.

"So the town thinks this barista at—"

"*The Roast*," Donald interrupted.

"Right, the town thinks this barista at *The Roast* is dating

Sidney just so she'll give him the recipe for...scones?" I held in a laugh.

They were cracked. Every last one of them.

"That's what Caroline told Paula at the market yesterday."

I shook my head. *Of course.* It had to be Caroline. She was the most cracked of them all.

The busier I was, the more normal I started to feel. It wasn't a cure by any means, but it was a band-aid. And even if I wasn't *actually* okay, when I was busy, I could pretend I was.

I could pretend that my husband was alive, that we moved to this small town, and that I had typical in-law problems and errands to run. When I had a task, I could pretend nothing else mattered.

Before going back to the house, I dropped in on Paula and brought her up to speed on the project, which I projected would be done by the end of the week if she was okay with me taking her documents home. She laughed.

"Honey, I would love nothing more than you removing all that garbage from my office."

She helped me pack up the papers into file boxes and load them into my car. "You know, it was real nice of Whit to offer your help with this."

"Actually, he's doing me a favor. I'd love to help more with the town while I'm here."

Paula sighed. "Look, I don't know exactly what happened with you and the McClearys, but as far as I'm concerned, any wife of Davis McCleary belongs in Connor Bay just as much as he did."

I gave her a grateful smile, but I needed to leave because if she said anything else about him in the past tense, I was sure I would lose it.

She squeezed my shoulder and went back into the studio.

When I got back to the house, Eric was preparing dinner in

the kitchen. He inclined his head to a glass of wine he'd poured for me.

"About earlier, Eric, I—"

"Don't worry about it, Liv. You're doing your best, and I'm really glad I'm here with you."

I wanted to tell him about seeing Davis's room and Whit's voicemails, but it was like I couldn't speak. Eric and I were good friends, but we'd never ventured too deeply into our inner workings. I wasn't sure whose fault that was. Probably mine.

"That'll be Whit," Eric said at the sound of the doorbell.

I fastened my hair into a clip as I walked over to the door. Whit had changed into a sweater and jeans, which made me think that maybe it got particularly cold by the lake.

"How are the cicadas over here?"

His mouth turned up at the corner. "Not too bad. Much better than in town, that's for sure."

I could cry. A full night's sleep was just a few hours away. No more of Eric's snoring and minimal cicadas. I couldn't wait.

"You don't like them?" Whit asked, passing me the bottle of wine he had brought as we walked into the kitchen.

"I've been having some trouble sleeping."

Whit's brows furrowed. "Is it just the noise?"

I glanced at him and realized he was looking at me like a doctor looks at their patient.

I waved him off. "Yeah, between the cicadas and Eric, I'm looking forward to passing out in my bed tonight." I laughed, but he didn't seem to relax. "Really, I'm fine."

He opened his mouth, but Eric cut him off. "Dinner's ready. Can I get you a drink, Whit? We've got a bottle of white open, or we can do the red…"

"White's great, just didn't want to come empty-handed."

"Good man." Eric clapped him on the shoulder as he held out a glass to Whit.

Dinner felt...normal.

Whit filled us in on some of the other members of the town. Eric and I explained our idea to boost tourism. Whit said he thought it was a great idea and that he'd be happy to help with anything we needed. He was most pleased to hear that Paula had warmed up to me so quickly.

Whit felt safe, like a lifeboat that tethered Eric and me to the town. I didn't feel like I was trying to tread water anymore.

"So you and Davis grew up together," Eric said long after dinner was over.

Whit glanced at me, and I gave him a small smile.

This is what I wanted. To know *him* better.

"Yeah, Davis and I were always close."

"How'd you feel about him moving to New York?"

Whit shrugged. "Davis had always done whatever he wanted. I couldn't fault him for wanting to try something new."

The truth was, I never cared enough to ask Davis about what he was giving up to be with me. In the back seat of my car, his lips against my neck, he asked me to marry him.

I laughed breathlessly because he was still thrusting into me. His hands were in my hair, and my nails scored lines down his back. Then he asked again. I couldn't tell you where we were parked or how we got there, only that car sex with Davis had to be the eighth wonder of the world.

Later, when I sobered up, I realized that the seat buckle had been jammed against my lower back and gave me a bruise bad enough that I couldn't sit or lie in a comfortable position for three days, and I hit my head on the side of the car so many times that a bump formed.

Even so, that moment in the car hadn't felt real. I couldn't even remember why I'd said yes, only that I felt like I never wanted us to end. I wanted us to be infinite, and we were...until we weren't.

Eric went to bed, and Whit and I were left on the couch. "Favorite thing about Connor Bay?"

He looked around the room like the answer was somewhere here. "The cicadas."

"Oh, shut up." I threw a pillow at him. "No, really. What's your favorite thing about the town?"

Whit's face grew serious. Not doctor serious, but enough to warn me that whatever he was going to say would be significant. "Can I show you something?"

"That depends. Are you going to answer my question?"

"I want to show you the answer."

He stood, and I followed him as he led us out the backdoor.

The lake at night was even more captivating than it was during the day.

I couldn't see too far in front of me, but the moon reflected off the lake. The stars blanketed the night sky, and I wondered how long we'd been talking to Whit. When he'd gotten here, the sun had still been out.

"You're not going to push me into the lake or something, right?" I asked, following him down the lawn.

He laughed. "Not tonight." Once he'd found a place that looked to be about halfway between the water and the house, he lay on the grass. I hesitated. "C'mon, Olivia."

I lay beside him, leaving maybe a foot between the two of us, and looked up. "Is this your favorite thing? The stars?"

"My favorite thing is that this town is small, and the stars demand that you remember that. No matter what, you are not the biggest thing in the universe. Your best friend dying doesn't change the fact that the sun will rise and set tomorrow like clockwork. Even though you feel like the world has tilted off its axis, it hasn't because the stars are still where they've always been."

I couldn't breathe.

People like Whit and Davis may not be the center of the universe, but they left pieces of themselves everywhere they went. They were as omnipresent as the stars in this town, and my chest ached again. I resisted the urge to rub at it like I typically did when it felt like my lungs would collapse.

There was some light outside, but if I held my hand out in front of me, I could barely make out its shape. For a long time, we stayed in a comfortable quiet.

I think part of me was pretending again. Pretending that he wasn't Keating Whitaker and I wasn't Olivia Carrington.

"Sometimes," I whispered in the cover of night. Only brave enough to say what I was about to because I was sure he couldn't see me. "Sometimes I play this game with myself where I try to figure out how Davis loved me more than he loved this town." *He had to if he left it for me.* "He's everywhere here, and I'm nowhere."

Whit didn't respond, but I knew he was listening because I heard the deep inhalation of breath. The kind of breath you take when you get a papercut—it happens just before the sting, but you know it's coming. Too bad I wasn't prepared for the ricochet.

"He was obsessed with your name, Olivia. *Liv,* in particular. You were such a conundrum to him. A person who radiated passion but wasn't living despite her name. He wanted you to *live,* Olivia. He wanted you to try new things and be who you are, not what you thought other people wanted. He would be devastated if he thought you felt trapped here because of him."

Whit had become a master at reading between the lines. My problem wasn't that I doubted Davis loved me; I knew he did. My problem was that I didn't know why, and I was trying to find an answer in a town that didn't want anything to do with me.

I wanted to tell him that I didn't feel trapped here. I wanted to say to him that I was living.

I wanted to, but I couldn't because it wasn't true.

I did feel trapped in this town because of my husband. I felt like I owed it to him to belong here. It was like I was frozen in the moment he was gone. I couldn't move forward, but I couldn't go back either.

I felt his hand cover mine between us, and warmth so comforting and electrifying sizzled up my arm and throughout my body. Without any conscious reasoning on my part, my hand turned, and I laced my fingers through his.

I wished I could pretend it was Davis's hand because no amount of grief and regret would make the feelings I was having okay. Davis was gone, but this still felt like a betrayal.

Whit didn't pull back, which made everything feel worse.

Even in the dark, I couldn't pretend it was Davis because I'd never been this honest with him. I'd never been this honest or vulnerable with anyone.

Maybe not even with myself.

"I have nightmares," I whispered. "Of the accident. Every night in New York, I'd go to sleep, and I'd be in his car again or wake up in the hospital with Eric there. Pretty soon, I just stopped sleeping. When I moved here, the nightmares stopped being as frequent, but I still can't sleep through the night. I don't know why. Maybe it is the cicadas, but maybe it's something else."

Whit's thumb drew circles against my skin.

"Come by the clinic tomorrow. I'll prescribe something to help you sleep."

"Okay."

Tears pricked at my eyes, but I blinked them away quickly.

Not yet.

When I finally decided it was time to go inside, I said good-night to Whit and walked back into the house. Upstairs, I showered and tucked myself into bed.

I listened for the cicadas but didn't hear them.

The only thing I could hear was the ringing that accompanied silence. I tried to listen to the sound of my breathing, but it only made me think about Whit's.

I flexed my hand like I could still feel his skin on mine.

My breathing started to hitch, and the lump in my throat grew painful.

Turning on my side, I squeezed my eyes shut and covered my mouth so Eric didn't hear the sobbing that wouldn't stop.

Today is not a good day. I'm so tired and I don't
know if I can be back in Connor Bay
without you. You're all over that town, and I
miss you...even if you were kind of an
asshole.
That probably solidified my place in hell, right?
I shouldn't call you an asshole. You're dead.
You can't do anything about it.

20

MAGNIFICENTLY CURSED

WHIT

I didn't bother watching Olivia go inside. I wouldn't be able to see her in the dark anyway.

My hand twitched, burning with the phantom feeling of hers in it.

What was I doing?

I rubbed my eyes with both hands.

If Olivia were anyone else, I would have asked her out the minute I saw her again. I didn't want to think about how that was the plan initially before Davis swooped in and changed everything.

"I'll be right back," I told him, putting my drink on the table and standing.

He looked up at me with an amused expression. "Where are you going?" I looked back at the girl at the bar, and Davis followed my gaze. "Whit, be serious." His voice was incredulous, bordering on a laugh. "You don't have a shot in hell with that girl."

I felt my cheeks burn with embarrassment and sat right back down. "Oh, yeah? And why not?"

A more confident version of myself would have ignored him, but she made me feel small in a bad way. This whole city did.

Occasionally, so did Davis.

"The only reason a girl like that would be in a bar like this one is if she was looking for something quick. You wouldn't know how to do a one-night stand if I wrote you a manual with diagrams."

I frowned at him and looked over at her again.

Nothing about her led me to think she was interested in a fling. In fact, I'd be more apt to believe whoever she was meeting was late, considering how often she checked her phone, and that the location had not been her idea. She was too...rigid for this.

Her clothes, her face, her body language. Everything about her was Upper East Side martini bars and overpriced appetizers.

Davis wasn't wrong about me not being into hooking up with no strings attached, though. That had never been my thing.

"And besides, you live in Baltimore, and you're going to move back to Connor Bay next summer. A girl like that won't do long distance, and she sure as fuck won't do Connor Bay."

Davis was my oldest friend, but that didn't mean he didn't get on my nerves every so often. This was one of those times.

It felt oddly reminiscent of a time when I told him I had a crush on Stacy Finch in high school. He laughed at me then, too...right before he hooked up with her.

I could have argued with him and said that I just wanted to go up to the bar and talk to her, which was about all I had planned anyway, but he'd cut me off at the start.

What was the point of talking to her if I wasn't going to be able to take it any further than that?

He was right that a girl who looked like that probably wasn't in a hurry to get involved with someone who didn't fit into her life, rather than the other way around.

"Why don't I go over there and see what her deal is? If she's your type, I'll invite her back over here and introduce the two of you."

Davis rarely did anything like this out of the kindness of his own heart. He was a good guy, but when it came to women he was interested in...

"And what's in it for you?"

"Well, if she's my type..."

He waited as if I could give him permission to go home with her on her behalf.

I could tell that she was the furthest thing from Davis McCleary's type. She probably ran a company and followed the stock market. Even so, at the end of the day, Davis would do whatever he wanted, so I lifted a shoulder. He took his drink and walked over to her at the bar.

Biggest mistake of my life.

"Whit? That you?" Daisy's voice rang into the kitchen from the living room.

I dropped my keys on the counter. "Yeah, Daze."

She headed to the fridge. "Where have you been?"

"Eric and Olivia moved in next door." She raised an eyebrow at me before grabbing a water bottle and shutting the fridge. "What?"

"You know what, Keating?"

Oh, it was Keating now.

She arched a blonde brow at me so high I thought it might detach from her face and smack me.

Why did she have to be so irritating?

"Daisy, I'm tired. Could you just tell me what your problem is?"

Her eyes bulged. *Definitely wants to smack me.*

"How about the fact you're in love with that girl?" My jaw ticked. "See."

"Don't be dramatic. I'm not in love with her."

I didn't want to have this conversation with Daisy. Not now, not ever. My sister was the worst kind of person because she was loud and she had a propensity to dig her nose into everyone's business—especially mine—but she was also observant. She never avoided calling people on their shit, and this situation with Olivia was no different.

Heaven forbid I make any comments on the way she lived her life, but she could freely share her opinions on mine.

She scoffed, her nose crinkling its favorite judgmental position. "Not yet anyway."

"And so what if I was? Would it be so awful?" I swallowed because I knew the answer I wanted.

I wanted Daisy to tell me that it wasn't a big deal for Olivia and me to get together. I wanted her to say that even though there's a lot of shit we'll have to sift through, Olivia and I could do it.

I wanted these things more than anything right now, but I knew she wouldn't be singing a chorus of *Whit and Olivia sitting in a tree...* any time soon.

"Of course, it wouldn't be awful, Whit," she says almost sadly. "You're my favorite person, and I want you to be happy. I want Olivia to be happy, too. But just because *I* wouldn't judge you for it doesn't mean this town wouldn't. Connor loved Davis, and... I'm starting to realize they do *not* love Olivia."

My brow furrowed. "What have you heard?"

"Lots of little things. Nothing worth repeating. If you two started something, I don't think the town would take it well, Whit. They've got to warm up to her. Maybe you could talk to

Marjorie and Levi about how the town has treated her. They must not know."

Right.

The only problem bigger than my own second-chance, missed-opportunity storyline was Olivia's desire for her in-laws to like her.

It was kind of hard to talk to Daisy about that since she didn't believe that Marjorie McCleary was actually the source of this town's disdain for Olivia.

Marjorie and Levi McCleary were like our second set of parents. Marjorie taught her to swim and helped her practice lines for the school play when our mom was too busy with work.

If you asked Daisy, Marjorie probably qualified for sainthood.

I think they wanted Davis to marry her, have a few kids, and take over the diner.

While the thought of that disgusted me to my core, I knew where they were coming from. They, mostly Marjorie, had an image in their minds of what Davis's life would look like, and Olivia wasn't in it.

"I'll talk to them," I said, dragging a hand through my hair.

Daisy turned to leave the kitchen, "Whit, I'll support you in whatever happens, but you need to be prepared for her to turn you down. Not because I don't think she couldn't fall for you, but because she came here for something, and this might be more than she bargained for."

"Yeah, Daze, I know."

She nodded and left me in the kitchen to think about all the ways this would screw me over, except I couldn't think of anything other than the fact that Olivia was probably having a nightmare 100 feet away from my house, and I couldn't be there.

BAD OMEN

OLIVIA

I dreamed about Whit that night and was sick the next morning.

SORRY ON THE FLOOR

OLIVIA

My head lolled against the wall of the bathroom when Eric knocked. The porcelain of the tub pressed into my shoulder blade, grounding me in a way nothing else had that morning. I couldn't bring myself to look put together. My hair was tangled, my day-old mascara smeared faintly beneath my eyes, and I hadn't slept more than a handful of fractured minutes at a time.

I was so tired.

Not just sleepy. Bone-tired. The kind of tired that seeps into your joints and makes even breathing feel like effort. Emotionally, mentally, physically — I was running on fumes. I was fighting a losing battle, and I didn't have any more soldiers left to send out.

If I wasn't dreaming about my husband dying — about the sterile smell of hospital air and the relentless beeping of machines — then I was dreaming about screwing his best friend. There didn't seem to be an in-between anymore. No neutral ground where I could just exist without hurting someone.

Any way I looked at it, I was betraying someone.

And somewhere in the crossfire, I was just a casualty.

"Liv. Are you okay?" Another knock. "Can I come in?"

I swiped beneath my eyes with my thumb, as if that would erase the evidence of the last hour, and reached over to turn the knob.

"Oh my god, Liv. What's wrong?"

Eric crouched beside me immediately, the back of his hand pressed to my forehead like I was ten years old and feverish. His expression shifted quickly from confusion to worry.

"Are you sick? Should I call Whit?"

I laughed humorlessly. "God, no."

The sound cracked halfway through, splintering into something frantic and uncontrollable. The laugh folded in on itself and tipped forward into sobs before I could stop it.

"Liv." He didn't hesitate. He pulled me into his chest, tucking my head beneath his chin, wrapping his arms around me so tightly that it felt like he was physically keeping me from unraveling. "You're scaring me. Talk to me."

"I'm going to ruin everything," I choked out against his shirt.

"Oh, Liv."

"I can't stop thinking about him, Eric."

"Davis?"

My sobs came harder.

Of course, he would think that. Of course, he would think my every second was plagued with thoughts of my dead husband and not his best friend.

He pushed me back just slightly so he could look at my face. "It's not Davis. It's Whit, isn't it?"

A sob slipped through my lips, and my bottom lip shook violently. I nodded.

Eric didn't recoil. He didn't look shocked. He simply pulled me back against him.

"It's going to be okay," he murmured, rubbing slow circles between my shoulder blades.

He held me so tightly that it felt like he was the only thing keeping me stitched together. It was the only reason I could force myself to say the rest of it out loud.

There, on the bathroom floor, I told him everything.

About the voicemails. About how I'd been listening to them at night like they were some kind of twisted lullaby. About Marjorie and how small she made me feel. About the night Levi picked me up from the bar and how ashamed I'd been.

Eric didn't interrupt. He didn't flinch. He let me empty myself out completely.

When I finally fell quiet, I felt scraped hollow.

"Let me hear one," he said gently, brushing a loose strand of hair behind my ear.

I shook my head. "I can't. It's an invasion of privacy."

"I don't need to hear all of them," he replied. "But if you're asking me to tell you what to do about him, I need a crash course in Keating Whitaker."

I hesitated. My instinct was still to protect the sanctity of those messages — like they were sacred artifacts I wasn't allowed to share.

But I was exhausted. And I needed Eric. I needed him to help me think clearly. I needed him to stay after this moment passed, not just physically but emotionally.

We moved to my bed. I reached beneath my pillow and pulled out the cell phone.

After my self-loathing cry ended last night, I played some of his voicemails until I passed out. It was probably why I dreamed of him.

I scrolled to a *Before* voicemail and pressed play. Whit's voice filled the bedroom.

> *Hey, just calling you back from earlier. I think I can make next weekend work. The cologne is Dior Sauvage, and I assume you won't be reimbursing me for the bottle you stole from my bag. It's fine if Liv can't make it; she probably has much better things to do than hang out with us. I'm glad you got around to talking to her about how you were feeling about the work stuff. Daisy's been on me about us all meeting up back home; maybe you could try pitching a Connor Bay visit sometime next month. Anyway, I'll confirm next weekend later today.*

Eric let out a quiet huff of amusement. "I knew Davis would never wear cologne on his own."

I swallowed. I didn't want to think about how one of my favorite things about Davis had originated with Whit.

"Another," Eric said softly. "From after."

Scrolling to more recent voicemails, I picked another. Whit's voice was different. Thinner. Tired. There was something frayed beneath it.

> *So it's been two weeks, and I'm on my way back from the funeral. You would have hated it. Olivia was there with Eric. She looked...as you'd expect. God, this tie is...*

A rustling sound came through the speaker.

*That's better. You were too hard on that guy. I'm
    pretty sure he's the only reason Olivia is
    standing. Your parents hosted the wake at
    the diner. Daisy didn't show; she's in Milan
    on some guy's boat. She said that was a
    better way to celebrate your life. She's prob-
    ably right. I don't know.*

He was quiet, but the voicemail wasn't over. Eric and I looked at each other.

*I don't know what to do, Davis. I don't know
    how we're all supposed to move on. I want
    to call her and ask her if there's anything I
    can do, but I know there isn't. I know there's
    nothing I can do that will bring you back.
    What if I just make it worse?*

The voicemail ended.

Eric stared at the phone for a long time. He nodded to himself slowly.

"Olivia," he said carefully, "a lot of people in this town have made your life much harder than it has to be."

I laughed. *That was an understatement.*

"Whit is one of the only people you can depend on in this town. It would be reckless for you to pursue something with him when you need him."

My chest tightened.

He paused, weighing his next words.

"But I think it's been a long time since I've seen you feel... anything as strongly as you have since you met him. I think it's time Olivia Carrington lived a little recklessly."

I stayed in bed the rest of the day.

Eric's blessing had done little to settle me at first. If anything, it made everything feel more real. Saying the words out loud had given the feelings shape, and shape made them harder to ignore.

He was right that being with Whit would jeopardize all my progress in the past few days. Even if I wanted to...be with Whit in some way, I also couldn't be sure Whit felt the same.

For all I knew, he was just being kind.

Just being supportive.

Just looking out for his best friend's grieving widow.

The thought hadn't occurred to me until that moment, and it made my stomach churn.

What if I had mistaken decency for desire?

What if the way he looked at me wasn't loaded with tension but with responsibility?

If I said something — if I crossed that line — and he didn't meet me there, I didn't think I could survive that humiliation on top of everything else.

I couldn't keep living in this in-between, though. The constant what-if was exhausting. It would almost be easier if Whit drew a line in the sand. If he made the choice for me.

Whit seemed like someone who did the right thing. Every time. If he turned me down, I would have to accept it. I would have to let it go.

I rolled onto my side and stared at the wall until the light shifted from afternoon to evening.

While Eric was out being productive and stable and everything I was not, I made a list.

All the reckless things I could do in Connor Bay.

Small things.

Bigger things.

Things that scared me.

Things that felt selfish.

Things that had nothing to do with anyone else.

Like every decision list I'd ever made, it wasn't long.

But it was thorough.

It was Olivia Carrington's version of reckless — organized, color-coded, and terrifying in its own restrained way.

The next morning, Eric had to head back to the city for client meetings, giving me ample opportunity to do something from my list.

While it wasn't the most obscene thing I could have done (that was arguably anything on the list involving Keating Whitaker), I did the next most surprising thing.

"Can you just...sit!" I told the golden-haired dog in the kitchen.

He tilted his head at me, ears perked, tail thumping hopefully against the cabinets.

"Hotpie, sit!" The golden abruptly lay on the floor. "That's close enough." I leaned down to feed the dog a treat from my hand.

I'd never had a dog before, and now seemed as good a time as any to get one.

I drove back to the pet store across from Stones Pub, and they gave me the address to the shelter that organized the adoption event. I told myself I was just going to look.

Hotpie was four years old. A Golden Retriever with soft eyes and a medical file thick enough to make most people hesitate. Some ongoing issues. Nothing catastrophic. Just expensive.

He needed someone financially stable. I needed something that was mine. Something that depended on me in a way that wasn't wrapped in grief or obligation.

He needed someone to bankroll his vet bills.

I needed someone who didn't know who I was before.

It felt, in a strange and slightly unhinged way, like a fair trade.

Of course, there was the little matter of my never having trained a dog before.

The shelter assured me he knew the basics. House-trained. Good with people. A lot of energy, though. Selective hearing, they'd said with a knowing smile.

I could relate.

I wasn't ready to leap into whatever was happening with Whit. I wasn't ready to test that boundary yet.

Hotpie felt like a manageable kind of chaos.

Later in the afternoon, I took Hotpie to the pet store in town and bought him anything he showed interest in. I even let the con-dog talk me into buying him two beds. Naturally, he needed one in my bedroom and the living room. Toys shaped like things he would inevitably destroy. A collar I changed my mind about twice before committing.

By the time we left, the trunk and back seat were filled with his new belongings.

There was no room for him.

"Looks like you're upfront with me, but you are not allowed to change the station. The last thing I need is for you to find a radio station that plays only Baha Men's greatest hits."

He hopped into the passenger seat with no objections and immediately placed one paw on the center console as if claiming the space.

I fastened his harness with hands that trembled slightly — not from fear, but from the weight of what I was doing.

This wasn't just about a dog.

It was about choosing something.

Choosing myself.

And maybe, if I was being honest, proving that I was

capable of wanting something again without it being catastrophic.

Being a dog owner, I decided as I pulled onto the road, was about compromise.

He got the front seat.

I got the illusion of control.

And for the first time in weeks, the quiet didn't feel quite so suffocating.

23

———

I CAN SEE YOU

WHIT

Olivia didn't come into the clinic the next day or the day after that.

In fact, I didn't see her until I went to the diner on Saturday.

She had her hair clipped up and an apron on with a notepad and pen sticking out of her pocket.

She had her hair clipped up loosely at the back of her head, wisps escaping around her face, and an apron tied around her waist. A notepad and pen stuck out of her pocket like she meant business. She moved quickly between tables, focused, efficient.

It occurred to me that I'd think Olivia was the most beautiful person in any room, no matter what she wore.

Preferably, one day that would be nothing at all.

In one of our bedrooms.

Until then, I couldn't stop myself from imagining what things would have been like if Davis hadn't intervened that night in New York.

Would she have made out with me at the bar the way she did with him?

Would we be doing long-distance now?

Would she have convinced her job that she could work remotely so we could settle down here?

Or would I be the one searching for an opening in a New York hospital, convincing myself I could survive a city like that if it meant having her?

I blinked.

Olivia was leaning forward over the counter, elbows braced, talking to Donald. He sat across from her on a stool, a sweating glass of Marjorie's sun tea in front of him. She laughed at something he said, and the sound hit me square in the chest.

She glanced up at me when I came in and looked like she'd seen a ghost.

Donald turned his head to see who she was looking at, and I gave him a two-finger salute as I walked over. I had a feeling she'd been avoiding me, and the look on her face all but confirmed it.

Maybe things had gotten too personal that night. Olivia exuded the energy that she didn't let just anyone see her inner workings. Maybe not even her closest friends. If she thought I'd judge her for anything she said that night, she was sorely mistaken.

"Keating, how are you?" Donald asked as I sat down beside him.

"Just fine," I said, plucking a menu from between the napkin dispenser and the salt and pepper shakers. "You been keeping Olivia busy?"

"I'd say she's been keeping me busy." He rubbed his chin. "Say, you hear about that dog that's been gettin' out? Destroyed Marjorie's azaleas yesterday."

I glanced over at Olivia, who'd covered her mouth to suppress her laughter as she brewed another pot of coffee. I raised an eyebrow and continued my perusal of the menu as if I hadn't grown up with it.

"Whose dog is it?"

Donald shrugged. "No one's sure. Just showed up one day."

"Decide on what you're having?" Olivia asked, gaze fixed stubbornly on the notepad in her hand.

"Pastrami on rye." She quirked an eyebrow but wrote it down. "What?"

Olivia shook her head and passed the order through the window to the kitchen.

"So," I said, trying to sound casual and failing miserably, "Daisy wanted me to invite you and Eric out to Duke's tonight."

"Oh." She turned her back to me, reaching for clean mugs. "Thanks, but Eric's in New York this weekend."

She said it over her shoulder, like looking at me would complicate the sentence.

"So, just you then?" I put the menu back where I found it. "It'll be fun. Don, help me out here."

Donald looked between us, clearly enjoying himself. "Go on, Olivia. Live a little."

Her eyes flicked up to mine.

Live a little.

I'd said that to her three nights ago.

We held each other's gaze longer than necessary.

"Okay, fine, but not too late. I'm taking the morning shift here tomorrow."

I smiled. "Scout's honor, I'll have you home by 10."

She rolled her eyes, but the tension in her shoulders eased just a fraction.

The bell above the door rang again.

"Whit! How great to run into you!"

I suppressed a groan.

Molly Erickson.

I glanced at Olivia, hoping for a shared eye roll, but she'd suddenly found something very important behind the counter.

"Hey, Molly," I said. "How are the boys?"

She let out an exasperated sigh as she sat down next to me. "Actually, that's what I was hoping to talk to you about. Colin started Little League last year, and the team just isn't what it used to be."

Ah, that was what she wanted.

"I'm sure Jim is trying his best," I said, trying to seem understanding.

Molly picked up the menu, and the corner of her lip curled up like it offended her. Molly Erickson also never came in here without her kids: two twin boys around 2, and the older one, Colin.

"Well, the parents were hoping you'd coach this year. Since you're back and you know..." She glanced at Olivia, and an even more judgmental look passed over her face. "Davis used to."

I frowned at her. Molly wasn't the first person to use this on me.

Davis used to.

Davis promised.

Davis would have.

It was as if my presence here meant I was automatically the substitute. The stand-in. The extension.

It was how the Tomlinsons talked me into helping with some painting, and the Haverfords got me to agree to clean out their rain gutters.

It was hard enough being my own person, and now I had to be Davis McCleary too.

I'd had practice with that when I was younger. Davis wasn't always the best friend, but he was a good neighbor. He was always helping people with groceries or delivering newspapers. I didn't understand why being respected in this town meant killing yourself to prove it.

Each time someone had asked for my help recently, I intended to say no, but then they'd bring up Olivia and I just wanted her name out of their mouth. I wanted them to stop blaming her for Davis's decisions.

So instead of standing my ground, I just agreed to their tasks. It felt much easier to do in the short term.

I didn't think Molly would bring up Olivia while she was standing right there, but her expressions gave me pause.

"I don't think I have the time," I said finally. "I'm alone at the clinic right now. Jim's probably your best bet."

Molly's eyes grew wide. I was sure that no one had ever said no to her before.

"But, Davis—"

"Davis was always much better than me at baseball and coaching. Trust me. Jim is the safest option."

She stared at me like I'd spoken a foreign language.

"Well. If you're sure."

Old Keating Whitaker would have folded like a house of cards at this second attempt.

But as I wanted to explain to Daisy the other night, I have to choose myself. I can't be Davis and Keating to this town. I needed to be my own person.

"I am. Maybe next year," I said, turning back to Olivia when she placed my food in front of me.

I looked up at her, but she avoided my gaze like that was her *actual* job.

Great.

Olivia walked into Duke's that night, hell-bent on making me lose my mind.

She wore a strappy red dress with white flowers on it and her hair down. It was the usual attire for women in this town during the summer. There were probably ten other women in this bar alone wearing something similar, but she was different.

I'd thought about what Daisy said.

About not being able to keep Olivia forever.

About what the town would say.

I didn't care.

I didn't care if we only got a handful of nights. I didn't care if the furthest we ever went was holding hands and watching the stars. I would take whatever piece of her she was willing to give me.

And I was done pretending otherwise.

"Thanks for inviting me," she said, slipping into the narrow space between Daisy and me along the wall. It was standing room only. Her arm brushed mine.

My entire body lit up.

"Sorry, I'm late. Had to take care of something at home."

Daisy pushed a drink toward her. Olivia didn't ask what it was before she took a sip.

"Eric's in New York?" Daisy asked.

Olivia nodded. "Back Tuesday. He handles most of the presentations."

"When do you need to be back?" Daisy asked, already flagging down another round.

Olivia turned her glass slowly between her fingers. "Maybe in two weeks. I need to check on the apartment. Clients probably want proof I still exist."

Daisy nodded and then waved to someone across the room. "One second. I'll be right back."

When Daisy was out of earshot, I said, "Do you want to talk about the other night?"

"I don't think there's much to talk about."

She didn't look at me as she said it, so there was *clearly* something to talk about.

"Olivia, I'm sorry if I crossed a line—"

"No." She shook her head, still locked on her glass. "You didn't do anything wrong. You're a good friend, Whit. I'm just in my head about so many things, and I— I think..." She took a breath, her eyes closed.

"You think?" I pushed her.

My throat was closing, and my head was spinning. This couldn't already be over. I hadn't even tried to convince her to give me a chance yet.

"I think I'm starting to have feelings for you, and I don't think the two of us hanging out is a good idea right now because you've been so nice, and I don't want to ruin things."

She blurted it so fast that I struggled to keep up, but I'd heard it. I heard hope and possibilities and—

"Olivia, I—"

She put her hand up. "I know that this is coming out of left field. You probably think I'm a terrible person for telling you this and that I didn't love my husband and—"

"Olivia."

My voice was firm, and it stopped her in her tracks.

"I don't think any of those things. I think you're amazing and so strong and brave. I know you loved Davis, and it hurts me to hear you say those things about yourself."

Olivia looked at me, equal parts relieved and nervous. "Thank you for saying that, but—"

"I'm not done, Olivia." She went still. "I'm not staying away from you. In fact, just recently, I decided trying to do that wasn't an option for me."

Her throat bobbed. "What do you mean?"

I stepped closer to her. "I mean, I have feelings for you, and they probably started long before yours did."

There it was.

All of my cards out on the table.

She stared at me like I'd just detonated something between us. Then she shook her head.

"You're just saying that. You're just saying that because I'm standing in front of you, and you feel bad—"

And then I kissed her.

I kissed her in the middle of a crowded bar, and she kissed me back.

She was everything I imagined. She tasted like cherry vanilla and was the most delicious thing I'd ever experienced. Her lips molded to mine, and her hands cupped both sides of my jaw, pressing me further into her.

My tongue swiped over her bottom lip, and she sighed into my mouth.

If *this* was all I got from her in this life, I'd have that sigh on repeat in my head until the day I died. In fact, I might die right here in this bar because it couldn't get better than this.

And then it hit me.

I was making out with Olivia in the middle of a bar.

I pulled back, breathless. Her eyes were glazed. Her lips swollen.

"Come on." I pulled on her wrist and took her to one of the unisex bathrooms at the back of the bar. The ones past the communal restrooms that only the locals knew about.

We slipped inside together. I pushed the door closed and locked it.

My hands braced on either side of her head, caging her in.

"Whit," she whispered, breath uneven. "We... we're friends. We shouldn't..."

Her words dissolved when I gripped her jaw and slid a thigh between her legs.

"Does this feel like just friends to you, Olivia?"

On a groan that slipped from her, I lifted her up against the door. Her legs wrapped around my waist while her hands tugged on my hair.

I pressed my mouth against hers, my tongue slid across her lips, and I never wanted it to stop.

24

UP AGAINST THE WALL WITH ME
OLIVIA

"Stop," I whispered. "We can't do this."

His breath was warm against my cheek. Too close. Too familiar. Too different.

"Olivia."

I had prepared myself for him to smell like Davis, but he was all Whit.

His cologne was leather, not bergamot. He used a cinnamon toothpaste, not the harsh mint one Davis did. Or maybe he was just an ardent Big Red gum chewer.

Even though one of my senses could distinguish between Davis and Whit, my head spun.

I pushed on his chest, but he didn't budge. "This is too far. We can't do this."

The self-loathing spread quickly, blooming in my chest like something poisonous. I had thought Eric's permission would insulate me from this. That if someone else acknowledged the possibility, I wouldn't feel like I was betraying the dead.

I was wrong.

I hated myself.

I hated my list.

I hated Whit for existing in a way that made this possible.

He was so beautifully broken in all the same ways I was. That was the problem.

He cupped my chin and dragged my bottom lip down with his thumb.

"If you think I don't hate myself too," he said quietly, "you're wrong. I hate myself for wanting you more than you could know."

I saw my reflection in his green eyes.

And I saw exactly how much I wanted him.

"It'll change everything, Whit."

"So what?"

"So what?" I pushed at him again, but this time, he stepped back and let me slide down his body. I ignored how it made me feel. "Whit, you know that we can't do this."

"Do I?"

God, he was infuriating.

"You were his best friend."

His eyes searched mine. Not defensive. Not ashamed.

"He's gone, Olivia. He's never coming back."

I swallowed the lump in my throat. I knew that.

I *knew* that, but it didn't change what we were...what they had been.

"What do you want, Olivia?"

Time seemed to stall around us. The music outside the bathroom faded into nothing.

What did I want?

What was I allowed to want?

"I'm not asking about tomorrow," he said softly when I didn't answer. "I'm asking about right now."

Brutal honesty came out as everything else flew out of my mind.

"You."

His eyes flared, jaw tightened, but he didn't move. I was grateful.

"What do you want from me?"

"Everything."

Whit didn't hesitate that time.

Before I could take a breath, his mouth was on mine as he lifted me onto the counter. One hand gripped my right hip, pressing me against him, and his other hand was around my throat. His thumb pressed against my pulse, and his fingers held my jaw in place as he continued his assault on my mouth. Everywhere he touched felt like it was on fire.

His stupid, perfect mouth knew exactly how to work mine over.

I hated him. I hated that he felt this good against my body. I hated that my hands tangled in his hair and anchored him to me.

I had never done this before. Never in a place like this. Never with someone who felt like both a mistake and the only right thing at the same time.

Certainly never in a public bathroom.

What was it about the men from this town?

"Stay here," he murmured against my mouth. "Stay right here with me. Don't think about anything else."

It was a whisper, but there was a force behind it that had me working to get his belt undone.

Whit's hands went under my dress and tugged my underwear down my legs. I'd just gotten his jeans undone when he put his hand over my mouth and two fingers against my clit. I moaned against his palm, rocking against his hand.

"*Fuck*, Liv."

He removed his hand from my mouth and gripped my hair, angling my face toward his as he pressed his mouth to mine again. His fingers stopped their circling and dipped lower, but didn't enter me.

"I'm so mad at you, Olivia."

He was mad?

I was furious that he could form words while he was doing this to me. I was livid he wasn't touching me with his mouth. I was irate—

"If I only get this one chance with you like this, I'm mad you made it happen in a bathroom where I can't hear you scream."

I couldn't find words to tell him that I was mad at myself for that, too. That was probably a good thing because I couldn't find an obvious reason why this only had to be a one-time thing. I couldn't risk losing him, too.

"If I fuck you in here, Olivia, are you going to be quiet?" I nodded at him slowly, trying to regulate my breathing. "I need you to say it, Olivia."

I nodded again. "I'll be quiet, Whit."

"Good girl."

He pulled me off the counter and turned me around.

I didn't recognize the girl in the mirror. My lipstick was smeared around my mouth, and my cheeks were painted crimson. Mascara was smudged under my eyes, and my hair had never looked so wild in public.

Whit's fingers slipped under the straps of my dress and pulled them down, exposing my chest. I watched him look at me in the mirror. His hands cupped my breasts, pinching my nipples between his thumb and index finger. My mouth opened, but I didn't make a sound. He arched a brow at me and pinched harder. I pressed my lips together, suppressing what I could only imagine to be something absolutely feral.

I felt myself get wetter when he looked satisfied that I wasn't going to make any noise. I needed him inside me more than I needed to scream his name. I would hate myself tomorrow either way, but at least I'd be satisfied if I did what he asked. He pulled me back a step so I could watch him pull the skirt of my dress up. One of Whit's hands held my dress against my stomach while his other hand parted me with his thumb and ring finger, holding me open. Whit's smile turned wolfish, and I wanted to collapse against him.

"Touch yourself." My eyes widened. "Olivia, you've given me a finite amount of time, and it's running out. There are too many things I want to do with you. Touch yourself." He said when I didn't respond immediately. I swallowed.

I'd never done this either. I'd never touched myself in front of anyone, let alone while we stood in front of a mirror. I moved my hand over my clit and closed my eyes.

"Eyes open, Liv."

My mouth dried, but my eyes snapped open, and we both watched as I pressed against the bundle of nerves exposed at the apex of my thighs.

"You're doing so well. You're everything I ever dreamed of." I bit my lip and worked myself faster. "You gonna come?" I mumbled a confirmation. "Good."

He moved so fast that I didn't have time to orient myself to what was happening. My stomach pressed against the counter, Whit's hand fisted in my hair and tugged my head back so my breasts jutted out, my neck exposed. He used his legs to nudge mine further apart as he tore open a condom wrapper with his teeth and the hand not holding my hair. He rolled it on and then pulled my skirt over my ass. His fingers skimmed over my skin before he gripped my hip again.

"Still going to be quiet, Olivia?" I sealed my lips in response. Then he thrust into me, and I regretted agreeing.

"Fuck. Olivia, you're so...*god*."

I was so full. My fingers tried to grip the counter, to hold on to anything as he continued to pound into me. "You're taking me so well. Such a good fucking girl." His hands tightened in my hair and on my hip.

I was transfixed. I watched my breasts bounce with each thrust, the heat of my skin spreading red across my chest, the way Whit looked at me. Then, it was all too much; Whit's pace became erratic. The orgasm that washed over me was unlike anything I'd ever experienced. It felt endless. As I convulsed around him, Whit angled my mouth to his.

He kissed me like I was the beginning and end of everything. I knew he had finished when he bit my lip, lost to his release.

When we both came down from our high, Whit helped me situate my dress again before he buckled his belt. He washed the lipstick off around his mouth and dried his hands with a paper towel.He made it almost to the door before I found my voice.

"Whit."

He stopped but didn't turn around.

"That can't happen again."

I hated myself for a new reason. One that I couldn't bring myself to entirely think about.

He didn't turn to look at me. "Whatever you say, Olivia."

"I'm serious, Whit. We can't do this."

Whit didn't say anything, but he left, leaving me in the bathroom freshly fucked...without my underwear.

Reckless indeed.

25

NOTHING GOOD STARTS
IN A GETAWAY CAR

OLIVIA

I locked the door behind him and all but collapsed against it. I drew the line at sitting on the floor of a public restroom. I could still feel him on my skin, and I wanted to bask in it and scrub my body clean at the same time. The sensation of him lingered everywhere — on my lips, between my thighs, in the ache of my hips. I didn't know whether I wanted to preserve it or erase it before it had the chance to settle into memory.

I had to go back out there. I'd left my purse at the table, which was the second dumbest thing I did tonight and the third dumbest thing I had done at Duke's period. Leaving my purse meant I had to walk back out into the real world, into noise and light and Daisy and Whit, like nothing seismic had just shifted beneath my feet.

When I gathered enough strength to look at myself in the mirror, my lipstick was unsalvageable, I looked ¼ raccoon, and my hair was... wild in a way that didn't belong in a crowded bar. My cheeks were flushed, my lips swollen, my eyes too bright.

After ten minutes of trying to look semi-decent and working up the courage to see him out there, I finally left the bathroom, heart hammering in a way that had nothing to do with what we'd just done.

Even though I knew nothing had changed in the real world, *I* was changed. I was fundamentally altered in a way that I couldn't undo. But the bar was the same—music too loud, glasses clinking, someone laughing at something stupid.

No one had looked at me as I made my way to the table. The world had not stopped. No one could see the imprint of his hands on my skin.

Whit was talking to Daisy, and she was shaking her head in disbelief. He had to be telling her what had just happened. She was probably planning a mob of her own to run me out of town for hopping from her childhood crush to her brother. She—

"Olivia! Can you believe this? Whit just told me that the Clearwaters want to cancel the Summer Festival." I blinked. "This ruins your pitch, doesn't it?"

"My pitch?"

She looked at me like I'd lost my mind. "The pitch you and Eric are doing? To get publicity for the town using the Summer Festival as an attraction?"

Oh right. I was doing things other than letting Whit fuck me in a bathroom of a crowded bar. *Right.* My cheeks were burning, and I could feel his gaze on my face.

"Why do they want to cancel?" Now that I had access to my purse, I pulled my hair into a clip.

Whit answered, "Avery Clearwater organizes it, and her health isn't what it used to be. No one else wants to organize it so—"

"I'll do it." They looked at me like I'd grown two heads. "I'll organize it."

Daisy shook her head. "Liv, that's really kind of you, but it's a lot of work. You'll need to organize the town, the vendors..."

"I don't think that'll be a problem for Olivia, Daisy. I think the hardest part will be that any plans you make need to be approved by the business council." Whit's voice rumbled through my body, and focusing on what he was saying was exceptionally hard. Every syllable felt like a private reminder of what we'd just done.

"Why would that be the hardest for her? Liv is great with people!"

Whit rolled his eyes. "Daisy, you know what the situation is. No matter how much you want to think people in this town love each other, things aren't always so rose-colored."

"Well, if Olivia agrees that's the problem, then I'm happy to extend my visit and help her plan the festival. I can go with her to the business council meetings and pitch the ideas with her. What do you think?"

Daisy looked at me encouragingly, and not at all how you would look at a friend who had just fucked your brother in the bathroom.

There was no suspicion. No accusation. Just warmth.

"Sure, Daisy. I'd love your help. Maybe you can talk to the Clearwaters and ask them how they'd feel about it. If Avery's up for it, I'm sure we could include her in our planning."

"That's a wonderful idea. I'll stop by their place tomorrow." I nodded at her.

It was getting hard to avoid Whit's direct gaze, so I grabbed my bag and was about to make an excuse to leave when Daisy said, "Actually, tomorrow night, I'm having some of my friends over for a girls' night. Whit's going to make himself scarce. Why don't you come? It would be great to have you meet some more people in town."

Daisy was being so nice to me that the thought of turning her down caused a wave of guilt through my core. I wanted to try, and she was giving me a chance. Eric would be gone for another two nights, and hanging out with Daisy sounded better than lying awake replaying the way Whit had looked at me in that mirror.

"Plus, those fathers on the business council do whatever their wives and daughters tell them. If you can rub some shoulders tomorrow, it would make the business council easier to win over."

Ah, we were strategizing. I knew how to do that.

"Okay, Daisy. Sure. I'd love to come." My cheeks heated again. I could just *hear* Whit's inner monologue.

Happy to make that happen again...and again.

"Great! Maybe swing by around 7? You know where it is."

I made a face. "I do?"

Daisy's eyes lit with confusion and swept from mine to Whit's. She laughed and looked back at me. "Well, I'd hope so. You moved in next door."

I did what?

I forced a laugh. "Right. Of course. I've moved around so much I just forgot. Right. I'm going to call it a night. See you tomorrow at 7...next door."

Why wouldn't Whit tell me that he lived next door? It seemed like a normal thing to mention. It didn't technically change anything, but it felt like something that should have been said. If it was harmless, why did it feel like I was suffocating? Like he was suddenly everywhere—in the clinic, at the diner, in the house beside mine, in my head.

We hooked up, and now what?

I told him I didn't want it to happen again, but was that true? And the part of me that might want it to happen again, was it because I wanted Whit or because I wanted a distraction?

"Olivia!" Whit's voice stopped me as I pulled the handle of my car door.

"Not now, Whit." Not when I was trying to figure out if I wanted him. Not when I could so easily be persuaded by his mouth alone.

"I'm sorry I didn't tell you we live next door."

The least of my concerns, honestly.

I stood between the door and the car, one hand on the door frame and the other resting on the roof of the car with my keys in hand.

"It's fine, Whit. I just need to go back to the house. I'm exhausted."

Instead of capitalizing on an easy innuendo, he frowned at me. "Let me drive you home. If you haven't been sleeping, you shouldn't be driving."

I shook my head, looking anywhere but at him. I couldn't be in a car with him right now. I couldn't be in a small, contained space with the memory of his hands still humming in my veins.

"We don't have to talk. Just let me take you home."

The bar light outlined him in shadow. I knew I could drive myself. I also knew he wouldn't stop asking.

"You came with Daisy. Shouldn't you drive her back?"

"She drove me, actually."

"What if I recite the alphabet backward? Can I drive myself home then?"

He laughed, and even from this distance, it reverberated through my body in a way that was deeply inconvenient.

"No."

"Fine," I said, tossing the keys in his general direction and walking to the passenger side.

It was as bad as I thought it would be. In fact, not talking was making it worse because I couldn't stop thinking about what we did. How sure he was when he touched me. How deeply inside my mind he got.

Stay here. Stay right here with me, Olivia.

How did he know I was overthinking?

"You didn't come by the clinic."

I glanced over at him. *Mistake number 854 (probably).* "I thought we weren't talking." He rolled his eyes. "I was avoiding you."

"Clearly," he scoffed.

"I will probably avoid you again."

"Counting on it."

My head whipped toward him. "What's that supposed to mean?"

"Olivia, your fight or flight response is to avoid entirely."

"I knew this would happen."

"You knew we'd fuck in Duke's bathroom?"

Fuck.

The word coming out of his mouth heated my body and tightened things that should not be paying attention to him. I wanted to hear him say it in all kinds of ways. Breathlessly. Assertively. *Desperately.* I was very aware that I wasn't wearing underwear in that moment.

I didn't respond, but he was smiling when I glanced at him.

"What's that face for?"

He licked his lips, and his smile widened. "If you were avoiding me because you thought we might do something like that, Olivia, then I'm sorry to say you're a liar."

"Excuse me?"

"That's not going to be our last time, and the next time won't be our last time either."

I should have smacked him. I should have lectured him on

consent, but I knew that was not what he meant. I could feel the certainty in the words. I was putty in this man's hands...his voice...his—If we weren't on the same page, we would definitely be doing it again. *Unless* I managed to avoid him.

"Whit, I need it to be our last time. Our *only* time," I corrected hastily.

"Why?"

"Whit."

"Olivia."

I shook my head, fighting the urge to chew on my thumbnail nervously. "I can't be in a relationship with you."

"Who said anything about a relationship?" My cheeks heated. "I mean, that's obviously my favorite option of all the options there are, but I know that's not where we're at yet."

Yet.

I didn't want to respond to that. What did he want from me if he knew we weren't in relationship territory? We both admitted to having feelings for each other, and clearly, we had chemistry, but...

"We don't need to figure this out now, Olivia," he continued. "Even though I would love nothing more than to crawl into bed with you tonight. I'm just putting that out there."

He added the latter part when I shook my head again in disbelief.

"Just don't avoid me, okay? We can pretend this didn't happen until you're ready to talk about it, but I'm in, Olivia. Whatever you want. You want to screw around when no one's watching? I'll map out every alcove in this town."

Don't think about that, Olivia, especially when he has your underwear in his pocket.

"You want to try being friends with no benefits? Okay with me. I hear you. But I don't want you to decide anything right now. Just think about it."

"Okay. I'll think about it."

Except in bed that night, when I thought about the two of us, I could only think about his hands on me.

I thought about how they felt against my skin and his fingers on my hip. How his hand wrapped around my hair and tugged in a way that I shouldn't have found pleasurable. I thought about how I wished his hands were pinching my nipple and pressing on my clit and not my own.

Then, I pictured him watching me get off in bed, and I crashed. I fell so hard into a wave of bliss that I let out an audible groan in the silence of my bedroom.

For the first time since moving to Connor Bay, I slept through the night.

*Davis, I never told you this. And I don't think
    I'd ever be brave enough to say it to your
    face.
I was so angry with you that night in the bar and
    even more angry when you went off and
    married her.
When you told me, I thought that she must be
    more like you than me. That I'd read her
    wrong in the bar.
Maybe Olivia was just as wild and reckless as
    you and we never would have worked. But
    then you started calling me about the two of
    you, and I realized that wasn't the case.
You went over to her that night and knew we'd
    be good together, and you took her home*

*anyway. I saw her first Davis, and it meant
    nothing to you.*
*I think...I think I've been angry with you ever
    since. I think I still am.*
*No, I know I still am because I saw her today in
    the market and it was electric.*
*It should have been Liv and I and I don't know
    how to get over it.*

26

I DON'T WANNA SHARE

WHIT

I knew I should have given Olivia space after the bar, but I couldn't let her go home without talking to her first. The only reason I left the bathroom after her declaration that we wouldn't hook up again was because I knew she'd need to go back to the table to get her keys.

I told myself I was being practical. Responsible. But really, I just wasn't ready for it to be over. Not like that.

When I returned to the table, Daisy was talking to Stacy Finch, but the look she gave me told me I'd get an earful later that night. It wasn't subtle. It was the look she used to give me when we were kids, and I'd tracked mud through the house five minutes after Mom mopped.

Daisy stormed into the house an hour after I got back from dropping Olivia off. I was in the kitchen making a drink. Lord knew I needed one. The silence after leaving Olivia at her door had been louder than any lecture Daisy could deliver.

"Keating Whitaker!"

Here we go.

"In here," I called, only because the longer it took Daisy to find me, the angrier she would get.

Her face was furious. I tried and failed to suppress a laugh.

"You think this is funny? Do you know how much damage control I had to do? Do you know how many people saw you take her into that bathroom to do God knows what?"

I shrugged, leaning back against the counter like this was no big deal. "I'd say...no less than 15."

"And you won't even say thank you. Typical." She took the drink from my hand.

"Daze, I didn't ask you to do that. In fact, I think it would have worked in my favor for a little gossip to run rampant."

The stare she gave me was lethal. "Yeah, you maybe. You're a man and a town favorite. Olivia is trying to make friends in this town, and sleeping with you isn't going to do her any favors." She jabbed at my chest with her index finger. "Next time, take her home first. For fuck's sake, Keating. This is so unlike you."

She wasn't wrong.

I'd never done that before. Not like that. Not in a public bathroom with half the town within earshot.

Tonight was straight out of Davis McCleary's playbook.

And the sick part?

He got her once doing it his way. So I figured maybe it would work a second time.

"Maybe things can be normal now that you've got it out of your system."

I gave her a look as I poured another drink. "Of course. *Of course*, screwing around made it even worse. God, Keating. Can't you pick someone else? Either of you. Literally *anyone* else."

"No offense, Daisy, but this isn't any of your business."

She clicked her tongue, sharp and impatient. "Keating, if

you think that what you do with that girl isn't this whole town's business, you are delusional at best and a complete moron at worst. She is under a fucking microscope right now. Do you think they'll take kindly to her being with her husband's best friend? The town's doctor? You stitched up Matt Dillard's son's face with those hands!"

I slammed my glass down on the counter harder than I meant to. The sound cracked through the kitchen.

"I'm so sick of hearing about Davis."

The words came out harsher than intended, but I didn't take them back.

Daisy gaped at me.

"I know who my best friend was, okay? I know who she was married to, but I saw her first."

God, it sounded so childish the second it left my mouth. Like we were arguing over a toy instead of a woman.

But I needed someone to know. I needed someone to understand that this wasn't some opportunistic rebound fantasy. This had roots.

She blinked at me in confusion. "What do you mean you saw her first? Davis met her in a bar."

I gripped the edge of the counter with both hands, head hung between my shoulders.

"We were there together. I saw her at the bar and told Davis I was going to talk to her. He talked me into letting him go over first. Said he'd wingman for me."

The memory still made my jaw clench.

"Oh, Whit...I—"

"He wasn't even into her long-term at first. When they left together, he texted me and said she was only into a one-night thing. I figured that was it. They'd hook up and never see each other again."

When I looked up, Daisy looked devastated. "And then Davis stayed, and they got married."

"And then Davis stayed, and they got married." I nodded.

"You never told him? About how you felt?"

I shook my head. "How could I?"

He was my best friend.

He was happy.

And I didn't know what I would've done if he'd chosen her anyway.

"Whit..." Daisy's voice softened, the anger draining out of it.

I rubbed a hand over my face. "Then he started complaining about her. Nothing serious, just like...little spats about how much she worked or that she made him go to work parties, and I just..."

Daisy stared at me, taking it in. "Whit, you can't...Olivia picked him."

"Only because he didn't let her pick me."

The second it left my mouth, I knew how it sounded. Desperate. Delusional.

She shook her head. "You can't know that, Whit. You can't know what would have happened if you went up to her that night. That's not how it works."

I knew she was right. This wasn't the first time I'd tried to play this out in my head. There was no guarantee I'd be with Olivia now if I'd met her first. But it didn't matter to me.

"I know that, Daisy, but I have a chance now. Now that she's here and he's not, I have a chance now."

I watched my sister's heart break for me. I could tell it was happening because her eyes were glossy, and her mouth was quivering in the way it did when she was fighting back tears.

"I know that makes me a bad person, but I don't care. I don't care that she was with Davis or what the town thinks.

Every time he talked about her, I felt like I should have been him."

The truth I'd never said out loud.

Daisy swiped under her eyes. "I can't say that I agree with everything you're saying, but I understand where you're coming from. I'm glad you get this chance with Olivia, but you need to be careful with your heart. Olivia married him, Keating. She loved him. You need to give her time, and you need to give this town time."

Time.

I nodded, even though the word felt like a threat.

Because the problem with time was that you never knew how much you had left.

27

OUT OF MY HEAD

OLIVIA

"What do I do, Hotpie?" I asked, trying to tug the rope toy out of his mouth.

It was embarrassing how strong he was and how *not* strong I was. He braced his paws against the hardwood like he was in a professional tug-of-war league, eyes bright with triumph, tail thumping.

We were making great progress on his training, but not so great progress on decisions regarding Keating Whitaker. At least Hotpie responded to commands eventually. My brain did not. As I tried to extricate the toy from his mouth, Eric called me on FaceTime.

"Okay, Hotpie, time to be really quiet. Remember what we practiced. Hide."

Hotpie dropped the toy and barked at me once—defiant, theatrical—before sprinting up the stairs. It had taken a full day of training, but we finally managed to associate "hide" with laying under my bed until I gave the okay. It was less obedience and more dramatic compliance, but I'd take it.

I was sure Whit was right that day outside the pet store;

Eric would never let me get a dog. He was a cat person through and through. Structured. Predictable. Dogs were chaos with fur.

I answered his call.

"Hey, how's New York?" I asked, plopping down on the couch and trying to look like someone who had not recently had sex in a public bathroom.

From the background, I could tell he was in the office. Stark white walls. Framed campaign boards. Overhead lighting that made everyone look slightly overworked.

"Same old, same old. I was just calling to check in and see if you needed anything from your desk. I can bring it back with me. I might come back tomorrow instead." I raised an eyebrow. "What's that look for, Olivia Carrington?"

I laughed. "Nothing. The Eric from a few weeks ago would take his time coming back to a town with no good espresso." I mimicked his grumpy voice.

"Ah, well. Things change. Like you, for example." His eyes narrowed. "You seem...chipper. When I left, you were quite distraught. What happened?"

I laughed again. "Nothing. Can't I just be happy?"

He gave me a look that said he'd known me for far too long for that to fly.

"Okay," I said. "But I think this information would be best conveyed in person."

"Olivia."

"I had sex with Whit."

I blurted, biting my bottom lip afterward to refrain from admitting anything else to Eric DiCarlo. Thank god it was Sunday, and I was positive no one was hanging around the office to hear this conversation.

There was a fast movement on the screen and the sound of a phone clattering to the ground.

It was then I heard a startled, "Excuse me?" When he picked up his phone again, his eyes were wide. "What are you saying? When? How?"

"Last night." If I kept my responses brief, I would be less likely to incriminate myself.

"Did he come over?"

I was blushing furiously now. *What was safe to say?* "No, I met up with him and Daisy at Duke's."

"So he brought you to his place?"

I relented. "No, it happened at the bar."

And down went his phone again. I was just full of phone-dropping surprises today.

Eric had his hand over his face as he came back into view. "Olivia, are you telling me you had sex in a bar? Is that what you're saying right now?" His voice rose an octave every few words, like a boy going through puberty. "That you and Whit were so charged with sexual tension that you could not manage to drive 10 minutes to a house with a bed in it. Is that what you're saying?"

I blinked and let out a surprised laugh. "I don't think I said *all* that, but I am saying that Whit and I had sex in a bathroom at Duke's. That is what I'm saying."

He shook his head, but he was smiling now, somewhere between scandalized and impressed. "For the love of God. I leave you unsupervised for less than four days, and you just... Was it good? It was probably good. His forearms do the veiny thing when he flexes them. Did you do it against the door so he'd have to hold you up? God, I bet you did."

"Eric!" While my best friend was pretty open about his sexual escapades, I preferred some privacy when it came to specifics.

"Sorry. *God*, I need to get laid; otherwise, I'll have to live through you."

I frowned. "Did you see Leo while you were there?"

Eric looked off-screen. We hadn't talked about Eric's ex-boyfriend since the night he came to stay with me in Connor Bay, and I had a feeling we weren't really going to talk about him now.

"Are you going to?"

"I don't know. I don't think we're compatible, so what's the point? He's so..."

"Pretentious?" I offered. It wasn't a secret that I didn't care for Leo much, but Eric liked him, so I tolerated him.

Eric tilted his head this way and that, which was his way of agreeing with me, even if he didn't want to do it out loud.

"Well, I'm supposed to be hanging out with Daisy and her friends tonight, so I'll get the scoop on the available guys in this town for you."

He shook his head as if trying to make sense of what I'd just said. "Hold on. Rewind. What?"

"Last night, Daisy invited me to hang out with her friends, so I'm going to her place. Which, by the way, is next door! Did you know they lived next door?"

Eric grinned slowly. "Wow, this is the small-town romance you deserve, Livie. Before you know it, you'll be sneaking over to his place to knock boots." His hand came into view as he wiped a pretend tear under his eye. "They grow up so fast."

My eyes widened, and my mouth dropped open slightly. "Eric, there will be no midnight booty calls."

Can you even call it a booty "call" when you're just shouting from your windows across the lawn?

"Why not?"

"Why not?" I exclaimed. "You sound like Keating."

He smirked. "What did Whit say about this? Kind of seems like he would be interested in a little late-night rendezvous."

I let out an aggravated sigh. "Why don't either of you see how bad this is?"

"Olivia," Eric said more seriously now, "when I left, you'd decided you were going to tell him how you feel. You did. And then you had sex. That doesn't sound like a disaster to me."

I rubbed my forehead, feeling the argument forming like a storm cloud. "Unless it's not a disaster for you specifically. Unless you're worried about something else?"

The shift in his tone pulled me backward in time.

Eric leaning over my shoulder in the office, pointing out a typo on an ad mockup.

"So, did Davis agree to come tomorrow?"

I frowned, adjusting the kerning on the lettering. "I didn't ask him. Does that spacing look okay? I feel like it's smushed. Maybe I'll go up an eighth."

"What do you mean you didn't ask him?"

I looked at Eric in his tailored suit with monogrammed cuff-links and then down at my pencil skirt and silk button-up. How could I explain to Eric that Davis wasn't the same as us? He didn't know how to schmooze or mingle with people in a marketing firm. Our coworkers' idea of an office party was renting out a quirky bar and pretending they had real personalities. Davis didn't fit, and he'd made it clear after the last one that he didn't want to try to fit.

"I mean, he didn't like the last one he went to, so I didn't invite him to this one. I think this mockup is done. I'll send it to Elise in design to print and put it together for your pitch tomorrow."

Eric clicked his tongue. "Davis should be there, Liv. He's your husband."

"I know that, Eric, but just because he's my husband doesn't mean he needs to come to every work function I attend."

Eric pushed me on it, and I gave in. I made Davis come. He insisted on driving.

Back on the couch, I realized the through-line: I had spent years trying to make everyone comfortable. Smoothing edges. Avoiding tension. Pretending compromise was the same as happiness.

If I had stopped trying to please everyone, maybe I wouldn't have felt so...split all the time.

It came down to fear.

Fear of what the town would think. Fear of being judged again. Fear that if I chose Whit and it didn't last, I would lose everything all over again.

"Just scared of something new," I admitted quietly.

Eric's expression softened. "I know. You've had a lot of change in a short amount of time. It feels like Davis was just here. But there's no timeline for any of this, Liv. You do what feels right. If Whit feels right, try it. What you do is no one's business...except mine. And, you know, Whit's."

I smiled despite myself.

"Saying yes to exploring something with him isn't signing a lifetime contract," Eric continued. "If he's open to figuring it out slowly, then figure it out slowly."

I nodded, more to myself than to him. "Yeah. Okay."

Then a thought struck me.

"Eric, I have to go. I think I have a doctor's appointment."

His grin widened knowingly. "Yeah, you do."

28

DEVILS ROLL THE DICE

WHIT

The ball was in her court, and that lack of control was driving me insane. I couldn't get her out of my head. I couldn't get the sound of her moaning off my internal record player, and I couldn't stop the phantom feeling of her tightening around me like my body had decided it no longer needed her physically present to remember exactly how she felt.

I rubbed a hand over my face. *Get a grip, Whit.*

I had to get through these appointments. Weekends were the busiest days in the clinic because most people in town couldn't afford to take time off during the week to see a doctor.

Pete had been a hardass about keeping to a 9-to-5 Monday through Friday, but he was older, and no one was about to argue about flexibility when the closest hospital was an hour outside of town.

The back-to-back appointments were killer, but they gave me room to breathe during the weekdays for the most part. I'd need to start looking for a partner in the clinic soon. I didn't know how Pete managed this on his own. Maybe I could hire an intern to—

"Come in."

I glanced up from my next patient's file as Stacy's blonde head popped into my office. Pete hired her after she finished her program. She was a fine medical assistant but could be... overly attentive.

"I'm sorry, Keating. There's a situation, and I tried to explain to her that you don't have any room in your schedule to see an extra patient today." Stacy let out an aggravated sigh as she pinched the bridge of her nose. "She said she didn't mind waiting for you to be free if you got done early with someone and that it would be quick, but she's been here an hour and a half. I thought she'd get the hint because—"

"Did you ask her to schedule an appointment for tomorrow? Surely it can't be an emergency if she can wait close to two hours."

Stacy shook her head. "I did. I told her we had plenty of openings for tomorrow, but she swore it would be quick and that she'd wait."

I raised a brow in confusion and shook my head slightly. "Who is it, Stacy?"

She clicked her tongue against her teeth. An irritating habit she'd developed since high school, and one she hadn't outgrown. "Olivia Carrington."

My throat went dry.

Olivia had been waiting for me.

For an hour and a half.

She'd been less than thirty feet away for almost two hours, and I hadn't known.

"Send her in."

Stacy's brows all but hit the ceiling. "Keating, you're booked solid. You're already late for your next appointment.

Both exam rooms already have people in them. Surely you have to be—"

"Send her in here then."

Stacy gritted her teeth. "Right away, Dr. Whitaker."

Ah. I was *Dr. Whitaker* now, I guess.

As she turned to leave, I stopped her.

"Stacy, one more thing. Next time Olivia Carrington wants to see me, you let me know immediately."

Her face pinched. "Understood."

Once the door closed, I surveyed the room like a trapped rat in a maze. I wasn't sure if I wanted to throw up, yell at Stacy, or clear my desk in case Olivia had come in for a quickie. *God*, wouldn't that be—

"Come in," I managed to say when Olivia knocked on the door as I tried to get a very NSFW image out of my head.

Olivia looked like the definition of ravishing in a white sundress with her hair piled on her head alongside her sunglasses, and the glossiest lips I've ever seen.

"I'm sorry to cause a delay in your appointments, Dr. Whitaker." She said with a tilt to her mouth as she sat across from me.

I would give up several organs to hear her call me that in a less...formal situation.

I leaned back in my chair. "Not a problem. What can I do for you, Olivia?"

Then I realized she might actually be here for a medical concern and straightened my posture.

"Did you want a prescription for the sleeping pills? I should really do a formal examination and tests and make sure—"

"I think I've found a solution to that problem," she said smoothly, crossing one leg over the other. Her dress shifted up a fraction of an inch. "No need for medication."

My eyes snapped back to hers.

"Something else then?"

"I've given some thought to our conversation last night."

I leaned forward despite myself as a faint red flush began to spread across her chest and up her neck.

"And?"

"And—"

The door swung open.

"Keating, I'm sorry, but if you're any later, you'll be here past five," Stacy said, walking in like this was a group meeting. She turned to Olivia. "Surely I can assist you. I am a trained medical assistant."

I stared at her like she'd grown a second head and sprouted horns.

"Stacy," I said evenly, "I don't think Olivia doubts your competence. But I'm beginning to question your decision-making abilities. If you can handle Olivia, you can handle checking on our next patient. You have their file. I can stay late. It's fine."

Stacy let out a breath and closed the door behind her.

Olivia looked amused, and I was just annoyed. "I'll add Stacy to my list of people who don't like me."

"It's not you. I'm just busy today, and she's...neurotic."

Olivia raised a perfectly sculpted brow at me.

"You're right. It couldn't be that she's interested in you, and she's upset that you're in here talking to me and neglecting poor Sally Henderson and her arthritic hands."

I laughed. "Well, I could get back to Sally and her hands if you'd tell me why you're here."

"And she seems comfortable walking in without knocking," Olivia noted, inclining her head to the door.

"You want her gone, Liv? Say the word."

Her mouth dropped open just slightly. Enough for me to know I'd shocked her.

Good.

"Though I doubt you came here to complain about Stacy Finch."

She looked down at her hands in her lap and then back up at me. A resigned calm had settled over her features.

"I'd like to try."

My breath caught. I could feel a cold sweat break out on the back of my neck. She waited almost two hours to—

Clearing my throat, I rolled my shoulders back. "I'm going to need you to be a little more specific."

Olivia smiled, suppressing a breathless laugh. I couldn't think. I needed her to keep talking because I wasn't able to.

"I told you I couldn't do a relationship," she said carefully, "and that's true, but I could do...other things."

The floor dropped out from under me.

"Like what?" I managed.

Her eyes widened. "Do you need a list?"

"I'd prefer schematics."

She laughed, and it was glorious. The most beautiful sound I'd ever heard.

"I want you to come over tomorrow night," she said. "I want you to spend the night with me. We can decide what this is then. I'll even draw you schematics. Maybe an infographic."

No thoughts. Head empty. Medical license in jeopardy.

"And tonight," I said, because apparently my brain was functioning again, "you're breaking up with your secret boyfriend so it's all kosher?"

Olivia stood from her chair with a smile. "If that's what you think Daisy and her friends are to me, then yes."

Right. Daisy invited her to a girls' night at the house.

"What if I came over after?"

"Is there an after to these things?"

II laughed. Usually, I woke up to find Daisy's friends passed out across our furniture like fallen soldiers. "Fair point. I'll see you tomorrow, Olivia."

"See you tomorrow, Whit. Sorry for disrupting your appointments."

She looked over her shoulder as she left, and I felt that look somewhere deep in my ribcage.

I let out a slow breath once the door closed.

I had a date.

Kind of.

With Olivia Carrington.

I could practically feel Stacy hovering outside when I finally opened the door. She looked torn between irritation and relief. She had a girls' night to attend, after all.

"Let's see if we can get back on track, shall we?" I took the file from her and walked down the hall toward the exam room.

And tried very hard not to grin like an idiot.

29

ANGELS ROLL THEIR EYES

OLIVIA

There was something ominous about knowing you were about to walk into a house filled with women who had known each other their whole lives. They spoke a language that was foreign to outsiders.

Facial expressions carried subtext. A raised brow could mean war. A sip of a drink could signal allegiance. Their body language held secrets I would never fully decode. Going inside felt like walking into a lion's den unarmed, and I wasn't sure what the mortality rate was. Judging by how few outsiders stayed long-term in this town, my guess was high.

I took a deep breath before knocking on the door. Aside from potentially being socially eviscerated, I had too many reasons to turn around and go back to the house, but I owed Daisy this much. My preferred method of winning people over one at a time was working, but it was slow. Painfully slow.

When I'd stopped by Paula's after seeing Whit to help her set up her new digital system, I mentioned the Summer Festival. She'd given me her full support without hesitation, which meant I had at least one vote on the business council. The issue was convincing the others that I was capable of running it. Daisy beside me was my only real leverage.

"Liv!"

Daisy answered the door in a green facemask, matching pajama set, and martini glass in her hand. I blinked.

"Come in, come in. Let me get you a drink." She wrapped a hand around my wrist and tugged me inside the Whitaker home.

"I uh...I didn't know this was a pajama situation."

She laughed. "It's a come-as-you-are situation, Liv. This is my most relaxed version, and if yours is a sweater, jeans, and booties, then more power to you."

I almost told her that my most relaxed self looked suspiciously like hers, but we'd already stepped into the living room.

Their heads, like owls, all turned toward me.

"Girls, you know Olivia. Olivia, hopefully, you've met Amelia, Stacy, Sidney, Claire, and Grace."

I gave them all a tight smile and an awkward wave, "Hi."

The Whitaker home was open and spacious. It could fit the seven of us with plenty of room in the living area for more. Though I hoped that this would be everyone.

I did not have a good track record in social situations like this one, and from the look Stacy was giving me, I did not have high hopes for this one.

"Sit, I'll get you a drink."

I slipped off my shoes and took the armchair beside Amelia.

I knew most of them in passing. Amelia was the florist's daughter. Sidney worked at the coffee shop. Claire was married to Matt Dillard. Grace worked at the bank. Stacy...

"So like I was saying," Stacy continued, placing her drink down, "Caroline Stenson claims her landline picks up other people's calls. That's how she knows everything."

My eyes widened in confusion before it clicked.

I knew it! I knew she had the town tapped! But who even has a landline anymore?

"Who has a landline these days, Stacy?" Claire asked from her place beside Stacy on the couch in front of a large window overlooking the Whitaker's front lawn.

Stacy shrugged. "That's just what she said."

"And even if they do," Claire pressed, "who's actually using them?"

"That's ridiculous. I'm not talking about this anymore. How do you like the town, Olivia?" Amelia asked from beside Sidney on the couch.

I gave her a small smile. "It's good."

"Different from the city, I bet," Claire added.

"Oh yeah," I said, letting out a small laugh. "But not in a bad way. Just different. How's wedding planning going, Amelia?"

If there was one universal thing among people getting married, it was that they loved to talk about their wedding.

Amelia was in the middle of relaying a problem with her caterer when Daisy returned with a drink for me, her green face mask rinsed off. She sat beside me on the arm of the chair and listened to her friends chatter.

This was good. I could do this. I could nod sympathetically and excitedly in all the right places.

Of course, it was too good to be true.

Stacy placed her drink on the table. "So, Olivia, what was so important that you waited to see Keating for almost two hours? Was your phone broken?"

She asked the last part with a laugh that someone unfamiliar with people like Stacy would take to be joking. I knew better. I also knew better than to look at Daisy, who I felt staring at me.

"Oh, just something he's helping me with. I didn't want to

talk about it over the phone." I waved it off as I took a sip of... the world's strongest espresso martini to grace my presence.

Daisy was either trying to fortify me or eliminate me. The verdict was still out.

Stacy raised a brow. "So you and Keating aren't...together?"

"I just don't see how that's your business, Stacy," Daisy remarked on my behalf. All of their heads whipped toward her on the armchair and back to Stacy.

Every head pivoted between them.

Stacy clicked her tongue. The sound scraped across my nerves. "Availability of the men in this town is everyone's business. Wouldn't want to tread on marked territory."

I blinked.

Marked territory.

I'd never heard a more objectifying statement than that one.

Sidney leaned forward. "I'm pretty sure Keating has rejected you enough times that it's actually not your business. And when he did ask you out, you chose Davis instead. So maybe that bridge is gone."

Whit and Stacy?

Davis and Stacy?

My brain tried to process too many timelines at once.

"Okay, I think we need a new topic that doesn't involve my brother," Daisy announced, standing. "What's everyone doing for the 4th of July?"

Daisy leaned forward to pick up our glasses and leaned over to whisper, "Drink up, Liv. It's going to be a long night."

She clinked her glass against mine, and we both took a long drink as Amelia explained that her fiancé, Dan, was working on getting Matt, Claire's husband, to agree to help with the fire-works show on the lake this year.

I'd forgotten about the 4th of July. It most certainly meant another barbecue that I wouldn't be invited to. I wondered if I could plan my trip to New York around that time to avoid it entirely.

"Do you guys think Whit and I should host this year?" Daisy asked, crossing her legs at the knee and finishing the rest of her drink in one go.

Sidney snorted. "Keating would rather die than host the 4th of July, Daze."

"Why is that?" I finished my drink, and Daisy took our glasses into the kitchen for refills.

"Keating doesn't do social events." Grace piped in, the first time she'd spoken all evening. "He's a big homebody. Work and home are his two favorite places, I'd guess."

Stacy groaned. "Tell me about it. These weekend shifts are the worst, but he's paying me time and a half, so I can't complain."

"And yet here you are," Sidney muttered under her breath, only loud enough for Amelia and me to hear.

Something about this conversation made me think about Molly Erickson's request for Whit to coach the kids' baseball team.

Had she asked him because she thought Whit would be a good fit or because he and Davis would always be thought of as a pair? They shared girls, why not town jobs?

Do not even go there, Olivia.

How could I not? Had Whit said no because he was busy with the clinic or because he was tired of being Davis's replacement?

If that were true...what were we?

Was I just another replacement narrative?

I'd thought choosing Whit was choosing something for myself.

But was I doing what everyone else did? Swapping one

McCleary for a Whitaker and pretending the equation was simple?

No.

Whit was his own person. He was quiet evenings and steady hands and starry skies. He wasn't Davis.

Maybe he needed someone to see that.

"Do you like going out a lot, Olivia?" Claire asked. "I mean, you were married to Davis McCleary."

I tucked my legs under me. "Not too often. I'm afraid I share Whit's homebody tendencies."

Grace adjusted her position on the floor pillow. "But you're from New York. And you met Davis in a bar, right? Then you ran off to Atlantic City? That's what we heard."

I wasn't the least bit surprised they had this information. Caroline Stenson probably hand-delivered a log of my whereabouts from the previous day to every one of Connor Bay's residents each morning—no need for a landline.

"Yeah, that's...that's true, but very out of character for me, to be honest," I admitted, glancing at the kitchen door frame, hoping Daisy would return soon to change the subject.

I didn't want to talk about this, not with them. Part of it was because I was sure half of them would judge anything I said, and the other half would question me more.

"Got a pizza delivery the size of a small child." Whit's voice rang out from the hall.

I couldn't help the smile that formed or how my heart sped up at the sound. God, it felt like I was in high school again.

32 and still growing up now, I guess.

Stacy was closest to the hall, so she unfolded herself from the other couch and went to help him.

"Thanks, Keating," she said, coming back into the living room with three boxes in her hands as Whit trailed behind her with three more.

"Ladies." He nodded at the group as his eyes found mine.

The way he looked at me made my skin heat. I swallowed, directing my attention to the pizza Stacy placed on the table. Now was the absolute worst time to show any interest in Keating Whitaker.

"Whit, take your box and go away," Daisy said, coming out of the kitchen with a tray of drinks for everyone.

He gave her a lazy salute before handing the bottom two boxes to Grace. He sent a wink as he passed me on his way to the kitchen.

"*Helping you with something.* Yeah, right." Stacy rolled her eyes before opening a pizza box.

My cheeks flamed for a different reason now.

"Ignore her," Amelia whispered to me, grabbing a slice of her own.

The thoughts came whether I wanted them or not. If Sidney had been truthful earlier, there was clearly a history between the two of them...the three of them.

Was there something there?

He cared about her enough to hire her.

But maybe Pete had, and he just inherited her.

He'd said he'd let her go if I was uncomfortable. But that would make me the villain.

I was getting good at breathing underwater here. At pretending I wasn't drowning. At adapting to a place that tested how long I could hold my breath.

Whit had felt like air.

But what if he was only temporary oxygen?

Was that what I wanted? Maybe Whit being with someone from this town was as inevitable as the sunrises he found comfort in.

Once everyone had food, the conversation turned to lighter

topics and taking strange BuzzFeed quizzes that I was sure no one did anymore.

Other than Stacy's ever-present glare, the night continued without incident, and I was pretty confident I'd won over Amelia and Sidney at the very least. That was something.

By midnight, Stacy, Amelia, and Claire had gone home, and Sidney, Grace, and Daisy had fallen asleep. I extricated myself from the blanket Daisy had given me and slipped on my shoes. I needed to get home to let Hotpie out.

But more importantly, so I could stare at my ceiling and think about how I had a date with my husband's best friend tomorrow.

"Going somewhere?" I startled, and my hand flew to my chest.

"God, you scared me," I whispered to him on the stairs. "How long have you been there?"

I turned toward him and immediately regretted it. Whit, shirtless in only pajama bottoms with slightly messy hair, was definitely...definitely something.

A big enough something that I was having trouble remembering why tonight had shaken my decision to try with him.

"Just coming down for a glass of water. I didn't expect you to be awake." His voice was low and did things to my body that I was pretending to hate.

Whit moved closer to me, and I stepped back until I hit the wall of the entryway. "Don't let me interrupt."

"You couldn't be an interruption if you tried, Liv."

He moved forward again and placed one of his hands on the wall just above my head.

Dipping his head, he whispered, "There's not a single thing I'd rather be doing than you."

The air was taut around us, and if I could stay in this moment with him, I would. If I could ignore the niggling thoughts in the back of my head whispering that this might not be worth the pain that will follow when it ends, I would kiss him right now.

But the thoughts were too loud, and the space between us, what little there was, was too heavy.

"Whit." I breathed.

"Come upstairs." His other hand came to rest against my neck. I was sure he could feel the erratic beating under his fingertips, but I couldn't bring myself to feel embarrassed about it.

I wanted to groan. "I shouldn't."

He pulled back, his brows furrowed. "Why not?"

A breathless laugh escaped my mouth. "You mean other than the fact your sister and her friends are asleep in the living room?"

He touched his forehead to mine. "We have really good insulation. They won't hear anything."

"Tempting," I replied, trying to regain control of my breathing.

Whit's mouth turned down just slightly. "Is something wrong?"

Oh, nothing; just feeling like I'm making the same mistakes all over again.

If there was one thing that tonight taught me, it was that I didn't know Whit. Not really.

Did we have chemistry? Absolutely.

Did I know anything about him? Only a handful of things, but we'd already slept together, and it was all happening so fast.

"No, just had a long day."

Now he was actually frowning, and he took a step back. "Are you sure you worked out your sleeping problem?" He had his assessment face on again.

I smiled at him. "Yes, *Doctor.* I'll see you tomorrow." I slipped past him and out the door before he could respond.

> *You won't believe who I just ran into. Benjamin Carter. Can you believe it? I haven't seen that jackass since Daisy dumped him in college. You really did a number on him when you found out he'd been seeing Claire on the side.*
>
> *I can't believe Daisy's still friends with her after that...Then again, Daisy's also still friends with Stacy Finch.*

30

I WAS MIDNIGHT RAIN

OLIVIA

Donald's porch got the perfect amount of sunlight in the morning. It wasn't so direct that eating breakfast with him outside was uncomfortable, and not so shady that you couldn't enjoy the warmth it radiated.

The day was so glorious that I didn't want to explain my breakfast food aversion, so I slowly worked through what was on my plate, chewing longer than necessary just to avoid conversation about it. Even the sound of kids racing down the street chasing after Hotpie felt like a gift.

On days I came into town, I participated in what I privately referred to as the children's bribery ring. They entertained my dog, and I paid them five dollars each to keep quiet about who he belonged to. This clause was critical to the agreement because Hotpie was an absolute menace. A playful menace who would never hurt a soul...unless flower bins and the occasional vegetable garden had souls.

"Heard Jeremiah is trying to start a petition to ban lawn gnomes from yards," Donald told me in between bites of the pancakes he kindly made for us.

I laughed.

Jeremiah was the town's oddity. He had more part-time jobs than I was sure the government would find legal. He did Tai Chi in the gazebo every Sunday morning; he was very bad. Every Monday, he sold T-shirts for bands that weren't real in front of Dillard's. Some of my favorites included *The Raspberries, AM/PM,* and *Def Coyote.* Tuesdays were an oddly quiet day for him, and only God knew what the rest of the week would hold for the exhilarating life of Jeremiah Allistair.

"Did one of Paula's look at him the wrong way?"

Donald snorted. "Not sure. Caroline said he thinks they might be planning a coup."

"The gnomes?"

"Indeed."

Donald asked me about Paula's and the Summer Festival and the potential magazine spread. Eric successfully convinced the *Coastal Living* journalist he knew to do a feature on the town. The full spread would run in the magazine after the festival, but they would do a shorter online article that would only take about a week to release. We had a little over a month before the festival, so we needed to make concrete plans. Once Eric got back, we'd make a formal timeline for everything.

He agreed to stay in New York until tomorrow to give Whit and me some space, which I was grateful for.

Since I liked trying my luck, I told Donald about my plans for the night.

"So," I said, sliding my sunglasses on when the sun shifted just enough to catch my eyes, "I have a date with Whit tonight."

Donald pushed his plate toward the center of the table and folded his hands together. He studied me with a soft sort of curiosity.

"Do you now?"

I nodded.

"Good for you."

It seemed genuine, so I smiled. "Little nervous."

"I'd imagine so. First date in a long while. Not sure what the town would think about it. Scared you're jumping into things with someone who your husband was close to." *Got it in one.* "The thing about getting to be my age, Olivia, is that you stop caring. What people in this town think doesn't matter."

I jiggled my leg nervously. "But shouldn't their opinions matter? Even a little?"

This isn't about them, Olivia. It's about you. You're worried about what they'll think—what Marjorie McCleary will think—because you haven't given yourself permission to move on yet."

The words landed quietly, but they were sharp.

"Maybe it feels fast to you," he continued, "but there is no timeline for grief. You probably woke up one morning, or it hit you in the afternoon after a second cup of coffee, that you might have feelings for someone. Then you found yourself missing Davis, but thinking about him didn't hurt like it used to. And maybe that day was when you got here, or maybe it was yesterday, but the point is that it's normal and healthy no matter how or when or why it happened. You deserve happiness, Olivia, but no one can tell you when it's okay to let yourself have it."

I nodded slowly. "I just feel guilty."

"Because of who he was to Davis." I nodded again. "We don't get a say in the people we fall in love with, Olivia."

"I'm not in love with Whit."

Donald shrugged, unbothered. "If you say so."

"I'm not."

"If you're not," he said gently, "and you don't think you ever could be, then why risk all of this? If Keating is just 'right place, right time,' why not choose easier? Why not decide not to do this? It would certainly be simpler to stay friends."

I didn't answer.

Because I couldn't.

After a long silence, he said quietly, "Because you can't be just friends with him."

That followed me the rest of the day.

It echoed while I collected Hotpie from the children, his tongue lolling happily. It lingered when I stopped at the store to pick up wine. It settled heavy in my chest as I vacuumed the living room and fluffed the couch pillows as if the arrangement might somehow change the outcome of the night.

Whit and I were inevitable, and I would take him for as long as he'd have me— for as long as I could bear it.

I thought I had forever with Davis, but the little time I'd gotten with him was sacred. The apartment we shared was holy ground.

But life didn't stop because one person's did.

I loved Davis with my whole heart, and maybe we weren't compatible on paper. Maybe he loved me in shades of daylight that contrasted my midnight, but that didn't make us any less real.

Davis McCleary was a great love of my life, but he didn't have to be my only one.

31

SUNFLOWERS IN THE KITCHEN

WHIT

Having a date with Olivia Carrington felt a lot like trying to catch your breath after a run. Your body felt alive, your head clear, but there was this sharp awareness that you might actually die if you didn't get your breathing under control.

In the kitchen, I drank water and tried to pull air into my lungs like it might anchor me. It didn't help. The breaths demanded to be felt. They insisted.

"Good run?" Daisy asked, coming into the kitchen.

I nodded, slowly pacing between the island and the counter, hands on my waist.

"Did it help with the nerves?"

I shook my head, taking a shaky breath. "Sounds about right. Did she get a dog?"

I braced my palms against the counter. "What?" It came out thin and breathless.

"A dog? I saw her walking along the water with a golden earlier today. She had her AirPods in, so I don't think she heard me call out to her. Did she get a dog?"

"Not...sure."

The image slotted into place immediately. The dog from Stones. It seemed wildly out of character for Olivia.

Then again, so did coming to my office and asking me on a date.

Olivia Carrington was proving to be far more unpredictable than I'd anticipated.

Daisy studied me, concerned. "Do you need your inhaler?"

My inhaler?

I hadn't needed one since high school. Did I even have one around here?

I used to get panic attacks. Was that what was happening? It didn't feel like a panic attack, but maybe it was?

I thought there might be one in the drawer at the end of the island, so I nodded to Daisy and pointed in the general direction.

It took four pulls before my breathing evened out.

"Thanks."

"You're really nervous about this date, aren't you?"

I shook my head, drinking deeply from my water bottle.

I shook my head, then reconsidered. "Not about the date. I think I'm nervous about after."

Her brows knit together.

"Olivia and I alone are—" She made a face, so I spared her the details. "It's when we're in public that things are...different."

"For you or her?"

"Both? We haven't really talked about any of it, but it feels like she's having all these second thoughts that I'm not privy to, and I don't want to push her."

Daisy nodded in understanding. "It'll work out, Whit. If it's meant to, it'll work out."

I hoped she was right.

At 6 p.m., I rang the doorbell at my parents' rental and laughed when I heard a faint barking that grew increasingly loud.

"Hotpie," I heard Olivia scold from the other side of the door, "if you're not quiet, he's going to leave, and you won't get any pets." The barking stopped, and my brows rose in surprise. "Good boy."

A moment later, the door opened.

Olivia stood there in a black dress that dipped low and wrapped at the side like it had been designed to test my ability to think. Her hair fell in loose red curls around her shoulders. I had the immediate, visceral urge to thread my fingers through them.

It was going to be a long night.

"Hi." She smiled, eyes drifting to my hands. "Those for me?"

I blinked like I'd forgotten how language worked. "Oh. Yes. God. Sorry. You're just—"

She laughed, cutting off whatever incoherent mess I was about to produce.

"Yes. These are for you."

I handed her the flowers Daisy had insisted I buy.

Olivia took them from me and opened the door wider, "Please, come in. These are lovely." I followed her into the kitchen.

"So, are we talking about the dog barking or..."

The corners of her mouth turned up as she filled a vase with water. "I got a dog."

"The dog from the pet store?"

She nodded as she unwrapped the flowers from their plastic.

"Oh, let me do that." Olivia looked at me curiously as I came around the island and bumped her hip out of the way. "I wasn't thinking. I should have prepped them before I gave them to you."

"The flowers?" she asked, leaning against the counter and watching me work.

I grabbed a pair of scissors from a drawer and trimmed the stems. "My mom says gifts that need to be assembled aren't gifts; just work with a bow on it."

Once I'd put them in the vase, I washed my hands and dried them on a kitchen towel. I looked up to find Olivia staring at me, the tops of her cheeks red.

"What?"

She shook her head slightly. "Nothing, I just don't think I've met anyone quite like you, Keating Whitaker."

"I hope that's a compliment."

"It is."

"How's Eric?"

She gestured for me to follow her into the dining room. "He's good. Gets in tomorrow. It'll be nice to have him back."

Olivia had set the dining table and laid out takeout containers of what smelled like Italian food. "Does he know about the dog?"

"Hotpie."

I took a seat at the head of the table, "Sorry?"

Olivia took the chair to my left. "Hotpie is the dog's name."

"Of course it is," I laughed. "Family name?"

"Naturally."

"On your mom's side?"

She shook her head. "Dad's. It was his father's father's optometrist's sister's goat's name."

I nodded, unfolding a napkin and putting it on my lap. "I was going to guess it was the pig's name, but very close."

Her mouth fell, offended. "Because 'Hotpie' sounds like it would be a pig's name? That's so rude, Keating." I liked hearing her say my name. "You'll need to apologize to Hotpie when you see him."

I laughed. "And where is he?"

"Oh, it's time for his evening snooze on the couch. He'll be here in about 10 minutes." She answered easily, opening a box and passing it to me. "I hope pasta is okay. I wasn't sure what you liked, so I got a little of everything."

"Absolutely. Thanks for getting all this." I said, spooning tortellini onto my plate.

Olivia twirled noodles around her fork and paused before putting them in her mouth. "How come you didn't want to coach the Little League team?"

My brows raised in surprise. I wondered why she was thinking about it, but answered her anyway. "Like I told Molly, I'm just stretched too thin right now. The clinic is taking a lot of time. Once I got here, Pete went MIA, so it's just Stacy and me. I'm thinking about trying to get an intern, but that will only help so much." She watched me ramble about my job like it was fascinating to her, and I felt my cheeks heat at the attention. "I haven't looked too closely at the books to figure out if we can afford another practitioner right now, but that would be the most helpful."

She nodded, looking back down at her plate. I knew she wanted to ask more questions from the way her brows drew together, but I didn't want to talk about Davis or about my aversion to taking his place...except wasn't I? *Wasn't I taking his place here with Olivia?*

I changed the subject. "How did last night go?"

She poured herself a glass of red wine and offered me the bottle. "Good for the most part."

"The most part?" I asked, pouring myself a glass.

She was quiet, and when I glanced up at her, she was staring at her plate, pushing noodles around with her fork. I set the bottle down.

"Olivia, this only works if we talk to each other."

She put her fork down and angled her head to look at me. "Did you and Stacy have a thing?"

Her face didn't appear to be challenging. I wasn't even sure how to describe it. My gut reaction was to ask what the other girls had told her, but never in any scenario had that gone well.

So, instead, I said, "I had a crush on her in high school."

"Just a crush?"

"I mean, that's all it was. I asked her out, and she turned me down."

I wanted to press her on what they said, but I could see she didn't want to ask me these things. I didn't want her to think I was hiding anything about my past from her.

"But she dated Davis?"

I nodded at her. "Yes."

"And he knew you liked her?"

I laughed. "Yes. It was just high school. Davis knew I liked her, but he warned me it wasn't a good idea. I guess he liked her and didn't want to tell me, or he didn't like her until I told him I did. I don't know." I lifted a shoulder in a half-shrug.

One thing about Davis was that you never knew his motivations for doing anything. Did he like her first, or did he ask her out because I wanted to? Did he join the baseball team in high school because he wanted to or because he liked to show me he was better? Did he—

"Did that hurt your friendship?" she asked, taking a drink of her wine.

I tilted my head, this way and that. "A little. We got into a scuffle and got over it. Davis and I had too much history to let Stacy Finch come between us."

Olivia Carrington, on the other hand...

She looked at me over her glass for a long moment. "I'm sorry I didn't try to meet you when he was alive."

I frowned at her. I didn't know where this was coming from. I couldn't tell if Daisy's friends had upset her or if everything was catching up with her at one time.

"Olivia, you don't have to apologize."

She put her glass down and pressed her hands against her eyes.

"I'm sorry. I'm ruining this."

I moved my napkin to the table and knelt beside her. "Hey." I ran the back of my hand along her forearm, and she sniffled. "Hey, hey, hey. Liv, it's okay."

She sniffled again and lifted her face to the ceiling, wiping under her eyes.

"I don't even know why I'm upset. You're here, and you're perfect, and I'm— *God.*"

She wiped under her eyes again.

We'd revisit the *you're perfect* thing later; it didn't seem like an opportune time to make her say it again.

"Talk to me, Liv. What's going on in that beautifully busy head of yours?"

She shook her head, standing from her chair. "I just need a minute. I'm sorry. I thought I was going to be okay."

Her voice was so defeated that it broke my heart to hear it. I could hear Hotpie's collar jingle from the living room as he presumably hopped off the couch. I was torn between giving her space and wanting her to talk to me. I couldn't fix anything if she didn't talk to me.

But even if she did, it was unlikely I could fix it. I couldn't bring him back. I couldn't go back in time and make him take a cab instead of insisting on driving. The truth was that the best I could do for her was to be here.

It was that thought that propelled me into the kitchen. She was leaning against the counter, rubbing her temples with Hotpie at her feet. I walked over to her, placed my hands on her shoulders, and brought her against my chest.

"I'm sorry," she mumbled into my shirt.

We stayed there for a long time. Sometimes Olivia shook with sobs, and I held her tighter, and sometimes she grew very still, and I stroked her hair. Eventually, she pulled back, her eyes rimmed with red, and apologized again.

"Olivia, stop apologizing. It's all okay." I rubbed her arms. "Why don't you take a beat, and I'll bring our drinks to the couch? We can watch something. I hear you like lousy reality shows in other languages."

She laughed and nodded. "Okay. I'll be right in."

I kissed her forehead and clicked my tongue so Hotpie would follow. I wasn't sure when we'd steered off course during the night, but I didn't think it was too late to right it.

Olivia settled against me on the couch a few minutes later with her glass of wine in her hand. I pulled her onto my lap so she didn't have to strain to see the television.

"So, how did you get into this whole thing?" I nodded at the people on screen trying to lug 20 pounds of what looked to be green Jell-O over a military training wall.

She laughed. "I found it to be the easiest way to learn languages."

"Do you know a lot of them?"

"Not that many. I learned French and Spanish in high school. I watched a lot of soap operas back then. Then, in college, I wanted to learn Mandarin, and that wasn't very successful."

"Huh. Interesting."

"You think it's weird, don't you?"

"Yeah, a little," I admitted, drinking the rest of my wine and putting the glass on the side table.

"Okay, well, what do you watch, Mr. Perfect?"

My brows raised. "I'm a detective show junkie."

She squinted her eyes, assessing me. "*CSI*?"

"*Law & Order*."

"Huh. Interesting." Her jaw ticked, trying to hide a smile.

We'd made it through two episodes of whatever we were watching and the rest of the bottle of wine before Olivia turned to me and said, "This is really nice." I smiled at her, and she ran her hand along my jaw. "I like this on you."

"My beard?" She nodded, watching her fingers slide through the dark facial hair. It wasn't long by any means, but it was thick and could become unruly quickly. "It's new. I actually have this scar on my chin. It does a good job of hiding it."

She hummed and continued her visual and physical exploration of my face. I closed my eyes and savored the feeling of her skin on mine.

Her thumb moved across my bottom lip.

"Can I kiss you?" she whispered.

I opened my eyes and found her watching me, waiting for a response.

I didn't know if it was the best idea, given that she had sobbed in my arms in the kitchen earlier this evening.

"Olivia, I need to know you're okay. That you're okay to do this with me."

She nodded slowly. "I am. I invited you here. I want you here."

"Olivia, I'm here, but I can be here for you without being with you if you're not ready for that."

I didn't want to upset her again, but we couldn't do this if she wasn't ready. Instead of a response, she stood and extended her hand to me.

"You're sure?"

"Keating, I'm not sure about too many things right now, but I am sure I have feelings for you. Please come upstairs with me."

It was the same offer I made to her last night, but it felt different now.

Not because *Olivia* was offering, but because I thought she was sure when she came to my office. She was confident and seemed so resolute, but I realized tonight that Olivia's air of confidence was a defense mechanism—one I was quite familiar with. A public-facing mask of confidence to protect herself from the town or anyone else who might be in danger of seeing her for who she actually was.

I took her hand.

32

GET IT OFF MY CHEST

WHIT

With my hand in hers, Olivia led us up the stairs. I knew we'd be in the room she chose a few days ago in less than a minute. A room I'd stayed in a handful of times when I needed space from my parents during holidays home from school. From that moment on, whenever I thought about it, I would have memories of Olivia and me instead.

I squeezed her hand when she paused in front of her door.

"Liv, we don't have to. We have time."

She looked at me sadly over her shoulder.

"You and I are both intimately aware of how much we can't know that."

I turned her and pressed her body against the door with my own.

"We have as much time as you want. It was an accident. I'm here. I'm right here, and I'm not going anywhere without you."

My hands traced the lines of her jaw, down her neck, and over her shoulders before wrapping around her waist. Her hands came to rest on my shoulders, and she stared at me like she was trying to memorize everything she could.

"What's your favorite color?"

My mouth curved. "Red."

"Like an apple?" She blinked.

One of my hands drifted up her body again and gripped the back of her head, knotting in her hair.

"No, like *this*." I tugged, tilting her head back to press my mouth to hers.

She tasted like the wine from downstairs, and it occurred to me that I would drown in her if I could. Olivia's fingers slid up my shirt and pressed into my lower back. Her fingernails would leave tiny half-moon indentations when they left my skin, and I hoped the traces would last forever so I'd have some reminder that this was real. That this was happening.

My tongue slipped into her mouth, and she groaned. I dropped my hand from her hair and cupped the back of her neck, my thumb snaking around to feel her pulse. She pulled back.

"Why do you do that?" Her breaths were ragged.

I frowned. "Do what?" She touched my hand on her neck with one of her own. "Your heartbeat is my favorite thing in this whole world."

Her eyes darted over my face, looking for something I wasn't sure she'd find. "I thought the stars were," she whispered finally.

"That was before you, Olivia. Everything I thought was important is nothing compared to you and this."

I pressed her skin; her heartbeat was erratic. She should really have a doctor check that. Lucky for her...

Her breath hitched. "I need you, Whit. I need you right now."

It was all I needed to hear before I lifted her against me and carried her into the room. She kissed me like I was her only source of oxygen, and I could come at the feeling of her mouth on mine alone. Her hands tightened in my hair, and mine cupped the backs of her thighs, keeping her pressed against me until my knees hit the bed, and I tossed her onto it.

I pulled off my shirt, and Olivia undid the tie at her side. She lay in front of me in only her black bra and underwear, highlighting the cream and rose tones in her skin. Leaving my jeans on, I crawled between her legs; I needed her mouth on mine again.

Kissing Olivia was like a drop on a rollercoaster. It climbed and then made your heart fly into your chest. It left your breathing ragged and your body pumping with adrenaline.

Her mouth was soft but unforgiving as it ravaged mine. She sank her teeth into my bottom lip. I sucked in a breath as my hand wound in her hair again and tugged it back. She released me with a groan, and I skated my nose down her jaw before sucking on the spot just below her ear.

She let out breaths that were not quite moans but gasps for air. Olivia's hands wound behind her, trying to remove her bra on her own. I caught her hands and pulled them above her head.

"Slow down. We've got plenty of time right here."

My words didn't seem to help because her hips ground against me, searching for any bit of friction they could get. I smiled against her skin.

"Alright, Liv, you win."

I kept her wrists together in one hand and reached behind her to unclasp her bra with my other, shifting the fabric further up her chest to reveal tightened peaks that begged to be in my mouth, but I was going to take my time with her.

My hand lightly drifted down her sternum, and she threw her head back further into the mattress, arching her back. I smirked down at her as I pinched a bud between my thumb and index finger.

"Whit." My name was a prayer on her tongue.

"Right here, darlin'. Always right here." I said, releasing her wrists to lean on an elbow while I took one nipple into my mouth and continued to tweak the other.

Her hands were in my hair instantly. She tugged me up to her mouth, and I obliged briefly before she pushed me back toward her chest.

"Whit. *Please.*" I dragged my teeth over the nipple in my mouth, and she gasped.

"You'll get what I give you, Olivia. If you're good, I'll let you come." Another moan slipped from her mouth. "Are you going to be good, Olivia?"

Her gaze met mine, and she nodded quickly. "Yes, Whit. I'll be good."

"Good girl."

My hand left her breast and slid down her stomach and over the damp fabric of her underwear. I pressed down on a spot that had her back arching again, her hands twisting in the comforter.

"Fuck."

Seeing Olivia Carrington completely undone like this would become a fantasy I got off to for the rest of my life, and I wasn't even inside her yet. My cock twitched at the thought. I kissed my way down her body and glanced up at her when I reached the top of the remaining fabric.

Her eyes were desperate, but she didn't say anything; she just watched me with wide eyes. And fuck if it wasn't the hottest thing I'd seen.

"Are you wet for me, Olivia?" I asked, my hands gripped the thin sides of the fabric.

She nodded. "God, yes. So wet, Whit."

Stepping off the bed, I pulled her underwear down her legs and dropped them on the floor.

"Will I get to keep those this time?" She asked, her eyes roaming over my torso and dropping to the zipper of my jeans.

I shook my head slowly, a grin spreading across my face. "Are you sassing me at a time like this, Olivia?" She pulled her bottom lip in between her teeth and shook her head. "Because if you were sassing me, that's not good girl behavior, and only good girls get to come."

Her gaze turned molten as her tongue darted between her lips, wetting them enough that they glistened. Before I could decide what to do with her, she slid off the bed, her chest pressed against mine. If I wasn't throbbing before, I was now.

"I'm sorry, Keating." She said, one hand resting against my stomach and the other working the button of my jeans. "I'll make it up to you."

My breathing all but stopped as she dropped to her knees in front of me and pulled my jeans and boxers down in one swift movement, leaving them at my ankles. I stood at attention under her gaze as she trailed her fingertips along my length. I twitched at her touch.

"Can I?" She asked, looking at me from beneath her lashes.

I wanted to press a fist to my mouth and bite it because *fuck.* Instead, I nodded at her request and watched as she gripped the base of me, wrapping her mouth around the head of my cock. My hands tangled in her hair, but didn't guide her. The feeling of Olivia's mouth on me was—

Her teeth grazed my length, and I bucked forward, deeper into her mouth. She moaned around me. "You look so good with me in your mouth, Liv." Another moan vibrated around me and triggered one of my own. Her tongue pressed against the underside of my cock, and I pulled out of her grip because if she did that again, I wouldn't last long.

"On the bed," I said when she pinned her wide eyes on my face.

She complied quickly, and not for the first time tonight, I thought about how perfect she was. I pulled my jeans and boxers the rest of the way off before approaching the bed.

I grabbed the backs of Olivia's calves and dragged her abruptly to the edge of the bed, eliciting a surprised squeak from her. Kneeling on the floor between her legs, my mouth was at the perfect height to devour her thoroughly and watch her writhe. I kissed her inner thigh as I made my way to her center. Her hands fisted the comforter in anticipation. I ran my tongue along her, and she let out a throaty groan that made me want to abandon this tactic altogether and bury myself in her, but I'd dreamt about her in this position for too long.

I consumed her like a man starved. When I sucked her clit between my lips, my name flew out of her mouth breathlessly. The sound went straight to my cock, and I had to squeeze it roughly so I wouldn't come right then. I inserted two fingers inside her and pumped leisurely while I continued to apply pressure to her clit with my tongue.

Olivia's moans changed. They became higher, more desperate, building until— There she went. She tightened around my fingers, and I felt her pulse against my tongue.

I groaned against her skin as I slowed my movements. Olivia let out a sigh as I removed my fingers. Rising, I looked at her splayed out on the bed for me.

She was so beautiful. Heat from her orgasm was evident in the red splotches across her chest and cheeks. Her eyes were half-closed, but she looked at me like she wanted me to do it all again.

"How you doing over there?"

She giggled, and I wanted to bathe in the sound. "Peachy. Do I get to make the rules at some point?"

I grinned down at her. "I think I can be amenable to that. What did you have in mind?"

Whatever it was, I hoped it involved me being inside her in the next 30 seconds.

The red in her cheeks deepened as my gaze lingered on her face, and then she shook her head. "Nevermind."

Consider my curiosity piqued. I crooked a finger in her direction. She rose quickly in response, kneeling on the bed in front of me. *Such a good girl.*

"What do you want, Olivia?" She shook her head. "Tell me, and I'll do it."

Olivia had been bold thus far, so I was surprised to see her so shy with me now.

"I'll do anything for you," I told her, pushing her hair back and kissing her shoulder before pulling back.

Olivia watched me carefully as I lifted her chin.

"Tell me what you need."

She wrapped her arms around my neck and brought our mouths together again. My fingers gripped her waist. I knew she could taste herself on my tongue, and I groaned. This couldn't be what she wanted a moment ago, but I wasn't going to complain.

The sound I made must have given her courage because she directed me in a way that had me on the bed with her on top of me. I pulled my mouth away, breathing hard and fast as I touched my forehead to hers. Her copper curls were a curtain around us.

"Is this what you wanted?" She nodded, her hands supporting herself on either side of my head. "You've never..."

Olivia shook her head. *Oh, fuck.* I did not want to think about the implications of that admission. Not now, not ever. But I did want her to ride the fuck out of me.

"There's a condom in my jeans."

She moved her hair to one side. "I'm on birth control."

Fuck me sideways.

"You're sure you want to do this, Liv?"

She frowned at me. "I don't have to be on top. I can—" She tried to remove herself from my body, but my hands gripped her waist tighter.

I laughed. "I meant the no condom, Olivia. Are you sure you're okay with no condom?"

"Oh. Yes, I'm sure." *Thank God.*

Her body had grown tense in the time between her last orgasm and now, and that just wasn't acceptable. I brought her mouth down and kissed her until her body melted against mine again.

I pulled us into a sitting position to help Olivia get situated.

"On your knees, darlin'."

She obliged, and hell if it didn't make me throb. I positioned her over my cock and guided her down onto it slowly.

"*Fuck.*" I couldn't help but groan as she began to envelop me.

Olivia let out a soft moan as she sank onto me, and I couldn't hold myself up anymore. She was so tight, and I just wanted to watch her bounce on my dick until pleasure seeped from our pores.

When she was seated to the hilt, I wanted to cry at how good it felt to be in her and thrust into her hard and fast at the same time.

She hadn't moved yet, but I was about ready to combust. "You can move whenever you're ready. Just do what feels right."

Olivia leaned forward onto her hands and lifted her body up and back down, eliciting a grunt from me. I palmed her breasts, my thumbs grazing her nipples.

Her eyes closed on a moan while she tried it again.

"Eyes on me, Liv. You should know better by now." My fingers tugged on her nipples in demand.

Her lashes fluttered as another moan escaped her parted lips, and her gaze locked on mine. She became more confident in her movements, finally collapsing onto my chest and bucking her hips against mine.

"Oh, *Christ*, Olivia. Don't fucking stop." I cupped her ass with both hands and forced her into a rhythm that had us both groaning uncontrollably. I moved a hand to her clit between us and rubbed it like it was my goddamned job. "Get there, Olivia. Right fucking now."

She let out a whimper and a breathless, "Oh my god, Whit," before she stilled on top of me as her body convulsed around me. The hand on her clit returned to her ass to move her against me as she rode out her orgasm.

I could feel mine building in the base of my spine. The thin sheet of sweat that broke out between us made her feel slick against me. Her hands dug into my shoulders, and I knew that I'd never get enough of her.

"Whit. *Fuck*." Olivia breathed against my skin in a low, raspy voice, coming down from her high.

It was enough to trigger mine, and I couldn't help but keep her firmly against me as I thrust into her for the final time.

Our mouths found each other as I finished. I knew, no matter what happened between us, neither of us could deny that we were made for each other.

33

PASSIONATE BUT FICKLE
OLIVIA

I blinked my eyes open to the sunlight streaming into the bedroom. I groaned when I sat up, my body sore. Then it all came back to me: crying at dinner, watching TV on the couch, Whit on top of me, me on top of Whit...

I pushed my hair back from my face and looked around.

There was no sign of the 6'2" doctor, but I couldn't have imagined it.

I was definitely naked under this blanket, so either I'd drunkenly forgone pajamas, or Whit fucked me into a brief coma.

I rubbed the sleep from my eyes, trying to orient myself. It had been a long time since I slept through the night as deeply as I had.

"Hotpie," I called from my place on the bed.

I could hear the dog's paws patter on the stairs as he raced up them and into my room. I patted the bed, and he hopped up. Holding the blanket against my body with one hand, I pet the dog with the other.

"Did Whit sneak out this morning, boy?"

My hand hit a folded paper attached to Hotpie's collar just then. "What's this, huh? Are the kids sending messages to each other via dog carrier?"

I removed it from his collar and unfolded it.

Definitely not kids.

Liv,

you were so wonderfully asleep i couldn't bring myself to wake you up. had to go into the clinic this morning, but i'll be back soon. if i'm not there by the time you're up, give me a call.

hope you're dreaming of me,
Whit

He wrote his number at the bottom of the note. To my great delight, someone had moved my phone to my bedside table and plugged it in to charge. I shook my head and touched a hand to my face.

How could he be this wonderful?

I dialed the number.

"Hello?" I opened my mouth to say something, but nothing came out. "Anybody there?"

I didn't know what I was doing now that I'd heard his voice. I should have thought about what I was going to say before I called. Though he did ask me to call him.

"I can hear you breathing. Is this a weird prank call? Am I in a *Scream* movie? I'm pretty good at horror movie trivia. I can give it a shot."

I let out a laugh and then clapped my hand over my mouth.

"Aren't you supposed to use a voice changer?"

"I'm not exactly sure of the rules. I've never seen those

movies." I said, sinking back into my pillows and chewing on my thumbnail, phone pressed to my ear.

He sighed. "Disappointed, but not surprised."

"That's how I felt when Donald told me the Garners finally got one up on the Tomlinsons' booth feud."

Whit's chuckle was low, and it ignited something deep in my core. "Are you still in bed?"

I licked my lips. "Mhm. Just woke up."

"Did you sleep okay?"

I shifted under the covers, tugging them higher around my chest even though he couldn't see me.

"Are you asking me as a doctor or as the person who spent the night with me?"

"Which answer will tell me if you're still naked?"

I let out an audible gasp. "Keating Whitaker."

"That's a yes," he said easily. "Will you be like that in an hour?"

I laughed. Talking to Whit was as easy as breathing. When it was just the two of us, it felt like there wouldn't be an end. It had been like that with Davis, too.

Maybe it was like that with all relationships. They get complicated when you're trying to include the real world in something private.

"Is *that* a yes?"

Even over the phone, he made me flush with heat. "I think something can be arranged."

Whit was at my door an hour later, but I had showered and dressed to his absolute dismay.

"It's probably a hazard to eat hot soup naked anyway." He

slid past me with a takeout bag in his hand, like he'd been here a hundred times already.

My brows rose as I followed him into the kitchen. "It's eighty-seven degrees outside. Why would you get soup?"

"I didn't," he said, grinning over his shoulder. "I'm just saying." Hotpie ambled down the stairs to investigate the commotion, tail thumping once against the wall as if he approved of Whit's presence on principle.

Whit moved with an aura of carelessness like he had all the time in the world. It was so different from Davis and me. We both had a restless energy. Davis and I talked with our hands, and all our movements were rushed—like we knew we were living on borrowed time.

Not for the first time since meeting him did I think Whit felt timeless.

"Okay, if not soup, what did you bring?" I asked, following him to the kitchen.

"Only the best pancakes on this side of the country." He set the containers down with a flourish and gave me a look like he expected applause.

I scrunched my nose before I could stop myself.

"Uhm, what is that face about?"

I crouched to give Hotpie a few pats, mostly so I could avoid Whit's immediate, devastating attention. "I'm not a pancake person."

Technically, I used to love pancakes. Breakfast used to be sacred in our apartment—Davis making a big show of flipping them, me pretending I didn't like syrup when I absolutely did, breakfast-for-dinner nights when work bled into everything and we tried to make it feel like it didn't. Somewhere along the way, it changed. Eggs, waffles, pancakes—my body rejected them now, like grief had decided breakfast was the enemy. Bagels were the only exception.

Whit stared at me like I'd confessed to hating sunsets. "Come again?"

"Breakfast foods are kind of...eh." I shrugged. "But if you say they're the best, then I will try them."

He pressed a hand to his chest in mock offense...at least, I hoped it was mock offense.

"Well, now I don't know if you *deserve* to try them."

I laughed, but he put a pancake on a plate and passed it to me anyway. The pancake was fine, but my body wanted to reject it. I proposed that lunch foods were underrated.

"What even are 'lunch foods'?" Whit angled his fork to put air quotes around the term.

I tried to remember times like this with Davis. Whether we got into "lively discussions" about the particulars of mundane items or spent any time getting to know each other without feeling like that was what we were supposed to do. Nothing came to mind.

Davis was a whirlwind romance with all the chaos of a tropical storm, but Whit felt like the slow change of the seasons themselves. I could see lazy mornings with him in bed in the fall and decorating a Christmas tree with him in the winter.

There was that feeling again. The overwhelming wave of guilt that came with thinking about Davis while being with Whit. I wished I could carry them both. I missed Davis, but Donald's speech had gotten to me. Just because I wanted to be happy didn't mean I needed to discount my relationship with Davis.

I could love them in different ways.

I stiffened. Was I falling in love with Whit? How could that be? I'd just met him. *Pot, kettle. Have you met?*

I'd known Whit longer than the time between meeting Davis and marrying him. That shouldn't matter. It didn't, but I'd gone through so many *what-ifs* in the past few months that I couldn't help but want to stop history from repeating itself.

Denying that Whit and I could be something if we let it happen was nearly futile, but after the panic attack that came out of nowhere at dinner yesterday...

"Whit?"

He looked over at me from where he washed our dishes.

"Yeah?"

I moved to lean against the counter beside him; he flashed me a grin.

"Just can't stay away from me, can you?"

Yes, that was my main problem, actually.

"I'm not ready to do this in public. Around town, I mean."

"*And* you want me all to yourself, Liv? Wow, you really know how to make a guy feel special." His laugh was easy as he said it.

I tucked my hair behind my ear. "Is that okay?"

He angled his head in my direction. "Absolutely. I told you last night. I'm not going anywhere." Whit flipped off the faucet and dried his hands on a towel.

The lack of hesitation, the sight of him in the kitchen, those forearms...

"Is that so?" I quirked a brow at him. He smiled confusedly at me as he tossed the towel back on the counter.

"What about..." I pushed off the counter, "...upstairs?"

In the time it took me to realize what was happening, Whit hoisted me over his shoulder. I laughed, and he smacked my ass, eliciting another noise entirely.

Insatiable was my new favorite word to describe Keating Whitaker.

34

THIS CITY SCREAMS YOUR NAME
WHIT

It had been a week since Olivia and I agreed to keep our relationship low-key.

When Eric returned from his trip last Tuesday, he told Olivia and me that their boss, Clark, had approved the pitch meeting. That news sent Operation "Revitalize the Town" roaring into action almost immediately. Olivia practically launched herself off the couch and huddled over her computer with Eric, the two of them leaning shoulder to shoulder as they began outlining their next steps. His suitcase sat abandoned in the entryway, forgotten within seconds of his arrival.

Before Eric got back, Olivia had mentioned she suspected he wouldn't react well to the dog because he was, in her words, "a militant cat person." But when he finally walked through the door and saw Hotpie, he just shrugged and kept talking.

In fact, it took nearly two hours before Eric even noticed there was a dog in the house.

Of course, the realization set Olivia off immediately. She launched into an impassioned tirade about how Eric had always been vehemently opposed to dogs. There were dramatic references to Stephen King's *Cujo*, statistics about dog-transmitted diseases, and a brief detour into the history of rabies outbreaks in the Northeast.

Eric listened patiently through the entire speech before laughing, kissing her on the forehead, and gently steering her back toward their laptops.

I knew what it was.

The only person more concerned about Olivia than I was happened to be Eric.

He'd known her longer than I had. He'd seen her before Davis, during her marriage to Davis, and in the devastating months after. If Eric believed she was moving forward—really moving forward—then Olivia could adopt a thousand Hotpies and he wouldn't question it.

A few days later, Eric arranged a phone interview for me with a journalist from *Coastal Living* about the Summer Festival. Daisy was confident we could convince the town council to host the festival even if they didn't love the idea of Olivia organizing it. The potential publicity was too valuable for the town to ignore.

So tomorrow night, at the town meeting, Daisy, Eric, and Olivia would present their proposal and see what happened.

As someone who owned a business in town, I wasn't allowed to help craft their presentation. Technically, that would be considered a conflict of interest. But I could attend the meeting, ask questions, and vote in favor of the proposal, which, according to Daisy, was actually more helpful.

After the town meeting tomorrow, Olivia and Eric would go to New York, and Eric would pitch their ideas in person. If everything went well, Connor Bay—and the Summer Festival— might finally get the kind of attention that small coastal towns usually only dream about.

The other reason I wasn't bothered by our more-or-less secret relationship was that Eric and Olivia had been working non-stop in preparation for the pitch.

She was up before dawn and only went to bed after I forcibly carried her up the stairs, once Eric had long since retired to his own room.

Hearing about Olivia's workaholic tendencies from Davis and actually seeing them were two very different things. I could understand where Davis's frustrations had come from—but the motivations behind our concern were different.

Davis had wanted more attention from her.

I just wanted her to be healthy.

I wasn't unfamiliar with long nights and impossible work-loads. I'd gone through medical school. I'd survived residency. I knew exactly how easy it was to convince yourself that sleep was optional.

But the truth was that sleep deprivation was the worst thing you could do if you actually needed to function.

On the bright side, she was out like a light once she hit the pillow most nights. And based on the energy she had for other things in the morning, I knew the nightmares had stopped.

I'd spent every night with her that week.

Eric was thrilled when she told him we were together, and then he was ostensibly less thrilled when she told him that we were keeping it under the radar.

So was I, but I knew where she was coming from. I knew it didn't have anything to do with me and everything to do with our situation.

The more time I spent with Olivia, the less bothered I was. Olivia was an all-consuming force, and with how viscerally she affected me, it was better that most of our time was spent in the privacy of our homes.

Eventually, we'd have to talk about the future. We couldn't sneak around forever.

I also ignored the possibility that she might not want to stay here in Connor Bay. It seemed like forever ago that Eric asked what was in it for me when I devised the plan to help them. Even back then, the end goal was to convince her to stay here.

The night before the town meeting, Olivia sat cross-legged in bed with her laptop balanced on her thighs while I read a battered true-crime paperback someone had left at the rental house. The book smelled faintly like sunscreen and salt air, the pages soft from years of beach reading.

Hotpie lay sprawled at the foot of the bed, grumbling dramatically whenever one of us shifted enough to disturb him.

"Come to New York with me," Olivia said suddenly.

I raised my brows. "Like..."

She laughed. "Sorry, I meant this week. For the pitch meeting."

I dog-eared the page I was on and set my book on the night-stand. "I'd love to go with you, but getting away on a weekend is a little hard for me."

Even as I said it, I was already mentally rearranging my clinic schedule. The idea of walking through New York with Olivia felt dangerously appealing.

Olivia glanced up at me from her laptop. "Right, sorry. I forgot about the weekend appointments. I should have brought it up sooner."

"I can try to move some of them around if we could be back Saturday night." I turned toward her, which was too much movement for Hotpie, evidently, because he huffed loudly and jumped off the bed.

"Oh, that's okay," Olivia said quickly. "I don't want you moving things around for me."

She waved it off and returned to her spreadsheets.

I studied her for a moment.

Her hair was twisted into a messy knot at the top of her head, and the neckline of her sleep shirt dipped just enough to reveal the curve of her breasts when she leaned forward over the keyboard.

"Olivia."

She raised her brows but didn't look away from the screen.

"Do you want me there?"

"Of course I do."

I dropped my voice, knowing how much her skin would flush at the sound.

"Show me."

The response was immediate. Color spread across her neck and climbed toward her cheeks. Her hands hovered above the keyboard like she'd forgotten what she'd been typing.

"Whit," she said quietly, "I have to finish this."

Her voice betrayed her.

"Okay."

Turning Olivia on had quickly become one of my favorite hobbies. It also happened to be the fastest way to interrupt her work habits.

I picked up my book again, pretending to read while sliding my other hand behind her to knead the tension in her shoulders.

"Keating."

She intended it to be a warning, but it was too soft to hold any weight. I moved my hand up to the back of her neck and squeezed lightly.

She groaned, her head falling back. *Three strikes, you're out, Carrington.*

"We have to be quick."

My book found its way to the floor, her computer on top of it, her on top of me, me inside of her.

I had a nipple in my mouth when she knotted her fingers in my hair and yanked my head back. I looked up at her with something that was probably closer to hunger than patience.

"I want you in New York."

God, this woman.

"Done."

She smirked at me, rolling her hips against mine. My hands tightened on her waist. Her eyes lit up, and I could tell she was on a sexually charged power trip. She could ask me to do anything right now, and I would, no questions asked. *Not sure how that's different from any other day of the week.*

"I want you there all weekend."

"Done."

"I want you on top of me."

Fuuuck.

"Done."

She didn't go back to work after that, but I did email Stacy to clear my weekend.

35

WANT THE HOUSE TOUR?

OLIVIA

The bell above the clinic door chimed softly when I stepped inside, the sound lingering in the quiet waiting room longer than it should have.

The place smelled faintly of antiseptic and old coffee. The kind of clean that reminded you people trusted their bodies to this building. Sunlight filtered through the front windows, stretching across the floor in long rectangles and illuminating the neat rows of chairs and the perfectly aligned stack of magazines on the coffee table.

For a moment, I wondered if the place was closed.

"Hello?" I called, my voice carrying down the hallway.

A door at the far end opened a second later, and Whit appeared. His sleeves were rolled to his elbows, and the collar of his shirt had softened from a long day of wear. A stethoscope hung around his neck like it had been there for hours.

When he saw me, surprise flickered across his face.

"Liv?"

The tension I hadn't realized I'd been carrying all afternoon loosened immediately.

"Hi."

He glanced at the clock on the wall before looking back at me, a faint crease forming between his brows. "Everything okay?"

"Yes. Nothing's wrong," I said quickly, stepping farther into the room. "I was just...in the neighborhood."

Whit leaned one shoulder against the doorway and crossed his arms, watching me with a quiet patience I imagined he used on patients who weren't telling him the whole story.

"You walked three blocks out of your way."

"Coincidence."

"Mm."

I dropped into one of the waiting room chairs and smoothed my hands over my skirt, suddenly very aware that I hadn't planned anything beyond showing up.

"Is Stacy here?"

"Lunch."

"And you're alone?"

His eyes narrowed slightly. "Why does that sound ominous?"

"It's not."

"Could be a continuation of your *Scream* bit."

I looked at him quizzically, but he waved it off. I exhaled and tipped my head back against the chair, staring up at the ceiling tiles.

"I'm nervous about the town meeting tonight."

The teasing left his face immediately.

He pushed away from the doorway and crossed the room until he was standing in front of me. Up close, the familiar details of him came into focus: the faint shadow of stubble along his jaw, the ink smudge along the side of his hand, the way his shirt pulled slightly across his shoulders when he folded his arms.

"It's not ridiculous," Whit said quietly when I muttered that it was.

The softness in his voice made me look up. He hadn't moved closer, but the clinic suddenly felt smaller, like the distance between us had shortened without either of us taking a step.

"They already hate me," I said.

"They don't."

I gave a small, humorless laugh and traced the seam of the chair cushion with my fingertip. "Some of them do."

The admission hung between us.

Whit didn't rush to contradict me this time. Instead, he shifted his weight slightly and glanced toward the hallway behind him, like he was mentally sorting through options the way he probably did when a patient came in with vague symptoms and no obvious diagnosis.

Finally, he looked back at me.

"Come on."

I frowned. "Where?"

He tipped his head toward the hallway, the corner of his mouth lifting just enough for me to know he had already decided something.

"You came all the way here," he said. "Might as well see where I spend most of my life."

"You're giving me a tour?"

"Yes."

I glanced past him into the corridor. The overhead lights stretched down the narrow hall in glowing rectangles, each door identical to the next. It looked exactly like every doctor's office I'd ever been in—quiet, orderly, faintly intimidating.

"Of the doctor's office."

"Yes."

I pushed myself out of the chair slowly, smoothing my skirt as I stood.

"That's incredibly romantic."

Whit huffed out a laugh and stepped aside, sweeping one arm down the hallway in an exaggerated gesture of hospitality.

"After you."

The first exam room looked exactly how I expected and somehow more personal at the same time. Bright overhead lights hummed softly above spotless white counters, and a row of labeled cabinets lined one wall with the quiet precision of a place where everything had to be exactly where it belonged. The same faint antiseptic scent from the waiting room lingered in the air, sharp and clean.

The padded exam table in the center of the room was covered with a sheet of crinkly white paper that looked like it would announce every tiny movement. A stainless-steel tray sat beside it, neatly arranged with instruments that gleamed under the fluorescent light.

"How thrilling," I said, glancing around.

Whit leaned back against the counter like he'd seen this reaction before, folding his arms as he watched me take it in.

"You're impossible to impress."

"It's the New Yorker in me."

"This," he said, gesturing around the room, "is Connor Bay medicine."

I tilted my head and pretended to study the space like a museum exhibit, even taking a seat on the doctor's stool to get a different perspective.

"I'm sure the germs are very cultured."

Whit huffed out a laugh and opened one of the drawers. The metal slid open with a soft clink as he rummaged briefly before pulling out a reflex hammer, the small rubber triangle swinging from the handle.

Before I could ask what he was doing, he stepped closer and tapped the side of my knee.

My leg kicked forward involuntarily.

"Hey!"

Whit's mouth curved with quiet satisfaction. "Excellent reflexes."

I narrowed my eyes at him. "You abused your medical authority."

"You walked into my clinic."

"That's not consent."

He laughed softly and set the hammer back in the drawer. "Next room."

The second exam room was nearly identical to the first, but that didn't stop me from hopping onto the table the moment Whit stepped aside to let me in.

As expected, the paper beneath me crinkled loudly as I settled there, the sharp sound echoing in the quiet room. I swung my legs slightly, my heels brushing the side of the table like I had every right in the world to be there.

Whit paused in the doorway with a bemused expression.

"Liv."

"What?"

"You're not a patient."

I lifted one shoulder. "I could be."

"You're not."

I leaned back on my hands, tilting my face toward the bright exam light above me.

"Hypothetically."

"Olivia."

"How long do you think we have before Stacy gets back?"

Whit didn't answer. The look and the head shake he gave me were enough of an answer. But still, something warm curled low in my stomach.

He pushed away from the doorway and stepped farther into the room, clearly intending to fix the situation by removing me from the exam table.

Instead, he ended up standing between my knees.

The moment stretched. The playful energy that had followed us down the hallway softened into something quieter, heavier.

"You're distracting," he muttered.

"That sounds like a you problem."

Whit straightened, but he didn't move away. He was close enough that I could see the faint shadow of stubble along his jaw and the tiny crease between his brows when he was trying to maintain composure.

For a second, neither of us moved.

"You came here because you're nervous," he said.

"I came here because I knew you'd make me feel better."

The words slipped out before I could soften them. Whit stilled.

Something shifted in his expression—something quieter and deeper than the teasing that had carried us through the rest of the tour. His gaze dropped briefly to my mouth before returning to my eyes.

"You shouldn't sit on the exam table," he said quietly.

"Why?"

"Because it makes me forget I'm supposed to be professional."

My pulse jumped. "You're doing a terrible job of sounding convincing."

Whit exhaled slowly and rested one hand on the edge of the table beside my hip, bringing him just a fraction closer.

"You're a menace."

"You like me."

"That's irrelevant."

But the way he was looking at me suggested otherwise.

The paper beneath my hands crackled softly when I shifted. Whit's eyes flicked down to the movement before returning to my face.

The room suddenly felt smaller. Quieter.

"You should get down," he said.

"Why?"

Whit's voice dropped.

"Because if you stay there much longer," he said, "I'm going to do something I absolutely shouldn't do in my own exam room."

His hand lifted and brushed a strand of hair away from my face, his fingers lingering lightly against my temple.

My breath caught.

"Whit—"

He kissed me before I could say anything else.

The movement stole the rest of the words from my mouth. One second he was standing there, fighting whatever line he'd drawn for himself, and the next his hand was at my jaw, warm and steady, tilting my face toward his.

It wasn't tentative.

The moment his mouth touched mine, the air seemed to disappear from the room, the tension that had been coiling between us finally snapping into place.

My hands found the fabric of his shirt automatically, fingers curling into the cotton as he stepped closer. The faint scent of soap and antiseptic clung to him.

Whit's other hand settled at my waist, the pressure gentle but grounding.

The paper beneath me crinkled loudly when I shifted.

I laughed into the kiss. Whit did too, the sound low against my mouth before he pulled back just enough for us both to breathe. His forehead rested against mine.

"You're a terrible influence," he murmured.

"You kissed me."

"You were sitting on my exam table."

"That's not illegal."

"It might be."

His thumb brushed absently along the curve of my waist.

Then the bell at the front door chimed.

Whit groaned softly.

"Stacy."

I grinned. "Saved by the receptionist."

Reluctantly, Whit stepped back, running a hand through his hair before straightening his shirt.

"Go."

"You're kicking me out?"

"Before she assumes something."

"What would she assume?"

Whit just looked at me.

The answer was obvious.

I slid off the table, smoothing my skirt.

"See you tonight, doctor."

Whit shook his head again, but he was smiling.

The nervous knot that had been sitting in my stomach all afternoon had loosened.

In its place was the lingering warmth of Whit's mouth and the quiet certainty that whatever happened at that meeting tonight, I wouldn't be facing it alone.

36

WHAT A SAD SIGHT
OLIVIA

Town meetings were held every other Wednesday at Paula's dance studio. The tumbling mats had been put away and replaced with rows of chairs in front of a lifted stage with a long folding table for the town council members.

I still wasn't entirely sure how many "councils" Connor Bay actually had. The town council was apparently different from the business council, but town meetings could be used to discuss business council agenda items. The organizational hierarchy was chaos. I had tried to map it out once on a notepad and abandoned the attempt halfway through when it started looking like the conspiracy board from a crime show.

The meeting was also surprisingly full.

There weren't enough chairs for everyone, so several people stood in the back of the room and along the doorways. A few leaned casually against the mirrors that lined the dance studio walls, arms crossed like they were settling in for a show.

I leaned over to Daisy, who sat beside me in the second

row. "Isn't that Angus?" I asked quietly, pointing to the man standing at the podium on stage.

She gave me a strange look. "Yeah. He's the mayor."

Sorry? "The mayor is a bartender?"

Daisy laughed. "Angus owns Duke's."

I had so many questions.

Who was *Duke?* What qualifications did someone who owned a bar possess that also made them capable of running a town? Had he run unopposed? Was it a landslide victory? Was it a prank everyone forgot to end?

"You look like you're doing really hard math," Eric whispered from my other side.

"This town is so fucking weird," I whispered back.

Eric snorted, "Tell me something I don't know."

Whit sat with arms crossed over his chest in a backward baseball cap wedged between Matt Dillard and Amelia's dad. He scratched his jaw absentmindedly as Matt explained something requiring many large hand gestures.

Angus banged a literal gavel and called the town meeting to order.

"Alright, we've got a packed schedule tonight. First, I'll start by saying that I hope you all feel good about yourselves because Jeremiah's lawn gnome petition got enough signatures. That means everyone is required to remove all lawn gnomes from their front yards sixty days from Monday."

The room erupted in laughter.

Eric pulled his lips into his mouth to refrain from saying something snarky. I shook my head, but I did feel proud of myself for signing it. He made a compelling case for the coup.

"Some other announcements..." Angus looked down at a sheet of paper in front of him. "Ah, yes. Whoever is paying the children to watch their golden retriever, please put a harness on the dog. It has been escaping its collar."

I coughed into my hand to cover my laugh as a chorus of grumbling broke out across the room about Hotpie.

Eric looked like he might actually explode as he pressed his hand over his mouth.

I glanced toward Whit, who had turned his hat around and tipped the bill down low enough to cover his eyes.

Angus moved through a few more announcements about adjusted summer hours for local businesses before arriving at the final item on the agenda.

"The last thing tonight is the potential cancellation of the Summer Festival."

The murmurs started immediately.

"Now, before everyone gets too worked up about this," Angus continued, raising a hand, "Daisy Whitaker would like to propose a solution. Daisy, the floor is yours."

Daisy stood and turned to face the rows behind her.

"Olivia and I would like to take over planning the festival," she said confidently. "I've already spoken with Avery about the possibility, and she's given me the go-ahead to take the lead. Avery confirmed everything with Angus this morning, so if there are no objections, Olivia and I can pick up where she left off."

A ripple of whispers moved through the room, but no one spoke.

I glanced toward Whit again. He had repositioned his cap and was glaring at someone over my shoulder.

I leaned toward Eric. "Who's Whit looking at? Can you see?"

Eric shifted slightly and looked behind us. "Uh... I think it's that girl he works with."

I rolled my eyes.

Daisy scanned the room, her gaze stopping in the same place as Whit's.

"Stacy."

Stacy stood from her seat, and we all turned to look at her.

"I'm just wondering why Olivia is the best candidate for this position. She's never been to one of these festivals and just moved here. I highly doubt that she'll know all the ins and outs of the festival traditions."

Daisy didn't miss a beat.

"Well, if I may speak on Olivia's behalf," she said, "she comes to us with extensive experience in financial planning, event oversight, and coordinating with third-party vendors. I've lived in Connor Bay my whole life and can guide her through the festival's traditions. There's no reason her involvement wouldn't be an asset to solving this problem."

She gestured toward the rest of the room.

"And I'm fairly certain many members of the business council would be happy to support her efforts, especially since several of you run the booths at the festival."

"Oh, I bet there's one in particular who would provide his *undying* support for Olivia," Eric murmured.

I elbowed him swiftly in the ribs.

"If there are no other concerns," Angus said from the stage, "I see no reason Daisy and Olivia can't take this on."

"She's not from here. Simple as that."

Marjorie's voice cut through the room.

I hadn't even seen her arrive.

Angus frowned in her direction. "Olivia lives here now, Marjorie. She's part of this town."

The whispers started again, louder this time, spreading quickly through the crowd.

Daisy sent me an apologetic glance. I wished, briefly, that Eric could handle this part. He was better at navigating rooms like this. But I knew it had to be me.

I stood.

The room quieted.

"I understand where Marjorie is coming from," I said. "I'm new here. You don't know me very well yet, and I'm still getting to know many of you."

I glanced around the room.

"In the short time I've been in Connor Bay, I've realized how important this community is and how much you all rely on each other. I'd really appreciate the opportunity to show you that you can rely on me, too."

I gestured toward Eric.

"And if you're willing, Eric and I would also like to share another proposal we have for the town."

An hour later, we walked out of the meeting with approval to plan the Summer Festival and begin working with local businesses on improvements aimed at increasing tourism.

Eric killed his presentation, and Angus put it to an immediate business council vote that passed unanimously...including a vote in favor from Marjorie.

I saw Marjorie and Levi walking toward the diner and jogged over to talk to them.

I was riding a high of support and was bound to crash. I should have seen it coming.

"Marjorie! Levi!"

Levi turned first, offering me a small, polite smile.

"Olivia," he said with a nod.

I smiled back. "I just wanted to say thank you for supporting the proposal, Marjorie. It means a lot to me."

Marjorie looked at me like I was the smallest, most irritating thing she'd ever seen. The way you'd look at a gnat that wouldn't leave you alone.

"It has nothing to do with supporting you," she said, making exaggerated air quotes around the words. "The way I see it, the sooner Connor Bay improves, the sooner you can go back to

New York. I'll vote for anything that gets you away from this town."

My breathing stopped.

My stomach clenched so tightly it hurt.

Levi sighed quietly and placed a hand on Marjorie's back, urging her forward toward the diner.

I could feel my skin prickle, and the tops of my cheeks redden. In this battle of fight or flight, I chose neither. I stood there, watching them finish their walk to the diner from right where they left me.

"Liv? What happened?"

Eric came up beside me. I felt the pressure of his hand between my shoulder blades, steady and familiar.

He was trying to comfort me.

But I couldn't—

I just...

It had been foolish to think Marjorie's vote meant anything.

She had fought Daisy and me on planning the festival in the first place.

I had been living in delusion if I believed Marjorie McCleary would ever see me as anything more than the reason her son was dead.

37

I'D NEVER WALK
CORNELIA STREET AGAIN

OLIVIA

Whit didn't ask me about my conversation with Marjorie the night before, but he knew something was wrong the moment he saw me. And even if he hadn't noticed right away, I would have given myself away eventually. I cried into his chest that night in bed until exhaustion finally dragged me under, my face pressed against his skin and my body folded into the crook of his arm like that was the only place I could exist.

Despite how hard it had been to fall asleep, no nightmares came.

I thought maybe it was because my waking life already felt like one.

When I opened my eyes in the morning, I was still pressed against Whit's side, my cheek resting against his chest. His arm was wrapped loosely around me, and his hand continued to move slowly through my hair in the same quiet rhythm it had the night before when I'd finally managed to turn my thoughts off.

I wondered if he'd slept at all.

I didn't move. I stayed exactly where I was, listening to the steady rise and fall of his breathing beneath my ear. Part of me wanted to freeze the moment exactly as it was—to trap it there, in that soft morning light, where the world outside the room didn't exist yet.

In the solace of that bed, it felt like only Whit and I existed.

No town meetings.

No whispered conversations.

No Marjorie McCleary looking at me like I didn't belong anywhere near her life.

Nothing else could reach me there if I didn't let it.

Eventually my stomach betrayed me, rumbling quietly against Whit's ribs. His hand paused in my hair, and I knew I'd given myself away.

I hadn't eaten dinner the night before, and my appetite still hadn't returned that morning. But I knew that if Whit didn't pitch a fit about it, Eric certainly would.

He'd seen me in the weeks after Davis, and Eric knew my appetite was always the first to go before a spiral.

I wasn't sure if I would spiral entirely, but maybe.

Whit pressed his lips gently against my forehead. "What's going on in that beautifully busy head of yours?"

A half-truth would suffice.

"Thinking about breakfast."

"I can pick up bagels."

I turned my head just enough to press a small kiss against his skin. "Okay."

By the time we boarded the plane later that morning, I had come to the conclusion that Eric must have overheard what Marjorie said the night before and relayed it to Whit. Eric hadn't mentioned it once, which was so unlike him that the silence itself felt suspicious.

Instead, he watched me carefully while I forced down half a bagel and washed it down with far too much drip coffee (*ugh*).

"Ever fly first class, Whit?" Eric asked, shouldering his messenger bag as we lined up for boarding.

"Can't say that I have," Whit replied.

"You're in for a treat then." Eric clapped Whit on the shoulder before pulling out his phone.

I looked at the two of them standing beside me.

Two of my favorite people in the world.

Two men who could not have been more different.

Whit's airport attire consisted of jeans, a white T-shirt, and a ball cap pulled low over his eyes. His carry-on was an Adidas duffel bag slung casually over his shoulder like he'd grabbed it without a second thought.

Eric's rolling suitcase was from one of our clients—a matte-black hard-shell case that somehow looked expensive even from across the terminal. He wore slacks and a crisp button-up shirt, like boarding a plane was just another extension of his workday.

Somehow I had landed somewhere in the middle.

I had the same suitcase as Eric, though mine was beige, but I wore jeans and a crewneck sweatshirt two sizes too big. I always got cold on planes, though normally I would have dressed more like Eric than Whit.

Looking at the three of us together, it struck me again how strange it was that we worked so easily as a group.

If the three of us could get along this naturally, why couldn't Marjorie extend the same grace?

Was I really the living embodiment of everything she hated?

My mom's gonna hate you.

If I had only known how right Davis was going to be.

The hotel was on the list of things Whit hadn't asked me about.

Maybe it was obvious to him that I didn't want to stay in the apartment I'd shared with Davis.

That decision had more to do with the fact that I wasn't sure I was ready to see that apartment again.

Even if I wasn't going to stay in Connor Bay, I didn't think I'd ever go back to that apartment. Maybe I'd never see it again and have Eric pack it up for me.

"Eric's going into the office today to check in on things," I told Whit as I hung my work clothes for tomorrow in the closet by the door. "I was thinking we could get lunch and then meet Eric for dinner."

Whit didn't respond from the other room.

"Does that sound okay?" I waited. "Whit?" I walked into the bedroom. "Are you okay?"

He stood at the window, looking out at the skyline. "You and I have *very* different lifestyles."

My cheeks heated, and my stomach dropped immediately.

Of course we did.

Marjorie had said it plainly enough the night before. People like me didn't belong in Connor Bay. We were too different.

I had slipped back into my New York self without realizing it—the version of me that booked expensive hotels without thinking about it, that ordered cocktails that cost more than a decent bottle of wine.

Davis never said anything directly, but I could tell that some of the things I spent money on made him uncomfortable.

It took me longer than I'd like to admit to realize that his minimalist lifestyle might not have been a preference at all.

It might have been a necessity.

In New York, I bought designer clothes and expensive

shoes without a second thought, while Davis couponed in our kitchen every Sunday.

"I'm sorry," I said quickly. "I should have warned you. We can switch hotels. Maybe somewhere in the Village. You could show me where you used to hang out when you lived here."

Whit didn't answer.

"Whit?"

"Hmm?" He blinked and turned toward me like he'd just returned from somewhere far away.

"The hotel," I said, shifting my weight onto my back foot. "We can stay somewhere else."

"Why would we do that?"

I blinked in confusion. "You just said—"

Realization crossed his face.

"It's not a problem, Olivia," he said gently as he walked toward me. "You and I come from different backgrounds, and honestly I'm a little in awe of yours."

He stopped in front of me.

"I was just thinking that in the four years I lived in this city, I never once felt at home here." He smiled softly. "And somehow I do now."

I studied him carefully.

"Who knew you had such champagne tastes?" I asked.

Whit laughed, and the sound softened something tight in my chest.

"We both know I'm talking about you."

I didn't, but I wanted to believe that. I wanted to think that Whit was so enamored with me that he could see past all the ways we were different.

"Are you sure it's okay?"

Whit leaned down and kissed my forehead.

"More than okay." He brushed his thumb lightly along my cheek. "Did you say something about lunch?"

38

SWEET NOTHING
OLIVIA

My favorite time of year was autumn, but summer was a close second.

Whit and I walked hand in hand down Bleecker Street in the West Village, the late afternoon sun stretching long shadows across the sidewalk. The Village always felt a little softer than the rest of Manhattan—quieter somehow, the buildings lower, the streets narrower. It was one of the few places in the city where you could almost pretend the pace slowed down.

I didn't spend much time there, but there were a handful of lunch spots I liked to slip into when I wanted a break from Midtown.

It just so happened that one of those places was also one of Whit's favorites.

"Maybe we've seen each other here before," I said as the hostess led us toward a small table tucked near the window.

"Unlikely," Whit replied as he pulled out the chair for me.

I laughed. "How can you be sure?"

Whit didn't even hesitate.

"I'd know if you were in the same room as me, Olivia. Then and now." His expression stayed serious, steady in that way that always made my stomach flutter. "If we had been here at the same time, we might be an entirely different story."

My cheeks warmed under his gaze.

Whit had a way of saying things that made the air between us feel heavier, like the words themselves carried weight. His declarations never sounded rehearsed or exaggerated—they slipped from his mouth so naturally that I sometimes wondered if that was simply who he was.

Or if it was who he was with *me*.

A buzzing started in my purse.

It was probably Eric or something at work. I went to grab it, but then paused. I shouldn't answer a call when we're out together, Davis hated that.

"No, it's just work," I said quickly. "I'll get to it later."

Instead of setting my purse beside me on the chair, I slid it behind my back like I was hiding the phone from temptation.

"Olivia," Whit said gently, "it's okay. I can answer emails if it would make you feel better."

I looked at him.

"If you're sure."

"We're in New York for work, Liv," he said with a small smile. "I assumed you'd need to actually do work."

It wasn't so much that Davis hated me working; he hated my inability to separate my personal and professional life.

He thought work was done in the office, and then at 5 p.m. on the dot, your brain should just stop thinking about your job.

Except, I had never been like that. I didn't think I ever could be like that. Whit seemed to understand that without me having to explain it to him.

"Clark wants us at the event tonight," Eric said when I answered his call.

I glanced at Whit, who was reading the menu across from me at the table.

"Okay, can do. What's the deal?"

Eric must have put me on speaker because his voice sounded distant. The clacking of his keyboard echoed clearly through the phone.

Clark and Eric hadn't mentioned any kind of event when we talked earlier that week. Which meant one of two things: it had come up last minute, or Eric had intentionally tried to keep me out of it.

"It's a client social at 583," Eric said. "So you'll need to break out something from your fancy closet. Bring Whit."

Definitely tried to get me out of it. Socials at 583 Park Drive didn't just "come up."

leaned back in my chair and started pulling a loose thread from the napkin in my lap.

The last time I forced someone to attend a work function with me hadn't exactly gone well.

Apparently I had a talent for bringing people into worlds they didn't want to be part of.

"I'm not sure he'd be up for it."

Eric's typing stopped.

"Shit. Sorry, Liv, I just meant— I just meant that Whit could come if he wants to, not that he has to. He went to school here, right? He probably has friends in the area to hang out with in the Village."

"It's okay."

Something in my voice must have shifted because Whit lowered his menu and looked at me, brows pulling together slightly.

"Just email me the details," I told Eric. "I'll be there."

"You got it. Have a good lunch."

I dropped my phone back into my purse. I had absolutely no interest in talking to anyone else right now.

There was a time when I didn't think twice about events like that.

I'd put on a nice dress, get my hair done, and show up beside Eric looking polished and effortless. I'd hang lightly off his arm while he talked with clients and investors. All I had to do was laugh at the right moments and look engaged.

It had been easy.

"Something wrong?" Whit asked.

I opened my menu, pretending to study it.

"No. There's just a work thing tonight I have to go to. Eric just told me about it."

"Ah." Whit glanced down at his watch. "I didn't bring a suit for that."

I lifted my head.

"But I could probably pick one up after lunch," he continued easily. "Eric seems like someone with a suit guy. I'll see if he can get me in with him."

He was already pulling out his phone when my brain finally caught up.

"You—, ah—, no, you don't..." I shook my head slowly, trying to form an actual sentence.

Whit looked up, his phone still in his hand.

"Unless you don't want me there?"

My mouth opened and closed like a fish.

"No, it's just... you can't honestly want to come."

"I can't?" His tone was amused.

I was glad someone thought this situation was funny.

"Do you?"

Whit laughed.

"Well, of course not."

"Okay," I said quickly. "So then you don't have to go."

Whit leaned back in his chair, completely relaxed, like this was the simplest conversation in the world.

"Liv, if my options are missing out on a night where you're willing to be seen in public with me," he said, "or screwing around with my college friends in NoHo, I don't think I need to explain which one I'd prefer."

I stared at him for a second longer than necessary.

It was such an absurd thing to say.

As if he were the one lucky to be included.

"...so you're coming?"

"Sounds like it." He leaned in, his voice low. "Besides, I think seeing you all dressed up at work might be fun. It'll make ravaging you later all the more...." Whit's gaze moved across my face and down my body, "...exciting."

My skin prickled immediately, heat rushing up my neck and across my cheeks.

The only response I could manage for the man who made it seem like loving me might actually be the most natural thing in the world was:

"Who uses the word *ravaging* anymore?"

Apparently, *Keating Whitaker*.

39

MAKE THE FRIENDSHIP BRACELETS

WHIT

The tailor's shop was tucked onto a side street off Madison, the kind of place I would have walked right past if Eric hadn't texted me the address twice and followed it with, *don't embarrass me by showing up at the wrong one.*

The windows were spotless. Everything inside looked expensive enough to make me stand up straighter the second I walked in. Dark wood. Cream walls. Low lighting that made the bolts of fabric look like museum pieces instead of something people actually wore.

A man in a charcoal suit looked up from behind a counter and gave me a polite nod.

"Can I help you?"

"Uh, yeah," I said, already feeling underdressed in the room. "I've got an appointment. Whitaker."

Before he could respond, Eric's voice drifted from deeper in the store.

"He's with me."

Eric stepped out from behind a rack of jackets, one hand

wrapped around a paper espresso cup, and the other holding his phone. He looked exactly like he belonged there in pressed slacks and a pale blue button-down with the sleeves rolled once at the forearm. It was deeply annoying.

"This is him," Eric said to the salesman. "We need something for tonight. Black tie adjacent, but not old money funeral. He has shoulders, so don't put him in anything too conservative."

I blinked at him. "What does that even mean?"

"It means I'm helping."

The tailor, whose name turned out to be Matteo, came around the counter with a tape measure looped around his neck and a look of quiet focus that reminded me a little too much of an attending physician before rounds.

"If you'll step this way, Mr. Whitaker."

I followed him toward a small raised platform surrounded by mirrors while Eric drifted to one of the leather chairs nearby and sat like he was settling in for a show.

"This is incredibly weird," I muttered.

Eric didn't look up from his phone. "You're welcome."

Matteo measured my shoulders first, then my chest, then the inseam, calling numbers to an assistant who materialized with a clipboard from somewhere in the back.

"You're nervous," Eric said casually.

I looked over at him. "I'm not."

He smiled into his coffee. "You should be."

"I've done residency."

"This isn't residency." He set the cup on the side table beside him. "This is a room full of rich people pretending they're not looking at each other's watches."

"That sounds easier than medicine, actually."

Eric snorted. "That's because you've never had to explain to a billionaire's wife why her spring launch underperformed."

Matteo stepped back to study the line of my shoulders. "He'll need the navy."

"Obviously," Eric said.

I looked between them. "I'm sorry, are either of you going to explain why I'm being spoken about like I'm not standing here?"

"No," Eric said.

Matteo gestured for me to step off the platform. "I'll bring others out as well. One moment."

He and his assistant disappeared into the back.

I glanced around the shop again, then at Eric. "You didn't have to come."

Eric leaned back in the chair, crossing one ankle over his opposite knee. "I know."

That was so very Eric that I laughed despite myself.

He looked up then, his expression easier than it had been in the café earlier. "Olivia's getting her hair done three blocks from here, and I had nothing else to do for forty-five minutes except answer emails and resent capitalism. This felt more productive."

"Watching me get measured for a suit is productive?"

"For me? No." He tilted his head. "For Olivia? Probably."

I studied him for a second.

Eric had a way of saying things about Olivia like they were obvious facts—simple, practical truths that didn't need much explanation. The unsettling part was that he was usually right.

Matteo returned carrying two jackets, one draped over each forearm like ceremonial offerings.

The first suit was too gray. The second made me look like I was either running for office or about to sell someone a time-share in Connecticut. Eric vetoed both with the kind of efficiency that made me understand instantly why he thrived in rooms like the one we'd be in tonight.

"No," he said to the gray. "He looks like a ghost."

Then, to the other one, "Absolutely not. Olivia would leave him at the bar."

I looked down at the jacket sleeves. "That bad?"

Eric finally smiled at me. "You asked."

The third one was navy. Dark enough to feel serious, but not so dark that it flattened everything out. Matteo adjusted the shoulders, tugged the sleeve, stepped back, then turned me toward the mirror.

I barely recognized myself.

Not because it made me look different, exactly. Just... sharper. Less like the guy who spent most of his week seeing elderly patients and more like someone who might actually have a reason to be in a room where champagne glasses were stacked like architecture.

Eric stood and came to my side, studying my reflection in the mirror.

"There," he said. "Now you look like someone Clark will try to hire away from medicine."

"That sounds threatening."

"It is."

Matteo moved in to pin the trouser hem.

"You nervous now?" Eric asked.

I met his eyes in the mirror. "A little."

He nodded once, like that was the correct answer.

"Good."

I watched him for a beat. "You're enjoying this more than you should."

"Not the suit." Eric slid his hands into his pockets and glanced toward the platform where Matteo was pinning the hem of my trousers. "The fact that she asked me to help."

That caught my attention.

"Why's that?"

Matteo crouched at my ankle, muttering something about a quarter break while he adjusted the fabric. Eric's gaze stayed on my reflection in the mirror, thoughtful in a way that suggested he was considering more than the line of the jacket.

"She hasn't asked me for help with anything in a long time," he said.

I turned slightly on the platform so I could see him more clearly. Eric shrugged like the observation didn't mean much, but there was a quiet weight to the way he said it.

"After the accident she got very good at pretending she didn't need anyone. Work. Life. Everything." His eyes flicked briefly to the suit jacket draped over my shoulders. "So yeah. This feels like progress."

I studied him for a moment, trying to decide if that was something he said lightly or something he had been waiting a long time to notice.

"You think that's because of me?"

Eric's mouth curved faintly, though it wasn't quite a smile.

"I think," he said carefully, "you make it easier for her to want things again."

Matteo stood and brushed his hands together before disappearing toward the back with a quiet promise to return with the finished alterations. Eric remained where he was, leaning against the mirror frame now, his arms loosely crossed.

"She's happier with you," he added.

It was the sort of statement a person probably ought to respond to. Instead, I looked back at my reflection. Hearing someone else say it out loud made the idea feel strangely fragile, like it might collapse if I acknowledged it too quickly.

Eric watched me for a second longer before speaking again.

"Just don't mistake that for things being simple."

I glanced over at him. He wasn't smiling anymore, though

there was nothing hostile in his expression either. If anything, he looked almost sympathetic.

"Olivia's very good at convincing people she's fine," he continued. "She'll make what she needs sound optional. She'll make what she wants seem like it doesn't matter." His gaze flicked back toward the hallway where Matteo had disappeared. "She's spent a long time taking care of everyone else. Sometimes she forgets she's allowed to ask for anything in return."

That sounded familiar.

I thought about lunch and the way she had tried to brush off the event as if it were nothing, even though it clearly mattered to her. The pattern was easy to recognize once someone pointed it out.

"I've noticed," I said.

Eric nodded once, satisfied.

"Good. Then you already understand the part most people miss."

Matteo returned a few minutes later with the final pins in place and instructions about when the suit would be ready for pickup. When I stepped down from the platform, Eric gave the finished fit an assessing look, the way he might study a contract before signing it.

"You clean up alright," he said.

"That's a terrifying compliment coming from you."

"Don't get used to it."

He settled the deposit at the counter before I could stop him, brushing off my protest with an absent wave of his hand.

"Relax. Olivia will reimburse me."

"That is not relaxing."

Eric only looked amused.

We stepped back out onto the sidewalk a moment later, the noise of the city rushing in around us again. A delivery truck idled at the curb, and someone down the block was laughing too loudly at something their friend had said.

Eric reached out and caught my arm just before I started down the block.

"She's worth the trouble," he said.

"I know."

He held my gaze for a second longer, as if deciding whether to say anything else, then nodded once and released me.

"Good. Then go meet your girlfriend before she decides that suit is wrong and sends you back in there."

I smiled.

"She'd do that."

"She absolutely would."

I started down the block before glancing back once. Eric was still standing outside the shop, leaning against the polished glass, typing on his phone.

"Hey," I called.

He looked up.

"Thanks."

He waved the word away like it embarrassed him.

Then, because he was Eric, he ruined the moment immediately.

"If you hurt her," he said conversationally, "I'll make you move back to Baltimore."

I laughed.

"That seems fair."

40

CHAMPAGNE SEA

WHIT

Every version of Olivia was my favorite.

Sleepy morning Olivia. Car ride Olivia. Late-night-work Olivia. They were all exquisite in their own way. Tonight, I got to add formal-event Olivia to my growing carousel of favorites.

While I went to get my suit, Olivia got her hair done somewhere across town. She'd sent one of her interns to meet me at the shop to collect her apartment key so they could deliver a dress to the hotel room before the event.

Watching the entire operation unfold made it clear that Olivia's life ran on a level of organization I'd never personally achieved.

I was taking my cues from Eric as to when to push her to talk about things.

I knew Marjorie had said something to upset her the night before. I also knew she had absolutely no intention of setting foot in her apartment on Fifth Avenue while we were here. But neither one of those things felt like my place to dig into—not yet.

"Can you zip this, Whit?" Olivia called from the bathroom.

I finished buttoning the cufflinks on my shirt as I walked over.

I took it back.

This version of Olivia was my absolute favorite.

Her hair had been pinned up in a soft arrangement that left the line of her neck completely exposed. The black dress she wore wrapped around the curves of her body like it had been designed specifically for her. It hugged her waist. Followed the slope of her hips.

The sight of her standing there in the mirror made something deep in my chest tighten in a way that had very little to do with romance and everything to do with wanting to drop to my knees.

"Whit?"

"Sorry," I said, pulling the zipper slowly up her back. "Ready?"

I was more than pleased when she didn't answer right away.

Instead, she watched me through the mirror.

Her eyes moved over me slowly, deliberately, tracing the lines of the suit Eric's guy had talked me into buying. The longer she looked, the darker her eyes became, the soft blue deepening into something closer to navy.

I wanted to ask her if we could skip the event, but I knew it wouldn't be an option.

I also knew she'd read too much into the request, so I leaned down to kiss her shoulder and walked back out.

I couldn't be trusted with her in an empty bathroom.

I'D NEVER BEEN to an event this extravagant.

A tower of champagne glasses rose in the center of the room like a piece of architecture. Men in tuxedos and women in formal gowns drifted through the ballroom in clusters of quiet conversation.

The combined net worth of the people in that room had to be close to a billion dollars.

Maybe more.

"So that's Luke van der Kleef," Eric said beside me as we stood off to the side surveying the crowd. "He owns cruiseliners."

He nodded toward a tall man currently speaking with Olivia across the room.

"Olivia and I ran a campaign for him last year that brought in a quarter million dollars over projection."

Definitely more than a billion.

That would explain the grin on Luke's face as he spoke to her.

Olivia laughed at something he said, tilting her head back slightly as she did. The motion exposed the long line of her neck.

My mind immediately betrayed me. I imagined my hand wrapped around her throat, the skirt of her dress pushed up over her hips as I bent her over the hotel bed.

If I didn't get it together soon, I'd be dragging her into the bathroom here before the night was over.

Olivia still looked perfectly at ease in conversation, but then she slipped one hand behind her back.

Her index and middle fingers crossed.

"That's our cue," Eric said immediately. "Come on."

Ah. The *"save me"* sign they'd mentioned earlier, in passing.

I followed behind Eric as he weaved through bodies to get to Olivia.

"Luke, so good to see you. How are the kids?"

Luke looked genuinely surprised when Eric appeared beside him. He shook Eric's hand firmly.

"They're good, thanks."

"Great to hear. Actually, I came over here because Clark is looking for Olivia. I hope you don't mind us stealing her."

Luke did look like he minded, but he shook his head. "No, no. Not at all. Olivia, always a pleasure."

Eric steered us back to our corner.

"Thanks for that," Olivia said, grabbing three champagne flutes from a passing tray and handing one to each of us. "He just invited me to Mykonos."

My brows raised, but Eric laughed.

"A non-transferrable invitation, I'd assume."

She gave him a look and then turned to me. "How are you doing? If you want to leave, feel free to head out. I'll call you when I'm on my way back."

Eric replied before I could. "Actually, Olivia, Whit charmed Eileen McNally earlier." Her eyes lit up in surprise. "She's talking to Clark about a Spring campaign for her new collection."

"What did you say to her?"

I shrugged. "Just small talk."

The truth was, I had spent most of the evening watching Olivia from across the room. I couldn't remember a single thing I'd said to the older woman.

Which was unfortunate because Olivia was looking at me like I'd just performed a magic trick.

"Well, whatever you said, we've been trying to get her to sign with us for the last year."

It sounded like adoration in her voice, and I needed to look anywhere but at her unless she wanted me to kiss her senseless in front of her clients.

Eric tapped his glass to hers before taking a sip of his own. "Must be his boyish charm."

"Must be," I said with another shrug.

Eric and Olivia continued making their rounds, drifting from conversation to conversation with the practiced ease of people who had done this many times before.

We finally left sometime around midnight.

Despite the extravagance of the entire evening, I didn't feel nearly as out of place as I might have expected.

I'd gotten through med school and residency, which definitely made me intimately familiar with the art of *fake it 'til you make it*. And I'd do just about anything to make it with Olivia Carrington.

41

JUST TO KEEP YOU

OLIVIA

Whit leaned against the elevator wall and loosened his tie, tilting his head left and right to stretch out the stiffness in his neck. The motion pulled the collar of his shirt open slightly, and I had to swallow before forcing my eyes back to the glowing numbers climbing above the door.

"Do you have those often?"

I frowned and turned to look at him. "Was it awful?"

Something crossed his face then—something I couldn't quite place. Not discomfort. Not exactly amusement either.

He straightened and reached for me, pulling me against him with an ease that made my breath catch.

"Absolutely dreadful," he said gravely. "It's quite distressing that you look this good and I can't do anything about it."

"Always such a smooth talker, Keating Whitaker," I said, my hands resting on his chest.

"Only for you, Liv."

"But really," I pressed, searching his face, "was it awful?"

Whit stroked my cheek with the back of his hand, the other settling easily at my waist. His fingers curled under my chin, tipping my face toward his.

"Not at all."

The elevator chimed before he could close the distance between us.

I stepped away instinctively as the doors opened.

Once inside the hotel room, I slipped off my shoes and placed my purse on the dresser. The quiet of the room felt almost startling after the noise and glitter of the ballroom.

I had a feeling that even if Whit had endured the worst night of his life, he wouldn't have told me.

But by every measurable standard, the evening had been a success.

The clients loved him. *Clark* loved him, and Clark didn't even *like* people most of the time. In fact, Clark had been so taken with Whit that he had practically told Eric and me he'd approve the Connor Bay proposal tomorrow after the pitch.

The thought made my chest flutter.

Whit had a place in this world beside me—not behind me. He could stand in those rooms, hold his own, and people would fall in love with him...just like I had.

I sat down at the vanity and began pulling the pins from my hair.

"Here, let me," Whit said softly, catching my hand before I could remove the next one.

I met his eyes in the mirror and smiled as he carefully slid each pin free. One by one, my curls loosened and fell around my shoulders.

Something about the tenderness of the moment made a quiet certainty settle inside me.

I knew then.

I think I'd known it all along.

I loved Keating Whitaker.

Not the cautious version of love that waited for proof or protection. Not the version that could hide comfortably in quiet corners.

I was in love with him.

I'd never met anyone quite like him. No one had ever treated me like I was both durable and fragile at the same time. No one made me feel as alive as Whit did.

"What's going on in that beautifully busy head of yours?" he asked, pulling the last pin out and massaging my scalp with his fingertips.

My eyes closed automatically.

"You can't be real."

Whit's lips brushed the side of my neck, and I tipped my head slightly to give him better access.

"I was thinking the same thing about you."

My lips parted when his teeth grazed a sensitive spot just below my ear.

His movements were slow and purposeful, as if he could spend his life in this moment. I was pretty sure I could, too.

Whit's hands found the zipper of my dress and tugged it down as far as it could go while I was sitting. His hands slipped under the straps and pulled the bodice of my dress down my chest.

His palms skated over my breasts and stopped against my stomach, his mouth still on my neck.

I forced my eyes open to find him staring at me in the mirror. It reminded me of the bathroom at Duke's, but this was more controlled. More intimate.

Whit took my hand and pulled me gently to my feet so he could finish unzipping the dress. The fabric slid down my body and pooled around my feet, leaving me standing in nothing but my underwear in front of the mirror.

I turned toward him and reached for his tie, loosening the knot slowly. He didn't touch me while I undressed him. He let me take the lead completely. But the way he looked at me did almost as much as his hands ever had. His gaze moved across my skin with a heat that made every inch of me feel alive.

The times we'd been together had been hot and heavy and fast. This was different.

This was the Whit who walked with his hands in his pockets and gave lazy smiles over his shoulder. The Whit who watched me from across the room when he thought I didn't notice.

This was Keating Whitaker in his purest form.

When we were both undressed, he kissed me all the way to the bed.

His hands weren't rough against my skin. They worshipped me. Even his mouth was soft and yielding against mine.

"You're so beautiful, Liv," he whispered, leaning his elbow and tracing his thumb over my bottom lip.

"So are you."

And *god,* was that the truth. I remembered seeing him for the first time and not being able to stop staring at him. A sculpted Adonis brought to life.

He pushed into me and thrust in a beautifully paced rhythm that brought me to a peak before I realized what was happening. Whit groaned against my mouth when he found his release.

He pulled me against his chest, and we lay there in a serene silence that only one thing could warrant breaking.

"I think we should have dinner with Marjorie and Levi," I said, looking up at him.

Whit's brows shot up. "Come again?"

"I want to do this, Whit. I want to be with you outside of our houses. I want to walk around town with you. But I want Marjorie and Levi to know first."

Even if Marjorie wanted me gone, they still deserved to know that Whit and I were together.

It wasn't about getting them to like me anymore; maybe it never was. It was about showing them and Davis respect.

If I wanted Marjorie to respect me, then I'd have to show her my cards—all of them.

Whit's eyes searched mine. "And if they don't react well?"

I rolled onto my back, staring at the ceiling.

I recalled a ceiling in a different city with glow-in-the-dark stars. A ceiling that belonged to someone who wasn't here anymore, but who I was sure still wanted me to be happy.

"I think we'll reevaluate," I said softly. "I don't need their permission. But I don't want them finding out from someone else."

Whit leaned down and kissed me before brushing his thumb across my cheek.

"I'll set it up."

I can't help that I'm in love with her, Davis. I'm
in love with every part of her, and I don't
even feel guilty about it anymore.
I know that you'd want us to be happy, and
maybe if you were here, you'd never forgive
either of us, or we wouldn't be together,
but you're not here Davis, and Olivia
makes me feel smaller than the stars ever
did. She is an all-consuming midnight, and

> *I can't help but want to be wrapped up*
> *in her...*
> *I don't think I'll leave any more voicemails after*
> *this one.*
> *I love you, Davis. I hope wherever you are,*
> *you're happy for us because I am so happy*
> *to have found her.*

42

LITTLE MISS UNSTABLE
OLIVIA

A little after *Before*

Duke's was a bar off the interstate, and the only one I could find that was within walking distance from my motel room at the *Juniper Breeze*, according to Yelp. It sat alone in the middle of a wide parking lot, the kind of place that probably looked exactly the same twenty years ago as it did tonight. From the outside it looked like a saloon—wood siding, dim yellow lights, a neon beer sign flickering in the window.

Inside, the floors and walls were covered in dark wood paneling that smelled faintly of old smoke and spilled beer. Every table was a high-top, and there was a wide space cleared in the center of the room that I assumed doubled as a dance floor on busier nights.

For a Saturday night, it was quieter than I expected for the closest bar to Connor Bay.

But then again, it was only seven.

I slid onto a stool at the bar.

I had only been sitting there a moment before a man with hair cropped close to his scalp on the other side of the bar came over and asked me what I was having. I missed *him*, so I ordered his drink.

"What Whiskey do you carry?"

He set a glass down and pulled another from beneath the counter. "Tennessee and Rye."

"Tenessee on the rocks with a twist, please."

He nodded and scooped ice into the glass. "Hard time?"

I laughed. *That was an understatement.* I told him as much. Then he squinted at me.

"You're not from here." He wasn't asking as he put the drink in front of me.

I shook my head. "Just in from New York."

The bartender let out a low whistle.

"New York, huh? What's got you hanging around here?"

I took a drink and bit back my cringe as the liquid burned, sliding down my throat. *How you drank this was beyond me.*

"My husband's from here."

He glanced at the hand gripping my glass. It was an automatic response when I told someone I was married. *Check for the ring.*

Except we'd never gotten around to buying rings. Sometimes, I would put one of my other rings on my left ring finger as a placeholder, but he hated it. He wanted to buy me one himself, but just never got around to it.

The bartender didn't say anything.

"He died," I said finally, looking at him over the rim of my glass.

His eyebrows lifted slightly as he looked me over again, this time with a little more understanding.

"Olivia, I presume."

Of course.

Everyone in this town knew who I was, and so far, it was only causing me exuberant amounts of trouble. I couldn't find a place to live. I couldn't walk into a store without being stared at...glared at occasionally.

I'd only come here once before, for the funeral. I didn't know how anyone could form an opinion so quickly. Then again, Marjorie McCleary had become my worst enemy, and the town seemed to revolve around her.

"In the flesh," I replied, followed by another long drink.

It wasn't so bad once you got used to it. His dark brows rose as he watched me finish my glass.

"Is someone meeting you here?" he asked, glancing down the bar to see if anyone was waiting on him.

I pushed my empty glass toward him.

"I'll have another." Then I added lightly, "I don't think it's safe to tell strangers about my plans."

Of course, he probably knew the answer already. I didn't have anyone.

What had *he* said that night? *Your life with your* one *friend.* It rang through my mind. It did cartwheels on the back of my retinas.

I had one friend in New York and zero in Connor Bay. I leaned my forehead into my palm and then ran my fingers through my hair when the bartender put a new drink in front of me.

"Just pace yourself," he warned, tapping the edge of the bar before he moved down a few seats to attend to someone else.

I did not pace myself.

In fact, the bartender paced me as much as he could, but eventually, a second bartender started her shift, and she couldn't care less about who I was and whether I had someone to drive me home later. I had walked over from the *Juniper Breeze.* I could find my way just fine.

"Alright," she said eventually, setting down another glass before pulling it back again, "I have to cut you off."

I frowned up at her.

"Orders from the boss." She jerked her thumb over her shoulder toward the first bartender. "And your ride's here."

I didn't have time to be annoyed about the first part because the second part made my brain stall.

"My ride?"

She nodded toward someone standing beside me and walked away.

"C'mon, Liv. Let's get you home."

Liv?

Lifting my head to the side to see who they'd called to get me, I froze.

My eyelashes fluttered, trying to clear my vision. He came closer, and my vision focused.

Levi.

His dad.

Not *him.*

Just his dad.

I sucked in a breath while he shrugged out of his jacket and put it around my shoulders.

"Liv, c'mon," he said gently. "It's okay. I'll take you over to your motel."

I snapped out of it then. "I have to pay…"

My hands floated uselessly in the air while I searched for my bag.

"I'll get it," Levi said, already reaching for his wallet.

I shook my head. "No, I've got it. You shouldn't."

I thought my words might not be coherent when he glanced at me worriedly.

"I'm fine. I've got it." I found my bag attached to my body and pulled out a card.

Levi frowned but put his wallet away. The first bartender came over with my receipt, and I handed my card over without looking at it.

"Thanks for calling," Levi said.

"Figured it was a family thing," the bartender replied, running my card and sliding the receipt back toward me with a pen.

After signing something slightly resembling my name, I slid off my stool and lost my footing. Levi caught me before I hit the floor. I muttered a thank-you and pulled his jacket tighter around my shoulders.

He guided me toward his car with a steady hand against the middle of my back.

This was an all-time low for me, for sure.

Having a bartender call my father-in-law to pick me up from a bar in the middle of nowhere.

Ladies and gentlemen, Olivia Carrington.

In the middle of a drunken daze, I tried to determine if I could sink any lower. When I couldn't, I started to cry. It turned out that was an even lower low.

"I'm sorry," I said through the tears as Levi rubbed slow circles against my back.

"Nothing to be sorry about, Olivia," he said quietly. "Nothing at all."

He was wrong.

I had so many things to be sorry about.

43

THE COMEDOWN OF CLOSURE

WHIT

Olivia smoothed her hair with her hands nervously.

The rest of our New York trip had been incredible. She'd taken me to her favorite restaurants and dragged me through half the shops in the West Village. We'd spent entire afternoons wandering the city with no real destination, and watching Olivia move through New York had been something else entirely.

In Connor Bay, she felt cautious—careful about where she stepped and how she spoke.

In New York, she belonged.

Another day and I might have convinced her to move there with me so we could spend every day like that.

But we were back in reality now.

Back in reality meant keeping our relationship quiet and sitting down to dinner with Marjorie and Levi.

When I'd called Marjorie to arrange it, she had shut the idea down immediately. It had taken Daisy stepping in and doing some serious arm twisting before Marjorie reluctantly agreed.

Levi answered the door when I knocked.

"Keating, good to see you. Olivia, always a pleasure."

Olivia offered him a tight smile. "Thanks for having us."

"Marjorie is just finishing up dinner; come in."

Olivia glanced at me, and I gave her a small nod of encouragement.

I wasn't entirely convinced this dinner would accomplish what she hoped it would. But if this was the step she felt she needed to take, then I was all in.

"Can I get you a drink? A beer, Whit?" Levi asked, already halfway toward the kitchen.

"Sure, thanks."

"Water's good with me, thanks," Olivia said quietly, wringing her hands together.

"It's going to be fine, Liv," I whispered, glancing around the house as I said it.

This place had been a second home to me growing up.

I'd broken my arm here when Davis pushed me down the stairs in a race to the ice cream truck. I had my first kiss right there in the living room when I was fourteen. I had my first beer in the kitchen at fifteen one night when Marjorie and Levi had gone to visit family and left Davis behind.

Every room in this house held a memory. Marjorie and Levi had to remember those things, too. Whether those memories would work in our favor tonight was another matter entirely.

Olivia exhaled slowly. "You're right. It will be fine. This is about us."

I smiled down at her, wishing I believed that as confidently as she was trying to.

"Here we go—two drinks," Levi said as he returned.

Marjorie entered the dining room behind him, carrying two

plates that were already assembled. Her eyes moved immediately to Olivia.

"No whiskey tonight, Olivia?"

Olivia's cheeks flushed red as she tucked her hair behind her ear. "It's not usually my drink of choice. Water's fine."

Marjorie raised her brows as she took her seat at the head of the table, which was our cue to take our seats. It also seemed like there would be no pleasantries at this dinner.

"Could have fooled me...and Levi...and Angus."

I looked between the three of them.

Levi suddenly became very interested in adjusting his napkin. Olivia focused on the food in front of her. Marjorie took a slow sip of her drink.

I had definitely missed something.

I knew Levi had picked Olivia up from Duke's one night, but maybe it had been a bigger deal.

"This looks delicious, Marjorie. Thank you so much." Olivia said, cutting into a piece of chicken.

Marjorie didn't respond.

The silence that followed wasn't just quiet—it stretched across the table like something alive. The clink of silverware from the kitchen suddenly sounded too loud. Even the old clock on the wall seemed to tick more deliberately.

Olivia tried to act normal. She cut a small piece of chicken and lifted it to her mouth, but I noticed she didn't actually take a bite. Her fork hovered there for a moment before she lowered it again.

Across from us, Marjorie watched.

Not openly. Not in a way anyone could call rude.

But she watched.

I had seen that look before when I was younger—when Davis and I had broken something in the garage or tracked mud through the house. The quiet assessment before the verdict.

"So," Levi said finally, his voice careful, like he was stepping across thin ice, "what brings you two to see us tonight?"

Olivia set her fork down. The tiny sound it made against the plate felt louder than it should have. She opened her mouth, clearly preparing to speak, but Marjorie beat her to it.

"They're together, Levi," she said flatly. "They're here to ask for permission."

My head snapped toward her while Olivia froze beside me.

For a second, I thought Marjorie might smile—might soften the comment like it was some kind of sharp joke—but she didn't.

Her head shook slightly, not angry so much as... tired. Like the whole situation had already confirmed something she'd suspected all along.

Levi coughed quietly into his hand and shifted in his chair.

"Is that true, Keating?"

I hesitated.

Not because I didn't know the answer, but because there were about ten different things Marjorie thought were happening right now, and I wasn't sure how to untangle them before she decided she was right.

"Well, not exactly—"

"It's not true that you're together?" Marjorie cut in sharply.

"No," I said, glancing briefly at Olivia before looking back at Marjorie. "That part's true."

"And did you not come here to tell us?"

"That's also true, but—"

"So then you must just not be here for our permission." Marjorie pushed her chair back from the table with a scrape that made Olivia flinch. "Message received."

"Marj, sit down," Levi said quickly, reaching out like he might steady the situation with sheer will. "Hear them out."

She shook her head once.

"No."

Her voice wasn't loud. If anything, it was worse than loud.

"I'd like them to leave. I'm not interested in hearing anything more, and I'm suddenly not hungry."

The air in the dining room felt heavy, like the oxygen had been pulled out of it. The smell of roasted chicken and potatoes hung in the room, suddenly nauseating.

Then Marjorie turned and walked out of the dining room.

No hesitation. No second glance. Just gone.

Her footsteps echoed on the stairs, sharp and deliberate. I'd heard that sound a thousand times growing up—Marjorie calling Davis downstairs for dinner, Davis running down them two at a time, the two of us racing each other to the front door.

Tonight the sound felt different. Each step landed like something shutting behind us. A door closing.

Another one.

And another.

Until there was nothing left to say.

A door slammed upstairs.

The sound carried through the house and settled in the room with us.

I looked back at Olivia. She hadn't moved.

Her hands rested in her lap. Her eyes were fixed on the food in front of her, but she wasn't seeing it. She looked like someone trying very hard to disappear into the chair she was sitting in.

The sight of it twisted something in my chest.

This house had once felt like home to me. Now it felt like we were intruding.

I wondered what Davis would say if he were sitting here now.

"We just wanted you to hear it from us," I said quietly,

turning back to Levi. "Not from Caroline or anyone else in town."

Levi nodded slowly. "We appreciate that, Keating."

His voice sounded older than I remembered. Tired.

His eyes drifted toward Olivia, and the expression in them softened in a way that made my stomach drop.

He understood.

Understood more than Marjorie was willing to.

"She'll come around."

I didn't know if he believed that, or if he was just trying to give Olivia something to hold onto in the middle of a moment that had clearly gone exactly the way she feared it would.

Levi pushed his chair back and stood.

"I'll get this packed up for you."

He disappeared into the kitchen, leaving the dining room strangely hollow.

The silence that followed wasn't comfortable. It wasn't even neutral. It was the kind of silence that settles over a place after something breaks.

Then Olivia lifted a hand and pressed it against her forehead. Her shoulders began to shake.

At first I thought she was just breathing unevenly. Trying to steady herself.

But then I realized she was crying.

Completely silent.

The kind of crying that tries not to exist. The kind that happens when someone doesn't want to make things worse by letting anyone hear it.

And somehow that made it worse.

Definitely a mistake.

"Well, that went well," I said once we were safely on the sidewalk outside the McCleary house.

The words came out dry, the kind of humor people use when there's nothing else left to say.

Olivia wrapped her arms around herself like she was trying to hold her body together. The porch light behind us cast a soft glow over her shoulders, but it did nothing to warm the tightness in her posture.

"I guess it could have been worse."

Her voice sounded distant, like she was replaying the dinner in her head and trying to convince herself it hadn't been as bad as it felt.

"What was that jab about whiskey?" I asked as we walked toward the car. I hadn't meant to bring it up so quickly, but the comment had clearly hit a nerve back at the table.

Olivia tucked her hair behind her ear again, the same nervous gesture she'd been doing all night.

"I got drunk the first weekend I was here," she said quietly. "Angus called Levi to come get me."

She let out a small breath that might have been a laugh.

"Not my finest moment."

I nodded, holding the door open for her to slide into the passenger seat. "Because whiskey with a twist was his favorite."

She glanced up at me, and I knew I was right.

I closed the door and walked around the front of the car, the thought settling uncomfortably in my chest.

I wanted to tell her she had nothing to be ashamed of. Grief makes people do strange things—things they'd never imagine themselves doing in any other circumstance.

Lord knows I had.

Like falling in love with Davis's wife.

The drive back to the rental was quiet.

Not the comfortable quiet Olivia and I had settled into

before, the kind where we didn't feel the need to fill every second with conversation.

This silence had weight.

I could practically hear the gears in Olivia's head turning beside me, every memory of the night probably being picked apart and replayed.

I didn't know what would comfort her right now. I didn't know if anything could. And the truth was, I didn't know if Marjorie would ever come around.

She had made it painfully clear that hating Olivia wasn't just a passing reaction—it was something she had settled into. Something she had decided to hold onto.

I couldn't imagine her wanting Olivia to be happy. Especially not with me.

When I pulled into the driveway of the rental house, Olivia didn't move right away.

She looked toward the house and chewed on her lip, like she was trying to gather the courage to say something she didn't want to say.

"I think you should stay at your place tonight."

The words landed harder than I expected. A quiet sadness washed over me, but I nodded.

"If that's what you want."

Olivia pushed the car door open. "It doesn't seem to matter what I want, Whit."

I wanted to tell her that it *did* matter what she wanted. Of course it mattered.

But saying that out loud would mean asking her to believe it too. Olivia was so wrapped up in everyone else's validation that she'd talk herself out of us before we'd even had a real chance.

I was caught between being selfish for myself and being selfish for Olivia. I wanted badly for those two things to be the same, but I knew that if she didn't fight for us of her own accord, we'd always be this way.

She'd always be one foot out the door, and I'd always try to make her stay.

I needed her to *want* to stay with me. We wouldn't work any other way.

The gnawing at the pit of my stomach told me that we might have to get worse before we got better.

44

TOO SOFT FOR ALL OF IT
OLIVIA

The kitchen at Daisy's house always smelled faintly like coffee and lemons, even late at night.

I wasn't sure which of us had started that habit—brewing a pot of coffee long after dinner and letting it sit on the warmer while we worked—but the smell had become part of the place. Part of the rhythm of evenings spent at her kitchen table with papers spread between us and Hotpie asleep somewhere underfoot.

Daisy sat across from me with her elbows on the table, chin resting in her hands, while she watched me in the quiet, patient way people do when they know someone is pretending to be busy. I had been staring at the same line on a vendor spreadsheet for several minutes without actually reading it.

"You're not looking at that," she said finally.

"I am."

"No," she replied calmly, "you're performing the act of looking at it."

I let my eyes drift across the page again, even though I couldn't have said what was written there if someone asked me.

Daisy leaned back in her chair, the wood legs scraping lightly across the kitchen floor.

"You went to dinner the other night," she said.

It wasn't a question.

"Yes."

"With Marjorie."

"Yes."

Daisy waited. She seemed to be very good at waiting. Perhaps it was the journalist in her. When I didn't add anything else, she lifted her eyebrows slightly.

"Well?"

I folded the spreadsheet in half even though there was no practical reason to do so. The crease ran straight through the middle of the page like a fault line.

"It didn't go well."

Daisy nodded once, as though that outcome had been part of the original forecast.

"Define *didn't go well*."

I rested my forearms on the table and stared down at my hands for a moment before answering.

"She asked us to leave before we finished dinner."

Daisy's eyebrows lifted again, though her expression didn't change much otherwise.

"Ah," she said.

"Ah?"

"I was hoping for yelling," she admitted. "Yelling usually means people still have energy left to argue."

"She does have energy," I said quickly. "She's just—"

I stopped. The words didn't line up in the way I wanted them to. Daisy watched me try to assemble the sentence and fail.

"Complicated?" she suggested.

"Yes."

"That's a generous word."

She stood and walked over to the counter, pouring herself a mug of the coffee that had been sitting there all evening. She took a sip without reacting to the temperature and came back to the table.

"You know what I think is interesting?" she said as she sat down again.

I had a feeling I wasn't going to enjoy the answer.

"You walked into this kitchen already assuming the entire evening was your fault."

"That's not what I said."

"You didn't have to."

Daisy possessed a remarkable ability to summarize my thought process with unnerving accuracy. Different than Eric, who could filter his words. Daisy was blunt.

I leaned back in my chair and rubbed my forehead.

"You weren't there," I said.

"No," she agreed easily. "But I know you."

The kitchen fell quiet again. Outside, somewhere down the street, a screen door slammed, and a car drove slowly past the house. Connor Bay was never particularly loud, but nights like this made the town feel even smaller.

"Whit doesn't deserve this," I said finally.

Daisy studied me over the rim of her mug.

"No," she said. "He doesn't."

The way she said it made my stomach tighten slightly.

"You think I'm hurting him."

"I think," Daisy replied carefully, "that you're trying to decide whether hurting him now would be easier than hurting him later."

I didn't like how quickly that landed.

"That's not fair."

"Fair?" Daisy let out a quiet laugh. "Liv, nothing about this situation is fair. Your husband died. Marjorie lost her son. Whit fell in love with you anyway."

She gestured lightly with the mug in her hand.

"We're well past the point where fairness is part of the equation."

I stared down at the folded spreadsheet again, tracing the edge of the paper with my thumb.

"I can't be the reason that family falls apart," I said.

Daisy's expression softened slightly, though she didn't contradict me right away.

"That family already fell apart," she said gently after a moment. "You're just standing in the space that's left."

The words settled heavily between us.

"I mean that kindly," she added. "But grief does strange things to people. It rearranges their lives in ways that make no sense to anyone else."

I looked up at her, the words sitting heavily somewhere behind my ribs.

"That doesn't make it easier."

Daisy shook her head slowly. "No," she said. "It doesn't."

The kitchen fell quiet again. The refrigerator hummed softly in the corner, and somewhere outside a car rolled slowly down the street, tires whispering over the pavement before fading into the distance.

Daisy nudged the folded spreadsheet back toward me across the table, the paper sliding over the wood with a soft rasp. I stared down at it for a moment without unfolding it. The crease I'd made earlier ran straight through the center of the page, dividing the neat columns of vendor names and supply lists into two uneven halves.

"You like him," Daisy said after a moment.

The understatement of the century.

"Yes."

She studied my face carefully, as though the answer mattered less than the way I said it.

"And he likes you."

"That has been made fairly clear."

A small smile tugged at the corner of Daisy's mouth, though it faded quickly.

"Then here's the part you're not going to enjoy hearing."

I had a feeling I already knew what was coming, but I waited anyway.

"If you keep deciding what Whit can handle," she said quietly, "you're eventually going to make the decision for him."

I frowned slightly, lifting my gaze from the table.

"What does that mean?"

Daisy leaned back in her chair again, folding her arms as she considered the question.

"It means," she said after a moment, "that protecting someone from loving you is still a way of controlling the outcome."

The words settled somewhere deep in my chest, uncomfortable in the way truths usually are when you hear them out loud for the first time.

Because if I was being honest with myself, that was exactly what I had been doing.

I pushed my chair back and stood, carrying my mug to the sink even though it was still half full. The movement gave my hands something to do. I rested them on the edge of the counter and stared out the window above it.

The harbor lights glowed faintly in the distance, scattered reflections trembling across the dark water. From Daisy's kitchen, you couldn't see much of the shoreline—just the faint outline of the docks and the slow movement of boats shifting against their moorings—but it was enough to remind you how close the ocean always was in Connor Bay.

At night, the town looked peaceful. Almost gentle.

It was easy, standing here in the quiet, to forget how loud everything felt during the day—how every conversation seemed to carry a history, how every familiar face came with expectations you weren't sure how to meet.

Behind me, Daisy pushed her chair back. I heard the soft scrape of the wood across the floor before she came to stand beside the counter, resting one shoulder lightly against the cabinet.

"You're thinking too hard again," she said.

I watched the reflection of the harbor lights ripple across the glass.

"That's kind of my thing."

"I know."

For a moment, neither of us spoke. Daisy followed my gaze out the window, her expression thoughtful in the reflection.

"For what it's worth," she said finally, "I think you two are ridiculous for each other."

I glanced sideways at her. "Ridiculous?"

"In a good way."

A small breath slipped out of me, something between a laugh and a sigh.

"I'm not sure Marjorie agrees."

Daisy shrugged one shoulder lightly. "Marjorie doesn't get to decide who makes you happy."

The words lingered in the quiet kitchen longer than either of us expected.

Maybe she was right.

Then again, maybe she wasn't.

The thought pressed uncomfortably against my ribs, settling there in a way that made it difficult to breathe too deeply. I couldn't shake the uneasy feeling that I had just taken the first step toward a decision I wasn't ready to live with.

45

NO COMMENT

WHIT

I hadn't seen Olivia much in the last week.

Technically, we were still sharing the bed most nights, but that was about the only thing that felt normal between us. Even then, she felt far away. She would slip under the covers long after I'd fallen asleep and leave before the sun came up.

Sometimes I wondered if she only allowed it because I kept the nightmares away.

Olivia had started working with Daisy and Eric at *The Bean* to plan the festival.

Since the dinner with Marjorie, Olivia's mood had been... brittle.

Not openly angry. Not even openly sad.

But brittle.

Around the rest of the town she was the picture of polite peppiness—efficient, capable, relentlessly helpful. She'd met with every single person planning to run a booth at the festival and compiled detailed to-do lists for all of them so they could stay on schedule. She'd convinced vendors to donate supplies in exchange for advertising space on flyers and in the paper.

She was even working with Angus to overhaul the town website so they could promote local businesses more effectively.

Olivia Carrington had thrown herself headfirst into saving Connor Bay. She just wasn't letting me anywhere near the parts of her that needed saving.

I was on my way to The Bean for the Coastal Living interview Eric had arranged. He'd convinced the journalist to come out to town so she could do the interview in person and get a tour before the festival.

When I walked into the coffee shop, Olivia was already seated with her.

She looked up as I approached, her expression smoothing immediately into that professional brightness she'd been wearing all week.

I smiled and slid into the booth beside her.

"Katie, this is Keating Whitaker."

Katie held out her hand. "Nice to meet you, Keating."

"I go by Whit, actually."

Katie scribbled something down on her notepad. Her blonde ponytail bobbed as she nodded vigorously.

"I'll be over here working on a few things, but Katie, let me know when you want that tour."

I squeezed her hand on the seat before she moved to the next table. That was about as much PDA as she allowed these days.

"Thanks, Olivia." Katie smiled at her. "Whit, I'm just going to record this if that's fine."

"Sure," I said, nodding. "Whatever you need."

"Why don't you tell me a little about yourself? Are you from Connor Bay?"

"Kind of," I said. "My family moved here when I was pretty young. My dad opened the clinic, and I'm taking it over now."

"So you're the town doctor," she said, writing quickly. "That's a big job."

I laughed.

"Uh, it's a busy job. But I think it's important that people have easy access to healthcare in their own town, so I work evenings and weekends sometimes to make that possible."

Katie jotted something else down.

"That's probably hard on your family."

"Oh, it's just my sister and me," I said. "My parents live down south now. And when we were younger, my dad had a partner at the clinic, so their hours were actually pretty reasonable."

She tilted her head at me. "So, no wife or kids?"

I shook my head. "No, not right now."

Katie nodded. "Can you tell me more about the town? What are some of your favorite parts?"

The interview continued for the better part of an hour.

Katie moved easily from topic to topic, asking about the clinic, the history of Connor Bay, and the upcoming festival. By the end, I was telling her about Paula's annual dance showcase, where her students insisted on performing wildly inappropriate musicals.

"Legally Blonde was a recent favorite," I said. "Something about child lawyers arguing courtroom cases was equal parts impressive and terrifying."

Katie laughed. "It sounds like your town has lots of quirky folks. I can't wait to see them at the festival."

She glanced at her watch.

"If you're not busy now, I'd love to do the tour. And I'm sure Olivia could use some time back in her day... if that's okay with you, Whit?"

I glanced at Olivia, whose jaw was locked in a tense position usually reserved for Stacy Finch. *Oh boy.*

"I'm sure Whit needs to get back to the office," Olivia said without looking at me.

I nodded. "I'm afraid she's right. I do have to get some work done. I'll leave you ladies to it."

"Actually," Olivia said quickly, standing up, "Katie, why don't I call Eric and have him show you around? I have to get back home."

"Oh, sure," Katie said easily. "That's fine with me."

Olivia had already pressed her phone to her ear. Katie gathered her things and smiled at me again.

"Maybe we could get coffee when I'm back, Whit? I'd love to chat some more."

Shoving my hands in my pockets, I gave her a polite smile. "Thank you for the invitation, but I'm afraid my girlfriend wouldn't appreciate that."

Katie blinked, surprised but not embarrassed. "Oh, I'm sorry. I thought when I asked...Sorry, I thought you were single."

I waved it off. "Not a problem."

At that exact moment Sidney walked by carrying a tray of mugs.

"Keating Whitaker," she said, pausing dramatically. "You have a girlfriend?"

I looked anywhere except Olivia, who I was sure was plotting my demise—potentially *our* demise—as I kept talking.

"It's new," I said. "We're just seeing how things go."

Sidney grinned and headed back toward the counter, almost certainly already composing a message to at least three different group chats. Hopefully Daisy would run interference.

Right on cue, Eric walked in through the front door. I assumed he'd been across the street at Paula's working on the festival banners—a task he'd aggressively claimed from Daisy after insisting he was excellent with Puffy Paint.

"Hey, Katie!" Eric said, walking over. "Good interview?"

His face fell ever so slightly when he looked at Olivia.

"Really good! Thanks so much, Whit." She held out her hand again, and I shook it. "Shall we?"

"Uh... yeah," Eric said, blinking once. "Let's do it."

He glanced between Olivia and me before opening the door for Katie.

"See you at home, Olivia."

I actually did have an appointment waiting for me, so the best I could manage was, "We'll talk later?"

She nodded, but didn't look at me.

Whatever the conversation would be, I knew there was a possibility it wouldn't end well.

46

UNLESS YOU'RE CHOOSING ME...

WHIT

I tried my best not to think about Olivia during the rest of my shift at the clinic, but she overwhelmed my thoughts anyway. Every quiet moment between patients pulled me back to her—the way she hadn't looked at me in the café, the tight line of her jaw, the careful distance she'd been keeping all week.

I didn't want to lose her, but we couldn't keep standing still like this either.

I loved her, but I needed us to be on the same page.

I wasn't afraid of loving Olivia. I was afraid of loving someone who kept one foot out the door.

Because if she decided to leave—if she convinced herself that leaving was the right thing to do—I wasn't sure there was anything in the world strong enough to make her stay.

If she wanted to go back to keeping things low-key, if she needed time, if she needed space—fine. I could live with that.

But this? This silence between us?

This not talking?

It wasn't working. It wasn't healthy.

And it sure as hell wasn't us.

When I stopped by the lakehouse, Olivia was in the kitchen leaning against the counter on the other side of the island. Her elbow rested on the marble, her hand pressed against her forehead like she was holding something inside her head together by sheer force.

The late afternoon light filtered through the windows behind her, catching in the loose strands of her hair.

I wasn't sure if she was angry, sad, scared. Maybe she was all three.

But even like this—exhausted, worn down, somewhere far away in her own mind—she was still the most beautiful thing in the room.

In any room I'd ever been in.

It was what I'd thought the first time I saw her. It was still true now.

Even while I could feel her slipping away from me.

With each slow tick of the second hand on my wristwatch, something in the room felt like it was fading. Like we were both standing on opposite sides of a crack that was widening by the second.

She hadn't said anything, but she didn't have to. I knew her that well.

I slid my hands into the pockets of my slacks, forcing my shoulders to relax. Maybe if I made my body look casual, I wouldn't feel so damn defensive. Maybe if I stood still enough, the moment would stop moving forward.

"Whit—"

The way she said my name told me everything I needed to know. I closed my eyes for half a second.

"Don't, Olivia," I said quietly. "Don't do this to us." I stayed where I was, rooted to the floor.

I didn't want to move an inch because I didn't want it to be real. I didn't want to move backward.

Her hands went to her hair, clutching her scalp, like they were the only things keeping her together.

That wasn't right. I was keeping her together. I was keeping her whole, and she was doing the same for me.

"There can't be an us, Whit." Her voice was so tragically broken, it almost didn't sound like her.

Something inside my chest twisted painfully.

How could she already be broken when she hadn't even tried to fight for it? For us?

"Yes, there can, Liv," I said, trying to keep my voice steady. "They know now. We can be together."

The sigh she let out sounded worn down, like it had been living inside her lungs for days.

"What are you so afraid of?"

God, I wished she'd look at me.

I wished she could see what I saw when I looked at her—how brave she was, how strong we could be together if she'd just let herself believe it.

"What we're doing to this town," she said quietly. "It's not fair. It's not fair to Davis, and it's not fair to us."

A brief flicker of anger flared inside of me. "Because you get to decide what's fair to me?"

Finally, she made eye contact with me. Except there was nothing there. A vacant expression. A mask over whatever emotions were buried deep inside her.

"I didn't mean it like that. It's not fair of me to ask you to keep us a secret. You shouldn't have to hide pieces of your life in shadows."

"You think I'm hiding you?" I asked quietly. "We might be a secret from this town, Olivia, but I'm keeping you like an oath. I have given you so many pieces of myself that I don't know who I am anymore."

Her gaze dropped back down to the counter. Like looking at me was too much.

"That's even more of a reason for us to end this."

I shook my head slowly. She couldn't even say it to my face. Like if she avoided my eyes long enough, it would make the words easier to believe.

"Stop," I said quietly. "You don't mean this. You're angry, or scared, or overwhelmed, but you don't mean what you're saying."

She couldn't possibly.

Her head fell into her hands again. "I'm so tired of people telling me I don't know what I'm doing."

"Can't you see that we fit Olivia? I fit in your life here and in New York. We work together. We're better together."

She shook her head but didn't say anything.

"I'm not *him*, Olivia."

That made her look up.

This time, there was something in her eyes. A flash of something raw. I'd hit a nerve.

"I know that, Whit," she snapped. "God, don't you think I know that? Don't you think I can see how different you two are?"

The venom in her voice hung in the air between us. Daring me to push her further.

So I did.

"Then stop making decisions about us based on how you feel about *him*."

Her lips pressed together so tightly they nearly disappeared. Her eyes filled, the glassy shine of unshed tears catching in the light.

"I'm trying, Whit. Can't you see I'm *trying*?"

No, I couldn't.

Because from where I was standing, she'd given up.

47

JUST NOT HOME
OLIVIA

My face felt hot. Even though I could tell Whit was angry—red splotches coated the tops of his cheekbones—his voice stayed level.

That somehow made it worse.

If he had shouted, if he had slammed something or stormed out, it might have felt easier to survive.

But I couldn't imagine that Whit had ever been the kind of man who destroyed things when he was angry. He held himself together even when the ground under him was breaking apart.

"Do you even miss him, Olivia?"

He sounded broken, and I caused it.

My hands gripped the counter for support. I didn't know how long I would last if I didn't have something to hold me upright.

"Of course I miss him," I said quickly. "He was my husband. Of course I do."

The words left my mouth, but that wasn't what he was asking. I knew he was asking me the same thing I'd been asking myself for three months.

"No. I mean, do you miss *him*? Is that why you came here? Because you missed him so much, you were desperate to hold on to any part of him you could?"

Whit didn't raise his voice. Not once. But every word felt like a scalpel.

"Or are you here because you feel guilty? Did you come because there weren't enough parts to hold onto in New York? Or did you come here because you only wanted to know your husband, really know him, after he was gone?"

Even though I was breaking him, he was still careful not to break me.

"That's not fair," I whispered.

He shook his head and looked away before he continued. "At night, when you can't sleep, Olivia, do you wish he were there or that things hadn't changed? Do you miss Davis, or do you miss you?"

The question hung between us. Heavy.

"I—"

Whit looked back at me then. His deep green gaze moved across my face slowly, like he was trying to read every thought I'd never said out loud.

"Because it's okay," he said. "It's okay to miss someone you loved, but don't pretend we can't be together because you miss your husband. Don't pretend we don't have something good and solid here because you're trying to be a good person."

His voice cracked just slightly this time, and my stomach twisted.

"I miss Davis more than I could possibly describe to you, but I am not a good person, Olivia. I wasn't when he was alive, and I'm not now. I'm not good enough to fight this. I'm not strong enough to let you go again."

He'd cut too deep, exposed too much. "Well, do you just want to be with me because I remind you of your best friend?"

The moment the words left my mouth, I wished I could take them back.

Whit blinked at me. For a second, he looked like he genuinely couldn't believe I'd said it. Then he let out a short, hard laugh.

"I saw you first, Olivia. That night in the bar with Davis. I was there. I was the friend he ditched for you."

The memory flashed in my mind—Ethyl's, the crowded bar, the neon lights, Davis smiling at me across the counter.

"I saw you sitting there at the bartop, and I thought..." He shook his head. "It doesn't matter what I thought, but don't you dare try to make this about him. What's happening between us belongs to you and me."

Between the dinner at Marjorie's and now, I'd listened to the rest of his voicemails. I knew he'd seen me at Ethyl's. I knew that Davis had confided in Whit about some of our "lively discussions."

I knew he'd wanted me long before I knew he existed, but it didn't matter.

It *couldn't* matter.

"I know, Whit," I said quietly.

His expression shifted.

"I know about that night." My voice felt rough in my throat. "I know about anything you told him in the voicemails you left. I heard them all." I admitted.

I hadn't decided to tell him until it was already happening. It was out now.

He visibly stiffened. "What?" I swallowed. "What did you say?"

My instinct was to shrink back. To apologize. But I forced myself to stand on my own.

If I was going to do this—if I was going to end this—I had to own every word. I had to because I wasn't doing this to this town.

They'd lost too much, and it was my fault. This town had me, and me alone, to blame for Davis's death. The fact I'd even thought for one moment that I wished Whit had approached me in the bar was already something I'd regret for the rest of my life—as if my time with Davis meant nothing. I was ashamed of thinking it for even a second.

"I said I heard the voicemails, Whit. All of them."

He took a step back from me, not that we were anywhere near each other.

"If that's true, and you're still doing this to us, then this conversation was over before it started."

This conversation was over the moment he told Davis he could talk to me at the bar. Regardless of how we felt about each other, this was what it was, him and I. We'd never get a do-over.

There was no fresh start just because Davis was gone.

I drew in a slow breath.

A clean break was the best thing I could give Whit.

The kindest thing.

"We're done, Whit," I said quietly. "I'm done."

His jaw flexed as he angled his head away from me toward the lake outside. You could see it from the windows. The water outside was calm, reflecting the fading evening light.

Whit nodded slowly with raised brows.

"Okay."

Keating Whitaker didn't look back as he walked out the back door, and I didn't stop him.

48

WHAT ABOUT WENDY?

OLIVIA

Before

Davis took a right onto East 76th Street. We had four more blocks to go.

I wasn't sure why he insisted on driving when taking a cab would have been much easier. Parking would be just as expensive as, if not more than, the round-trip fare.

I didn't want to argue with him.

I was so tired of arguing with him.

"We don't argue, Liv," he'd always say. "We have lively discussions."

But we'd been having a lot of lively discussions lately, and I didn't know why. I hadn't been working any more than usual. We went out of town together last weekend to see a baseball game in Boston.

I was trying to get us back to where we'd been a few months ago, but it seemed like he wanted so many things that I couldn't give him.

He wanted the Olivia he met at Ethyl's, and I didn't know how to tell him that the Olivia from back then wasn't an everyday occurrence.

The Davis in the bar—the one with the easy smile and the way he leaned against the counter like the whole world was just beginning—that version of him had pulled that version of me out.

But eventually we had to return to the real world.

The real world where I had a job and responsibilities and clients who expected me to answer emails at midnight. I couldn't spend every weekend partying in dive bars like we were still strangers flirting over cheap whiskey.

"My mom called earlier this week," he said, stopping at a red light.

The glow of the traffic signal washed over his face, painting it red. It made his expression look more serious than usual—but he'd already been in a bad mood all evening.

"How is she?" I asked, half distracted as I replied to a text from Eric asking where we were.

I turned on my location tracker for him.

God forbid he spend any time alone with his partner at a work event. Maybe that was why he wanted me to make Davis come, so Leo had someone other than Eric to complain to about our firm. I rolled my eyes at the thought.

"I think we need to spend some time in Connor Bay soon," he said. "The diner could use some help."

The words left his mouth so nonchalantly I wasn't sure he'd actually said them—as if they weren't going to change everything about our lives.

I put my phone in my jacket pocket. "What does that mean?"

He glanced at me from his periphery. "It means what I just said."

My jaw tightened. I hated when he did that—when he answered questions like they were stupid.

"But how long is 'some time' in Connor Bay?" I asked, turning toward him fully now. "A weekend? What is soon? Tomorrow? Next week? Next month?"

My eyebrows were practically in my hairline.

He started tapping his fingers against the steering wheel, and I could feel the irritation radiating off him.

Well, I was annoyed, too. Davis paused his tapping to drag a hand through his already tousled blonde hair.

"I don't know, Liv. Maybe a while."

I held my tongue before I asked what *a while* meant. We both knew how that would go.

"Well, I just don't know if that's feasible for me." I tucked my hair behind my ear and turned my body towards the windshield instead of him.

Davis turned his head to look at me.

This was the longest fucking red light of my life.

"What do you mean it's not 'feasible' for you? You're my wife. You have to come with me."

My brows dipped on my forehead, and my head whipped toward him.

"I can't just quit my job and move to Connor Bay, Davis. That's ridiculous."

"Ridiculous?" he repeated, his voice rising now. "My parents need help, Olivia. What am I supposed to tell them— no?"

He'd started talking with his hands. We'd been elevated from annoyed to angry.

I shook my head in disbelief. "You can go help them, Davis, but I'm not quitting my job. Why should I have to?"

"Why did *I* have to move here?"

"Because I wasn't fucking moving to a small town when my life is here."

"Yeah, your life with your one friend," he scoffed, and a sharp pain cut through my stomach.

A low blow.

"I left my family for you, Olivia! I married *you*, not your fucking job. Now, what? It's like you're just tolerating my existence."

My breath caught.

"I have to schedule an appointment to get you to pay attention to me. I wake up; you've already left for work. I wait for you outside your office after work; you're working late. You finally come home, and I have dinner for you; you already ate at the office. What the fuck am I supposed to do with that?"

My breath hitched. We'd had renditions of this argument before, but nothing as blunt or aggressive as this one.

"You asked to marry me. I didn't force you into that. You didn't ask me about work or tell me about how close you were to your family. You didn't tell me moving to New York wasn't right for you, Davis!"

Great, now I was yelling.

"And if I had, would you have said no? Is that what you're saying? If I didn't move here, we wouldn't be together?"

I looked out the window instead of answering him.

"Glad to know I was just *convenient* to you."

My jaw ticked again. I didn't like this Davis. I didn't like the version of him that made me feel like our unhappiness was my cross to bear alone.

"I'm not doing this with you tonight. We'll talk about this tomorrow." I said finally.

"Fine."

The light turned green, and Davis accelerated. We never made it to the other side of the intersection.

We never made it to tomorrow.

I BLINKED MY EYES OPEN. Bright lights flooded my vision.

To my left, a rhythmic beeping of a machine made my head throb. Another machine sounded like it was exhaling.

Something was on my face. I lifted my hand weakly. Tubes that led to my nose.

"Olivia!"

I glanced at where the sound came from. I could make out Eric's features. I knew I was in the hospital. There was an accident. The beeping grew faster, louder.

"Davis." I breathed. "Is Davis okay?"

Eric's face was still fuzzy in my vision, but I could see him shaking his head. My stomach dropped.

I was going to be sick. My skin felt cold and slick. Hands gripped mine, and I felt like I was choking.

Somewhere, someone was screaming. Loud, broken sobs, but I couldn't make them out because my throat was closing up. I couldn't get air in my lungs.

"Shh, Olivia. Olivia, it's going to be okay. Please, calm down."

His hands touched my face, my cheek pressed against his shirt, and then his arms cradled my head, but I still couldn't breathe.

Two people rushed in.

"We're going to sedate her," one of them told Eric.

Good, I thought. It would give whoever was screaming some relief. Maybe then they could help me breathe.

When I finally got air into my lungs, the screaming stopped, and my body felt heavy.

And somewhere in the quiet that followed, I realized the truth.

It was me.

I had been screaming.

49

GOOD FAITH TREATIES
OLIVIA

When you'd finally lost everything, it really put things in perspective.

Eric stopped trying to get me to talk about what happened, and I stopped sleeping through the night again.

I had new nightmares and monsters under my bed.

Sometimes I woke up convinced someone was in the room. Sometimes I woke up gasping, my chest tight like I had forgotten how to breathe. Sometimes I didn't sleep at all.

It wasn't fair. Nothing in the past year had been.

I hadn't been fair to Davis. His death hadn't been fair to anyone. And then when Whit had put me on that impossible pedestal—when he looked at me like I was something worth protecting—I'd been terrible to him too.

I told myself I had stopped feeling.

But that wasn't true.

Every thought of Keating Whitaker sent pain shooting through every nerve ending in my body, sharp and immediate like touching something that burned.

And I was angry. I was so angry that I couldn't just stop caring about Marjorie McCleary.

I hated that I ruined something that could have been a masterpiece because I wanted to save face.

I hated that I had boiled myself down to being Davis's wife, like that was the only role I was allowed to occupy in the world. Like I was nothing without him.

I had been alive before him. And even though I never expected there to be an after him, my heart was still beating. The days were still arriving, one after the other, whether I wanted them to or not.

Two days before the festival, the anger finally bubbled over.

It was probably because I had run out of things to work on.

Daisy, Eric, and I had spent weeks planning every detail of the festival. Booths were built. Vendors were organized. Flyers were printed. Every task had been checked off, every contingency planned.

For the first time in weeks, there was nothing left to fix.

And with my hands idle, the rage had somewhere to go.

I dragged myself from my bed early that morning, and Hotpie shot up with a bark as I threw on clothes that probably didn't match and drove to the diner.

It was empty when I arrived because *of course* it was.

"Olivia, you look like you've seen better days." Marjorie regarded me from behind the counter. "Finally decided to show up to work. How generous."

Red flooded my vision. The words spilled out before I could stop them.

"Okay, you know what, Marjorie? I'm *sorry* Davis is dead."

Her head snapped up. Some part of me couldn't believe I'd said that out loud.

"And I'm sorry we got married without telling you," I continued, my voice shaking despite my efforts to steady it.

"But I am not sorry we got married. I am not sorry I loved your son with all my goddamn heart."

Her face turned hard, and she gripped the counter. "This is *my* diner, Olivia, and you don't get to come in here and talk to me like this."

"Oh, I know this is *your* diner, just like I know this is *your* town, and Davis was *your* son." My throat tightened. "I came to Connor Bay because I thought that's what he would have wanted."

The anger that had fueled me that morning began to crack, something more fragile pushing through.

"And I've been trying to get you to... I don't know...forgive me? Accept me? I don't know what I wanted from you. Maybe just convince you not to hate me. But everything I've done has just made it worse."

I bit back angry tears.

I would not cry in front of Marjorie McCleary. She didn't get to see that.

"Just tell me," I said finally, my voice cracking despite my efforts. "Tell me what I can do to make you not hate me. Because I am tired, Marjorie. I am so tired of trying to prove myself to you. I ended things with Whit if that's what you want. You won't see us together."

My body shook as the words poured out of me. The things that I'd bottled up from the beginning—since setting foot in this town.

Her mouth pressed into a thin line as she watched me carefully.

It seemed like an eternity before she said, "I don't hate you."

The shaking stopped, and I was frozen. My breath caught in my throat until I could finally get something out.

"What?"

She looked away and then back. "I don't hate you, Olivia. I don't particularly like you, but I don't hate you."

She paused. When she spoke again, her eyes had gone glossy.

"I wanted to hate you because it would get rid of how much guilt I feel about wishing it was you who died in that accident."

I felt my skin pale. The adrenaline that raced through me this morning was waning. I didn't feel any anger toward her about that admission.

Sometimes, I wished I had died then, too.

"You being here is a constant reminder that he's not," she continued, her voice cracking. "I don't care that you're with Keating. Davis would want the two of you to be happy. I know that. I just...I want my son back, and I can't have that."

All this time, the quiet war we'd been waging with each other had never been about me. I felt that throbbing in my chest again. It was the same one I used to get when I thought of Davis. My heart was breaking all over again.

Grief over what could have been.

Marjorie could have liked me once. Another casualty of the accident. A relationship that never had a chance.

I waited for her to calm herself down. I didn't think that she wanted me to console her, even if my hand twitched to reach out to her.

She dragged a hand under her eye. "Be with Whit, Olivia. If you make each other happy, be together. You never needed my permission. I'm sorry you thought I hated you, and I appreciate your help with the diner, but seeing you is hard for me." Marjorie took a shaky breath. "It's really hard."

I knew what she meant. It was hard for me to look at her and Levi when all I saw was him.

I nodded numbly in understanding.

It was a floating feeling like I was watching this play out from somewhere else.

This had never been about me. I could have been *anyone*—Stacy Finch, Daisy Whitaker, another girl from New York—and Marjorie would have treated me all the same.

She took another shaking breath. "I don't know when it will get easier, but I am sorry for treating you the way I have been. Davis would be horrified. I just need some time."

Time.

I wanted to laugh. I wanted to scream.

Didn't she see that no one had time? People could be there one minute and be gone the next.

If I had the energy, I would have tried to explain this to her, but I was so tired. I was so angry and tired and broken that I didn't have anything left to give her.

I couldn't leave this town. I couldn't leave *him*. I wouldn't.

Time wasn't a resolution, but it was something. There wasn't a single action item, but it was enough. It was enough for me.

"Thank you for being honest with me," I said finally. "And I really am sorry, Marjorie. For everything."

50

HEARTBREAK IN REMISSION
OLIVIA

People could be there one minute and be gone the next.

I fucked up.

I fucked up so badly.

I should have never said those things to Whit. I should have told him the truth—that I was scared. I should have told him that Marjorie affected me more than I could explain. That every look she gave me made me feel like I didn't deserve to be here.

But none of that mattered because I didn't say any of those things. I was a coward.

Maybe I was afraid of losing him the way I lost Davis. Maybe I was afraid of loving someone enough that losing them would destroy me again.

Or maybe I was just afraid to admit that I was afraid.

"Hey, where'd you go?"

Eric's voice rang from the living room. My back hit the front door, and I slid down it.

"Liv?"

The sobs started then. Broken, endless sobs that had become part of my norm.

How could I have done that to him when I knew—we both knew—how precious time was? How little promised time anyone had?

Whit was here. He was real and breathing. And I had let my fear, my guilt, and every insecurity I had about Davis rule something sacred between us.

"What happened?"

Eric knelt in front of me as he had in the bathroom that morning only a few weeks ago. Here I was again, crying over Keating Whitaker, but for an entirely different reason.

It took a while, but I managed to get everything out. Eric sat beside me, holding my hand and nodding.

When I was done, he smiled at me sadly. "Everyone gets scared, Liv. It's okay. Whit will forgive you."

That was the worst part.

I *knew* Whit would forgive me. Whit was good in a way that made forgiveness seem effortless. He would listen, he would understand, and he would take me back without asking for anything in return.

But what could I possibly promise him after that?

What guarantee could I give him that I wouldn't panic again?

That I wouldn't bolt the next time things got complicated?

I asked Eric as much.

"You don't need to prove to him that you won't panic again," he said thoughtfully. "But I do think you need to talk to someone, Olivia."

He squeezed my hand lightly.

"You need to prove to him that your first instinct isn't always going to be to run. He needs to know you're going to stay."

The word settled somewhere deep in my chest.

Stay.

I wiped beneath my eyes and nodded slowly.

"I think I can do that."

Eric smiled.

"I know you can do that, Livie. You're the strongest person I know."

I KNEW what Whit wanted from me because he was a good person. Eric wasn't exactly right when he said that Whit wanted reassurance that I wouldn't book a one-way ticket to New York if we got back together. What Whit wanted more than anything, was something that he'd only done recently. He wanted me to pick myself over everyone else.

For him that meant turning down Little League, impromptu trips to New York, and *me.*

What I had done that day in the kitchen was pick everyone else over us. I picked Marjorie, Davis, the town....I had made it easy to discount our feelings for each other because I felt...I wasn't sure.

I didn't understand why I had this uncontrollable desire to put everyone's needs in front of my own. *Why couldn't I just be happy?*

Perhaps that was a question I would need to work out an answer to over time. A more concrete question to answer now was *could I be happy* here?

A tug jolted in my stomach. I hadn't even wanted to discuss coming here with Davis, so how could I just offer that to Whit? What made Whit different than my husband? Hadn't I loved him?

Glad to know I was just convenient to you.

Davis had said that in the car, and it didn't feel right at the time. I loved my husband so much that it felt like I couldn't breathe sometimes, and I didn't need to ask myself why. I knew in my bones that our time together was worth everything that happened after. But there was something in there– in what he said that wasn't entirely wrong either.

Glad to know I was just convenient *to you.*

That was how Whit was different from Davis for me. I loved Davis, but I was willing to go on without him. If he had wanted to help his parents, he would have gone and I would have stayed in New York. I would have missed him, but not enough to resign myself to Connor Bay...not enough to leave everything behind. But now, I wasn't willing to leave here without Whit and if keeping him meant I had to stay, I would.

Davis and I were a great right place, right time love story, but Whit and I were one for the ages.

I wanted to mold my life to fit Whit's and I knew he'd do the same for me. I hadn't been flexible with Davis– hadn't wanted to be– and I wanted him to give up more than I was willing to, but that wasn't what forever love was about.

Forever love was about making room for each other. It was work functions and dinners at home. It was early mornings and late nights. More than anything, it was an overwhelming and unmistakable feeling of being home.

I had been wrong before. Whit wasn't timeless, he was omnipresent. He was *home.*

I thought of the boxes in my apartment the day Davis moved in. *You were going to make space for me.* I made space for Davis in my closet and in ways that didn't matter, but I wanted to make so much space for Whit that he could take the whole fucking house if he wanted.

I'd stay in Connor Bay for Whit because he picked me even when I didn't pick myself. I'd stay because I was finally home.

51

IT'S BRIGHTER NOW

WHIT

Daisy shoved me into my seat at the entrance to the festival, right beneath the shade of an overgrown tree that had probably been there longer than half the town.

She put me in charge of the ticket booth.

"There," Daisy said, dropping a metal cash box onto the table in front of me. "You just sit here with this cash box and these tickets."

She shoved a roll of red admit tickets into my hand.

"It's one ticket per person. Eight dollars for adults, five for kids. Got it, Whit?"

I glared at her. I supposed I should have been grateful for the easy job, but if I was being honest, I would have rather been sulking at home.

"Great. Jeremiah will relieve you in two hours."

I didn't even have it in me to tell her that no one should trust Jeremiah with a cash box.

By the time Daisy disappeared into the crowd, the festival had already started filling in around me. Music drifted through the air from the stage at the center of the square, the smell of fried food and kettle corn floating on the breeze.

It should have been a good day.

Connor Bay looked exactly the way it always did during the festival—colorful booths, kids running around with painted faces, locals catching up with each other like they hadn't seen each other in years instead of days or hours.

But none of it felt real.

I hadn't seen Olivia since we'd split up...since *she* split us up. I wanted to be angry with her, but couldn't even bring myself to feel *that*.

Every time I tried to work myself into anger, something else got in the way.

Understanding.

She gave me so many warning signs. Between wanting to keep us a secret and shutting down after the dinner with Marjorie and Levi, maybe we were doomed from the start.

I couldn't believe she'd heard the voicemails.

How long had she known how I felt? How long had she had pieces of me I didn't even know I'd given her?

I wasn't mad about that either. I was glad that she knew how I felt about her. How I'd always felt about her.

Maybe I had been living in a delusion of what we could be.

The worst part about this whole thing was that if she changed her mind, I'd take her back in a second.

How little self-respect did I have that I'd let her do this to us and then get over it with no questions asked?

I rubbed a hand over my face and tried to shake off the thoughts of her.

I knew the only reason I'd need very little convincing was because I understood where she was coming from.

I just wished she could see herself how I did. I wish she'd stop caring about what the people in this town thought of her.

Connor Bay was small, and Olivia and I could be larger than life if she just let us.

"One, please."

Her voice froze me in place. I should have been used to that. She'd always had a way of disarming me.

"Can we talk?"

"I'm working, Olivia. I don't think now is a good time." I tore one red admit ticket off the roll. "$8."

"Whit, please."

I looked at her, and it almost killed me. I stared at her.

She looked the same as when I saw her in the grocery store the first time in Connor Bay. The dark circles under her eyes told me she hadn't been sleeping. Her pert, slightly upturned nose was red. Same as the rims of her eyes.

It was a devastating scene. I was already crumbling, but I knew I had to be strong.

I knew that this would happen over and over again if she didn't work through this on her own. No matter how much I wanted to tuck her into me and keep her safe from the world, I could never protect her from herself.

"Please." She tried again. It was just a whisper.

"You have until the next person comes."

"I'm starting therapy." She blurted, and my mouth fell open.

I did not see that coming.

"I know I need to work on some things. And I talked to Angus about a job in town. He's going to look at the revenue at the end of the month and see if there's room in the budget. I want to stay, Whit. I want to stay here with you in Connor Bay...if you'll have me."

Warmth spread over my body because this was what I wanted. She was saying all the right things. She was finally prioritizing herself. And she wanted to stay. She wanted to stay *here* with *me*.

Focus, Whit.

"Why now, Olivia?"

She tucked her hair behind her ears. "I talked to Marjorie. I realized that...well, not everything is about me. Not everything is my fault, but I take on the blame for a lot of things. Marjorie and I probably won't ever be what we could have been if Davis were still alive, but I understand her more now. But most importantly, I realized that you were right. I shouldn't let the accident taint how I feel about you. I can't live in that moment forever. I won't."

I looked at her again, roving my gaze over her face: her eyes turned glassier as the seconds ticked on, her slightly parted lips, her arms limp at her sides. I was trying to memorize everything about her at that moment because I hoped it was the last time I'd ever see her like this—suspended in a moment in time when she wasn't sure about me.

It was a strange thing to want to memorize, but I knew there would be times when we'd draw lines in the sand and argue over things like work and, *god*, maybe even kids one day. I knew that as long as she didn't look like she did right now, that we'd make it out okay.

I swallowed, but Olivia continued before I had a chance to say anything.

"And don't think I'm not willing to grovel. Whatever you want. I'll watch all the seasons of *Law & Order* or read those god-awful true-crime paperbacks from the 60s. I'll work for it, Whit. I swear to God I'll spend the rest of my life making this up to you."

Her breathing quickened like she'd run out of air.

"Please say something, Whit."

"You're taking cooking classes."

Her laugh broke into a sob. "Whatever you want."

"And obedience classes for Hotpie."

"Okay." She nodded, wiping under her eyes with the backs of her hands.

"And Eric can't live with us," I said sternly.

"Next door will be fine." She laughed, walking around the table to get to me.

"And I'm not keeping us a secret." I stood from the chair.

"I'll pull out my landline and call Caroline Stenson myself right now. The town will know immediately."

She paused in front of me, pointing her thumb over her shoulder toward Caroline's fortune-telling booth.

I pulled her against me and brought my hand against her neck. Her pulse was steady, strong. Just like her.

"Oh, I think they'll know sooner than that."

"Wait." I paused a fraction from her lips. "There's something else," she said, pushing against my chest with her palms. I raised my brows expectantly.

She took my face in her hands. "I love you, Keating Whitaker. You make me feel bigger than the stars."

A slow smile spread across my face. I pressed my mouth against hers and kissed her for all the times in the last week that I couldn't and all the times before that.

52

MADE IT TO SEPTEMBER

OLIVIA

Whit's laughter echoed off the walls of our empty bedroom.

We just closed on a new house—a place on Elm near Donald and an easy walk to the clinic. We didn't even have a bed yet, but somehow, I ended up underneath him.

We were home.

He peppered kisses all over my face. I laughed, trying to push him off.

"Whit, stop. I need to go to work."

He rolled his eyes, but his lips were turned up at the corners.

"Fine, but at 5, you're mine again, and I don't care what Angus says."

He tapped my nose with his index finger and rolled off me.

Things had been good...great even, since the festival. Angus created a position for me here as Director of Tourism. It was a quarter of what I made at the firm in New York, but it didn't matter. I got to be here with Whit. Eric convinced Clark to let him be permanently remote from Connor Bay and negotiated to bring me on as an occasional consultant.

The diner was doing well, and Whit was turning his parents' house into a second rental. We'd been staying there while we waited to hear back about our offer on this place. After the feature in *Coastal Living,* it seemed like everyone wanted to visit Connor Bay. Rental properties were the best investment we could make, and we didn't need all that space. Daisy was off in some European country, but she had gotten into sending postcards even though they always arrived after she'd left the place they were sent from.

My heart felt full when I looked at Whit. Not just now but every time.

"Keep looking at me like that, Liv, and you're never getting out of here."

I laughed. I did that a lot with him. He kissed me. We did that a lot, too.

He got up and tossed my clothes to me.

"Think Nando will give us that bedframe you bought for the apartment?" I raised a brow at him. "You're right." Whit pulled his shirt on and buttoned his jeans. "I've got some appointments, but let's meet at the diner for dinner."

I nodded before pulling my dress over my head.

"Sounds good."

Whit came over and tipped my chin toward his face, pressing his lips against mine.

"See you at the diner. Love you," I said when he pulled away.

He hummed in agreement and gave me another kiss before leaving.

"Love you, too," he shouted as he bounded down the stairs, and I giggled.

Only Keating Whitaker had the power to make me *giggle.*

Marjorie and I still weren't best friends, but we were cordial. That was enough for me. We hadn't made much progress since she asked for time, but I also hadn't pushed it. Maybe we'd never have a good relationship, or maybe we would when she got curious about her son's life in New York. Maybe she'd want to talk to someone who knew that part of him someday. But even if she never did, I no longer felt frozen in time.

I was moving on, and Marjorie's anger had nothing to do with me anymore. Maybe it never had anything to do with me. Marjorie was angry at the world and the cards she'd been dealt. Some days were better than others. Grief was like that. It demanded to be felt, no matter how long ago it started. Just because you learn to live with it doesn't mean that what happened before wasn't real.

I loved Davis, and I loved how much he loved me. But I *love* Whit and how much we love each other.

ACKNOWLEDGEMENTS

I'm used to writing Acknowledgements in scientific papers, not so much at the end of my books, but I'm sure the skills are largely transferrable...right?

To my husband, thank you for loving me even when I don't love myself.

To my editor, Lauren, the first person who reads every word I write, thank you for existing on my best days, my worst days, and all the ones in between. How lucky the world is to have you in it.

To my lovely beta and arc readers, thank you for your unconditional support and excitement about this book.

I'd also like to thank my funders: cold brew and Coca-Cola, only consumed through aesthetically pleasing glass straws (you know the ones). Without you two, I surely would not have been able to get through long days of writing.

Finally, I'd like to thank *you*, dear reader. Thank you for wanting to read about how two beautifully damaged characters find their way home. Whether it was the promise of Taylor Swift references, a small-town romance, or a love of my books that brought you here, thank you for reading. I couldn't do it without you.

BEHIND THE BOOK

Taylor Swift's *Lover* ends with an outro that perfectly depicts something that floats through my mind sometimes, often, always.

> I wanna be defined by the things that I love
>> Not the things I hate
>> Not the things I'm afraid of (I'm afraid of)
>> Or the things that haunt me in the middle of the
> night
>> I, I just think that
>> You are what you love

She then went on to release an album with a collection of songs inspired by a collection of restless nights. Even now, I think *Lover* and *evermore* are her two saddest albums.

Maybe, dear reader, you won't agree with that, but if you do, then you might also think it's because nothing is scarier than thoughts of what could have been and the things you love being taken away.

Eastern Standard is my third book, but it's the one that I spent the most time on. Not in terms of how long it took me to write it but in how often it swarmed my thoughts. I saw Whit and Olivia in my mundane routines and my comfort shows. I saw them even when I tried not to.

Writing books is always an emotional experience for me. Sometimes I don't know what characters will do until they're doing it or how angry they are at each other until they've said something that feels like a swift punch to the gut (no pun intended).

I *never* know how often my own insecurities and personality quirks will end up on the pages. In *Eastern Standard,* it was a lot: Olivia's overthinking, Whit's broody thoughts but outward pathological people-pleasing tendencies, Eric's blunt dialogue, and Daisy's desire to wrap things up in a nice, neat bow even if you have to forcefully shove everything into the box for it all to fit.

After long talks with my editor and husband, I think you might occasionally feel that some things Whit and Olivia do are out of character for them, but that's the point. In real life, people do things for reasons we don't understand or they can't explain—like marrying a guy you met at a bar, for instance. You don't have to do things just because they fit the nice, neat boxes of what you think people want from you. There is no standard version of yourself or anyone else.

That's *Eastern Standard.*

ABOUT THE AUTHOR

Sierra Spencer is a romance author who writes with sparkly gel pens as much as she does a sharp-edged quill. Combining all the feet-kicking and giggling of a happily ever after with the dichotomy of flawed and complex characters, Sierra writes stories that demand to be felt. When Sierra isn't composing heartfelt and cozy love stories, she writes about developmental science as an Assistant Professor. She lives in Pennsylvania with her friend-to-enemy-to-lover spouse and their dog. She enjoys cooking, game nights, and a good data visualization.

Get updates on sierraspencer.com or scan the QR code below to subscribe to the Sierra Spencer Newsletter!

ALSO BY SIERRA SPENCER

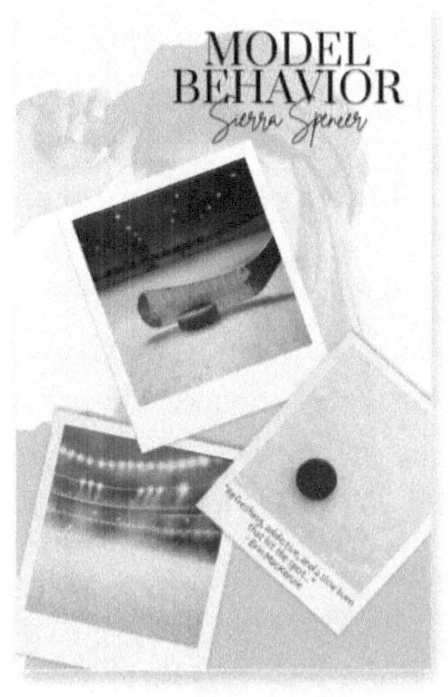

Serena MacPherson's mind races faster than the camera shutters as her photo gets taken. Flashing lights and magazine spreads are her life. Liam Richter has smoother skills on the ice than off it, and he'd rather avoid the limelight at all costs. When Liam gets talked into doing a photoshoot to announce his new residency as hockey captain, he leans into Serena's help on set —literally. Their on-camera chemistry has rumors flying about them. Surely, there has to be something real about it.

Model Behavior is for the readers who know finding someone doesn't necessarily mean finding yourself, but it's nice to have company…

Developing Feelings brings a creative and adoringly romantic twist to the world of academia while testing out the age-old question: can I fake it till I make it?

After leaving academia on not-so-great terms, Harper Sinclair started her own business helping new faculty build their research labs (with some interesting part-time jobs in between). When Jonathan Hoffman, a new rising-star faculty at UCLA, solicits Harper's services, Harper expects this will be like any other job. And it is. Until this adorable academic wants more than Harper's design ideas.

Jonathan has been inspired by Harper since he was a graduate student. Now that she is working with him, will she live up to the Harper he knew before she left academia? And will his imposter syndrome keep him from making a move? Meanwhile, the seemingly impenetrable Harper has done more than develop Jonathan's lab, she's begun to develop feelings.

Rose Thorne is a lover of all things romance novels. Whether you need a recommendation for an enemies-to-lovers, tutoring, sports romance, a fantasy novel that includes forced proximity and a *'who did this to you?'* trope, or a book that has less plot and more....spice, Rose has got you covered. Despite her extensive skills in matchmaking (see: a planned meet-cute that landed her best friend the love of her life) her own love has left much to be desired. Determined to work on her relationship drought she sets her eyes on Nate Cameron, a known player with the occasional tendency of reading romance novels. The catch? Nate Cameron has sworn off relationships and is much too determined to stay single.

Like birds of a feather Nate's best friend and captain, Chase Matthews, also has no time for distractions. Especially not the relationship kind—which he's always viewed as an overall waste of time. When Rose learns of his fear of commitment she's determined to change his mind...and strike a deal. If she's able to get Chase to realize that relationships are worth it, then he has to convince Nate to give her a shot. Can Rose's romance book clubs and fake dates convince Chase to give love a chance? Or will she have to admit that romance and relationships are best kept in fiction?

A VERY STANDARD CHRISTMAS

TWELVE DAYS OF CHRISTMAS
LYRICS BY FREDERIC AUSTIN

On the twelfth day of Christmas, my true love
sent to me

Twelve drummers drumming,
Eleven pipers piping,
Ten lords a-leaping,
Nine ladies dancing,
Eight maids a-milking,
Seven swans a-swimming,
Six geese a-laying,
Five golden rings,
Four calling birds,
Three French hens,
Two turtle doves,
And a partridge in a pear tree

My brother, Whit, used to be my favorite person. Then I met his fiancée.

Olivia's one of those people who wears her heart on her sleeve, and loves so fiercely you half expect her to combust. That's probably why she's marrying a doctor—good health insurance.

"I'm so glad you're here," Olivia says to me, opening the door to the nail salon.

Her best friend, Eric, laughs and holds the door open over my shoulder. "You've already told her that like twenty times, Liv."

Olivia's face reddens as she pushes her sunglasses to the top of her head. They're her signature accessory, even indoors.

"I know...I just...I'm—"

"So glad I'm here?" I offer, pulling her against me in a side hug. "Me too. Thanks for inviting me to your dress fitting. It's gorgeous, Olivia."

I mean it. Olivia is a knockout. She looks good in everything, but wedding bliss looks especially brilliant on her.

We check in for our manicures, the smell of nail polish and acetone stinging my nose, and the receptionist tells us to pick a color.

Thirteen days from her wedding, Olivia is still "auditioning" potential nail colors. She goes with an OPI classic, *Funny Bunny,* and a nail tech gestures her over to a chair.

"Writing anything good lately?" Eric asks me, stretching his legs out in front of him.

Eric is another one of my new favorite people. I met him when I met Olivia. They're sort of a package deal.

When Olivia moved to Connor Bay from New York, he followed her, citing the best friend codebook. He's blunt, funny, and just so ruthlessly comfortable in his own skin.

I wonder what that's like.

I lift a shoulder and investigate one of the fire engine red nail polishes. *Cajun Shrimp,* the label on the bottom of the bottle reads. I put it back on the shelf.

"The usual."

The usual: another fluff piece. Winter essentials, cruises to dodge family holiday gatherings, nail polish colors that go best with a Christmas wedding, or anything else you might imagine a travel journalist turned lifestyle magazine columnist would write.

"Tell Eric about the idea you had, Daze!" Olivia says from her manicure chair. "The twelve dates one!"

She's more excited about it than I am. *Clearly.*

"Twelve dates? Color me intrigued," Eric laughs, crossing an ankle over his knee.

His pant leg rides up and reveals his Lemony Snicket tattoo. You know the one with the eye from those books. I asked him about it once, and he pretended like he had no idea what I was talking about.

"I don't know if I'll do it," I sigh, grabbing a second polish off the rack and walking over to the station beside Olivia.

Eric makes himself comfortable in the empty chair on Olivia's other side.

"Well, now I have to know," Eric pushes.

Olivia fills him in, because of course she does. "She doesn't have a date to the wedding yet, so she was thinking she should try twelve dates themed like the Twelve Days of Christmas and then pick her plus-one from the finalists."

Eric gasps, delighted. "A bracket."

"Please don't make a bracket," I say, but I know he is already making a bracket in his head.

Olivia's brow creases as she inspects her first layer of polish. I pick up the second bottle I grabbed from the rack and place it beside her. She gives me a curious look when she sees the color, and I flash an encouraging smile.

"Wait," Eric says, scandalized. "Daisy got a plus one? Why didn't I get one?"

Olivia asks her tech to swap colors and gives him a look I can't see, but his dramatic eye roll tells me enough.

"When you get a real boyfriend, you can have a plus one," she declares.

He lifts both hands in mock surrender, but adds, "Daisy doesn't even date someone more than once, and she gets a plus one? I'm just saying, it's unfair."

"When you get married, you can invite whoever you want," I tell him, even though he does have a point. I'm not exactly a serial monogamist.

My romantic history is basically a graveyard of first dates, spaced 6 months apart, and mutual ghostings. It's fine. Better even. No mess, no expectations. People know what they're getting with me. I keep things fun. Which is why I don't understand the stupid little ache in my chest every time someone points it out, like part of me is tired of being treated like a commercial break instead of the movie.

The closest thing I have to a boyfriend is my roommate, Finn—part-time drummer, full-time pain in my ass—who friend-zoned me in elementary school when he rejected my very thoughtful Silly Band marriage proposal.

Which is fine. I'm not bitter. Especially not when he leaves his drumsticks on the kitchen counter or steals my shampoo. We're just friends...who occasionally share a bed when it's convenient.

Casual.

Totally casual.

Eric narrows his eyes like he can hear the italics in my brain. "Not to be that guy, but you're running out of evenings to make those twelve dates happen before the wedding."

He's right. The calendar is aggressively December. Lights in every window. Pine everywhere. That sharp, hopeful smell of cold New England air and strangers being nice.

"Details," I say breezily. "I thrive under pressure."

Olivia's sunglasses slide a little when she beams at me. "It'll be fun! We can help pick the themes. 'Partridge in a Pear Tree' could be a pear martini somewhere with rooftop igloos. 'Two Turtle Doves' could be ice skating—"

"—and 'Three French Hens' can be you flirting with a sommelier," Eric adds. "This is practically community service."

"Community service for whom?" I ask.

"Me," he says. "I need live entertainment."

My nail tech takes my hand and studies my cuticles like they're a crime scene. "Shape?"

"Whatever says 'I'm stable enough to attend a wedding without making a scene,'" I say.

"Squoval," she decides.

Olivia grins at me. "You'll find someone great. You're... you."

"What a ringing endorsement," I say, but my chest does a small, traitorous warm thing. Olivia thinks I'm a person whose happy ending is a when, not an if.

I keep my eyes on the wall of polish while the tech files. I pretend I'm not thinking about last night—how I sat on the couch, writing about stocking stuffers, while Finn tapped out a soft rhythm on his thighs like they were an invisible drum set. How he'd stopped, just for a moment, to ask if I needed anything before he went to bed. How I said no, but followed him into his room anyway.

Nope. Not thinking about it.

"Okay," I hear myself say, which is wild because my brain is still in last night. "Twelve dates. Twelve days. Holiday theme. A very efficient hunt for a plus one."

Eric claps once. "A montage! I adore a montage."

Olivia squeals, then covers her mouth like it's illegal to squeal in public. If it is...arrest me, officer, for I have sinned. "We'll help you pick outfits and locations. Oh my God, can we double-date one night when you're home? Whit won't mind."

"Whit will mind if your montage ends in Daisy eloping with a guy named Partridge," Eric says, swapping to the chair beside me. "But I support you spiritually."

My phone buzzes on the table with a text from Finn.

FINN

> You still alive or did the acetone fumes get you? Need an ETA so I don't eat your leftovers.

I type back with my free hand.

> You mean my leftovers you already ate?

Semantics. Do you want me to start pasta?

"Is that—" Eric leans over, nosy. "It is. Drummer Boy."

"He's making dinner," I say lightly. "It's called roommate survival."

"Mm," Eric says, deeply unconvinced. "Does roommate survival often include...naked cardio?"

"Eric," Olivia hisses, equal parts scandalized and delighted.

I stare at the polish wall like I've never seen colors. "Can we not get me kicked out of a nail salon? I actually live in this city, unlike you two."

Olivia giggles, then sobers, eyes soft. "You'll tell us if this gets...not fun, right?"

It's on the tip of my tongue to say everything is fun. That I am fun. That I am very good at being the fun one. But I look at my brother's future wife—at the way she's looking back at me, like I'm not a walking punchline—and I nod.

"Cross my heart," I say, and she grins like I just gave her an early wedding present.

Olivia studies her nails while the tech smooths on the last coat of the sage-green polish I picked for her.

"Well, that's a familiar color," Eric says, leaning back in his chair.

Olivia's mouth curves—small, knowing—before she glances at me. It's quick, but it's there. A thank you without words.

I drop my gaze to my phone like it's nothing. You don't grow up with that eye color, judging your every move, without being able to recognize the polish that matches exactly.

Before I can tuck my phone away, Eric plucks it out of my hand.

"Hey—"

"Research," he says, thumbing past my texts. "If we're doing Twelve Dates, we're starting now."

I reach for it, but he swivels his chair out of range. "Your Tinder bio is tragic, by the way."

"It's fine," I say. "It's functional."

"It's beige," he counters, typing like a man possessed. "There. Matched with a guy named Colin. His profile pic has pears in it. This is fate."

Eric bumps my knee with his. "Date One tomorrow. Partridge in a Pear Tree. Rooftop bar. Pear martinis. Ugly sweater optional, but encouraged."

By the time the top coat goes on, we've decided on four potential date themes, an outfit for each, and a strict no-partridge tattoo policy. Olivia pays even though I argue, because she's in a pre-wedding haze where she thinks show-ering people with love is the same as tipping.

Outside, the Boston air has that bite that signals snow. Eric pulls me into a hug, and I go willingly. He smells like bergamot and chaos.

"Call us when you get home," Olivia says, serious under the sparkle.

"I live with a drummer," I say. "Home is loud. Besides, you two are the ones with the drive back to Connor Bay. You text me when *you* get home."

"You know, Daisy. Now that you're more set at the maga-zine, you *could* move back to Connor Bay," Olivia says, waggling her eyebrows suggestively.

The idea of moving home feels more like a last resort than a promising new adventure, even if the population got an upgrade when the two of them arrived.

I laugh. "Then who would keep Finn Parker from home-lessness?"

"Isn't that their thing? Starving artists and all that?" Eric asks.

I tilt my head in mock-consideration.

Finn had actually taken me in when I hit rock bottom earlier this year. My life had lacked meaning. My doctor brother had gotten engaged to a New York marketing executive, and I...had nothing. No one.

Travel had consumed my life for so long that my roots were nonexistent. I told Finn as much at Whit and Olivia's engagement party this past February.

"Come stay with me in Boston," he said with a lift of his shoulder. "Slum it with me in Back Bay."

I didn't think he was serious, but he'd offered again a week later on one of our usual calls, and I didn't have a reason not to say yes. And thus, our roommate-ship was born.

Olivia sighs deeply. "Well, if you change your mind..."

I smile and nod. "I know. I *know*," I emphasize when she gives me a look that says she means business. "I'm happy here for right now."

Eric wiggles his fingers. "Give Drummer Boy my love."

"Noted," I say, and start walking. I take a picture of a department store window strung with fairy lights and send it to Finn.

On my way home!

Have you ever had a pear martini?

He replies with a pear, a skull, and...the Italian flag? Then:

...not to my knowledge

Pasta in ten. Don't be late or I'm eating your share on principle.

I smile at the screen, then tuck it away.

It's just for fun...but maybe it'd be nice to be more than the fun one.

By the time I get home, the apartment smells like garlic and whatever Finn puts in his pasta sauce that he swears isn't sugar but absolutely is. He's on the couch in sweats, socked feet propped on the coffee table, a bowl balanced in one hand, and his laptop open on the other side.

His thick, dark hair is a little mussed—like he's been running his hands through it while working on a song—and the cuff of his hoodie is pushed up just far enough to show a small tattoo near the crease of his arm. Another one peeks from between his thumb and forefinger when he twirls his fork. Tasteful little flashes of ink, the kind you only notice if you're really paying attention.

"Welcome home, Hallmark Heroine," he says without looking away from the screen.

"Not a Hallmark heroine," I say, tossing my coat over the back of a chair. "Those women have better hair."

He forks up a heap of pasta, finally glancing at me. "So what's this I hear about pears and birds?"

I narrow my eyes. "Eric texted you?"

"Eric texts me a lot. Mostly memes. Sometimes threats." He sets the bowl on the coffee table and leans back, smirking. "But tonight he texted me, and I quote," he pulls out his phone for accuracy, "'prepare your loins, your roommate is speed dating the Twelve Days of Christmas.'"

I groan and drop onto the armchair across from him. "It's not speed dating. It's...an experiment."

Finn tips his head. "An experiment in what? Avian mating rituals?"

"In finding a wedding date," I say, grabbing the throw blanket from the back of the chair and wrapping it around myself like armor. "I don't have time to actually date, so twelve holiday-themed first dates, one of them gets the plus one."

He looks at me for a long beat, something unreadable in his eyes before it's gone. "Sounds...festive."

"It'll be fun."

"Uh-huh." He picks his bowl back up. "Does this count as night one because you really didn't give me time to prepare, and while I haven't had a pear martini, I'm not in a hurry to change that."

"Nah. Don't get any ideas. This one's platonic."

Finn smirks around a bite of pasta. "Right. Totally casual. Should you take one end of this noodle, and we'll meet in the middle, Lady and the Tramp style?"

I kick at his foot in front of the coffee table, and he catches my ankle, squeezing once before letting go and humming "Bella Notte" to himself.

It's nothing. It's always nothing.

Except my pulse is doing a thing it shouldn't.

www.ingramcontent.com/pod-product-compliance
Lightning Source LLC
Chambersburg PA
CBHW051130130726
47988CB00005B/1782